**Jahn looked out the gun port of his rover as
the chaos of battle raged outside.**

A Spartan appeared right in front of him and he
opened fire, unconsciously gritting his teeth as
the body jerked wildly and fell underneath the
tires of his vehicle.

Suddenly an explosion jolted him to the
bone, and the metal beneath him warped from
the force of a concussion grenade beneath the
rover. The cockpit around him spun as the
rover went up and crashed down on its side.
Jahn's head slammed into metal.

"Get out!" he shouted. He punched the emergency exit switch and the hatch blew open, revealing the pale, cloud-sprinkled sky above. He
immediately began pushing members of his
crew outside, following the last one close behind.

Two suns blazed down on the slope as the
battle raged. Speeders and rovers turned in
tighter and tighter circles as soldiers on foot
tried to incapacitate them or jam flame
grenades through the gun ports.

He saw Spartans and Peacekeepers shooting
at each other point blank, and then shooting
the corpses. Shouts of anger and pain rang out.

There's no turning back now.

SID MEIER'S
ALPHA
CENTAURI™

BOOK I of III

Centauri Dawn

MICHAEL ELY

POCKET BOOKS

New York   London   Toronto   Sydney   Singapore

An *Original* Publication of POCKET BOOKS

POCKET BOOKS, a division of Simon & Schuster, Inc.
1230 Avenue of the Americas, New York, NY 10020

Copyright © 2000 by Electronic Arts

ISBN: 0-671-04077-4

First Pocket Books printing December 2000

10 9 8 7 6 5 4 3 2 1

POCKET and colophon are registered trademarks of Simon & Schuster, Inc.

Printed in the U.S.A.

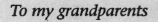

To my grandparents

Acknowledgments

The number of people who helped on this manuscript could pack a colony ship to a distant star. Here are a few of them:

First of all, thanks to Tim Train for reading my draft of the manuscript with an eagle eye and making many insightful comments. Thanks also to Brian Reynolds, for creating such a rich game world which served as a basis for the book, and to Sid Meier, Jeff Briggs, and everyone at Firaxis for bringing the game world to life in such a compelling way.

Many thanks to Marco, my editor at Pocket Books, for all his help and support, as well as Rob Simpson for his insights. And thanks to everyone else at Pocket Books that I haven't met (yet) who helped get the book to the shelves on time.

And a special thanks to all of my friends, family, and loved ones for supporting me through it all, especially YS, who let me write when I needed to write, and talk when I needed to talk.

Death thus raged in every shape; and, as usually happens at such times, there was no length to which violence did not go.

—Thucydides, 431 B.C.

prologue

The United Nations Starship Unity.
Mission Year 2100
Journey's End

"PRAVIN."

The voice came again over the quicklink strapped to Pravin Lal's wrist. He looked up from the body of his dying wife, whose quiet gasps seemed to echo the shrieking and groaning of the ship around him, and activated the device. "Captain?"

"Yes, it's me."

"Where are you, John? Are you okay?"

"I'm in the center of the ship. I've been shot."

Pravin braced himself as the floor rumbled beneath him. A maintenance door flew open and a thin crewman, his face drenched in sweat, locked eyes with Pravin and shook his head. Pravin saw the fear of death in the man's eyes.

"We're trapped, John," Pravin said into the quicklink. "We've made it into the landing pods, but the jettison system is wrecked. We can't break away from the *Unity*'s superstructure, and I can't send anyone to help you."

"It doesn't matter," said the captain, and Pravin felt his heart sink. He gazed again at his wife, Pria, a

victim of shredder bolts pumped into her back by
mutinous crewmembers, and the panic started to
rise inside of him again. They would not reach the
new world. Even as he watched her, the superstructure of the *Unity* spiraled toward the atmosphere of
Chiron, Alpha Centauri system's lone habitable
planet, out of control.

*The ship will burn, just as Earth burned. The last of
humanity . . . escaping nuclear Armageddon just to per-
ish out here. . . .*

The metal of the ship screamed around him, and
Pria's breath now rose and fell in shorter gasps. He
touched her soft hair, and the moment felt
strangely intimate amid the chaos around him.
"We are all going to die here."

Captain Garland's voice came back, shaky and
weak. "Maybe not. I'm in a maintenance duct near
the ship's axis. I think I can . . . cut the pods loose."

"You can free the landing pods?" Pravin imagined his friend in the center axis of the ship, where
the seven landing pods were joined, and suddenly
the possibility of survival returned. But then he saw
his own hand, wet with Pria's blood, and felt a
wave of grief.

*Even on our journey to the new world we try to kill
each other. Do we deserve to survive?*

He thought of the anger and hate that had taken
hold of the increasingly desperate crew, and the
suffering of the human wreckage they had left behind on Earth. And he knew his friend was thinking the same.

"Is it worth saving?" came the captain's voice
through the quicklink. "They may never stop fighting . . . we'll never be at peace."

"No," mumbled Pria, in a daze. Pravin touched at her pale, still luminous face, his heart beating faster as hers slowed down. They'd both believed in the future.

"Never?" he asked. "It's up to you, John."

"No," answered the captain. "Because once I do this, Pravin . . . the rest will be up to you."

Deep in the center of the ship, Captain John Garland broke the link and tried to calm himself, his breath echoing loudly in his pressure suit. He could taste blood in his mouth, and feel it inside his suit.

Above and around him the inner surfaces of the ship spun, open to the star-flecked universe beyond. The planet, Chiron, passed like a living jewel in space, then receded past the ship and appeared again as the *Unity* tumbled, closer and closer.

His earlier thought continued to haunt him. *Maybe there will never be peace.*

But, if there's a chance . . .

He struggled to rise but could not, and so he crawled through the narrow accessway toward the first rung of the ladder that led toward the core of the ship, where the seven landing pods were locked together, and where the explosive bolts that should have launched the pods into space still waited, dormant. He reached up to grab the rung, focusing on his gloved hand, on the feel of the ladder, trying to ignore the inner surfaces of the ship spinning wildly around him. He reached for the second rung, and the third, pulling himself toward the ship's core.

With every step he left something behind . . . the dream of peace, memories of the wife and the children he had left behind on Earth, his anger and hate at those who had usurped his crew, the shame at his own failure, his fear, his guilt. Piece by piece, step by step, he felt the weight lifting from his shoulders.

Until, at the last rung, his ego seemed to drift away, his very identity dissolving into the mass of humanity around him, and the space beyond.

He let out a breath and lifted his hand, which now held his last concussion grenade. He activated it and watched the countdown calmly. He measured the last moments of his life with it.

At one second to go he squeezed the grenade in his hand and slammed it into the nearest explosive bolt. And then he let go of the ladder.

Captain Garland drifted away from the *Unity*'s core as the explosion he planted rocked the center of the ship and blasted through the explosive bolts like a chain of lightning. He saw the seven landing pods fly out and away from the now-useless superstructure of the *Unity*, free at last.

His last sight was of the landing pods scattering, their thrusters firing one by one. He imagined them, arcing their way down to the new world, bringing humanity's curses with them, and humanity's gifts.

To Chiron.

chapter one

Mission Year 2101

JAHN LAL AWOKE TO A BUZZING IN HIS HEAD. IT TOOK him a moment to realize that the buzzing really was *inside* his head, and not in the dim metal room around him, and then his heart began to pound.

It's in my mind.

He began to tremble, and he looked around, realizing that he lay in something like a glass coffin. Tubes and wires snaked down into his arm, which was thin as a rail, and a plastic tube jammed down his throat choked him.

What's happening to me? Last thing I remember I was on Earth, in the cryochamber, the suspension gel welling up around me. . . .

He began to panic. Someone in a blue uniform loomed above him for a moment, his face a mixture of affection and concern. Jahn felt a warm hand touch him and then the figure hurried on.

That was my father.

Jahn took a deep breath. He could hear his own blood rushing in his ears, but beyond that he could hear shouts and scuffling, and then he heard screams. One word stood out.

"*—mindworms—*"

His heart pounding, he tore the IV tubes from his arms, then grabbed the thick plastic tube in his throat and pulled it out. He gagged at the taste of bile and the hideous sensation of the tube sliding out. His vision blurred and nausea wracked him, but the buzzing sound seemed to have retreated a bit, like a cautious animal.

He put his hands on the side of the coffin, which he now dimly recognized as a cryocell, the one that had held him in stasis on the forty-year journey from Earth to Alpha Centauri.

The new world. Is this the new world?

Somehow he hooked his limbs over the rim of the cryocell and pulled himself up. Nausea wracked him again.

His vision was still blurry, but he could dimly make out a small room with some equipment piled in a corner. He knew he wasn't on the *Unity* anymore; he couldn't feel the vibration of the ship around him. In fact his limbs felt heavy, and the air tasted stale. It could all have been a side effect of the cryosleep, but somehow he knew it wasn't.

I think we made it. We actually made it!

There was the stomping of feet and more shouts from somewhere nearby, and then a rushing sound, like fire from an exhaust. He felt an odd sensation of heat from somewhere, and thought he saw the orange light of flames in the narrow metal hallway outside. The hissing sound swelled in his brain, then began to die out.

I really don't feel well.

He slumped to the ground, his hand touching the glass of his cryocell and then sliding down it.

As he fell into unconsciousness he saw a vision of the burning rings, the rings of fire that consumed the cities of Earth, right before the launch of the *Unity*. And those rings now contracted around him.

The next day

Mindworms.

In his cramped pressurized room, Jahn lifted the small weights that would help to recondition his body following his near-disastrous cryosleep, remembering the word he'd heard during the chaos that accompanied his awakening. Part of him wondered if he'd dreamed the whole thing. But no; after he'd come to, his caretaker Paula scrupulously avoided answering his questions. Something bad had happened

He heard someone enter the room and looked up to see his father, a tall, slender Indian man in the pale blue uniform of a ship's surgeon, even its high-tech fabric now somewhat tattered from wear. Jahn rose quickly, letting the small weight fall back to the metal floor.

"Father!"

"Jahn," Pravin Lal answered with a smile, and moved toward him. They embraced. "I am so glad you're well."

"I'm doing better." He backed up and looked at his father, at the lines of worry etching his face. "What happened here?"

"A mindworm attack. Indigenous animal life. Most of the time they leave us alone, but there is a field of native plant life nearby that they sometimes . . . nest in, I guess you would call it. We don't know. Sometimes they stir all at once, seeming to boil up from the ground."

"They were inside my mind. A buzzing . . ."

"If you only heard a buzz, you're lucky, Jahn. The worms were right outside the base. Most of the people saw, and heard, their worst nightmares. We think they're empathic." He shook his head. "But forget about all that. You need to rest."

"I am resting," said Jahn with determination. He glanced at his reflection in the glass of the cryocell. He was a tall man in his late thirties, with a light brown complexion typical of his ancestry. His muscles, once lean and strong, were now thin from disuse, but he would fix that. Long black hair was pulled back in a ponytail. He was his father's son, but with a special toughness, the toughness that came from being raised in chaotic times.

Pravin touched his shoulder. "You know that your cryocell was damaged on the ship and that you're lucky to be alive. Don't push too hard. I'll bring you up to speed in good time."

"Will mother be visiting?" asked Jahn, looking back at the weights.

"You will visit her, in time," said Pravin, and when Jahn looked up his father had already left through the narrow curtain that served as his door.

Kilometers distant, Corazon Santiago watched as her medics stood over the crude metal hospital crib, yanking tubes and cords from the body inside. She clenched her teeth as they went about their work with brutal efficiency. Finally, one of them turned to her.

"What would you like us to do, Colonel?" The man's face remained cold and stern as he watched her, although there was no hint of disrespect in his manner. Just an expectant waiting.

Instead of answering, she stepped forward, gesturing for the medics to stand aside. They backed up slowly, mildly confused by the change in procedure. She looked into the cold metal crib at the body inside, pale and weak, with a blue tint to the skin. The face contorted with pain, and the baby's back was arched, as if against a blade in the spine. But the pain this child felt came from within, from some kind of inherited weakness.

"Put him on life support," she said, never taking her eyes from the boy's tiny limbs. She started to add something more, but did not. Instead she turned away and left the room, feeling the dark stares of the medics in her back.

She walked quickly down the hallway outside the hospital room, heading back to the command center. Five Spartans jogged by her, heavy lead weights hanging from their wrists and ankles, but they all managed a salute as they passed. She noted the sweat pouring down their faces with approval.

"Colonel," said a voice behind her. She did not stop, but waited for her second-in-command, Diego, to fall in step next to her. "Permission to speak freely."

She turned, cool eyes appraising him from a face that was smooth and stern. He shifted back a step; Santiago had been forty years old when she first entered cryosleep for the *Unity* exodus. Her body retained a youthful vitality and strength from rigorous training and periodic genetic treatments. Her jet black hair was pulled back from her face, giving her a clean, efficient look. She was nothing if not an intimidating presence.

"What is it, Commander?" she asked.

"That child, sir . . . why did you save him? He barely survived his birth, and his condition has grown worse over time. He won't survive long on Chiron. And if he does survive, he'll only be a liability."

She stopped and turned to look at him. "I know that, Diego. But he is dying. What would you have me do?"

He held her gaze. "I know you have the strength to do what is necessary, Colonel. Letting the boy live will look bad to our people. I fear it will be seen as a sign of weakness, and will undermine your authority."

"I built this base, and I defy anyone to challenge my authority, Diego. This child . . . he is only one life, nothing more. He will not bring down the Spartans."

"I know he is only one life, Colonel, but he represents a different way of life. A way of life you know we can't sustain. It is too hard in this world to coddle the weak."

She leaned toward him, her dark eyes burning into his. "Do you think that I am weak, Diego? Do you question my resolve, or my prowess?"

He glanced away. "No, sir. But not every king bears a prince."

She held his gaze, and he shifted uncomfortably. "He is my son, Diego. He has a strength in him. I believe he will do good things for us." She waited, watching him, as several moments passed. Another five Spartans ran by, their heavy breathing echoing off the walls of the narrow hallway. "Do you have any further objections?"

Diego bowed his head slightly. "No, Colonel. Permission to continue in my duties."

"Granted," she said, and accepted his salute. He turned and hurried away, and Santiago continued toward the command center, her pace a little slower than before.

Two weeks later

Jahn Lal awoke in his cryocell, which he still used as a bed. He waited for his eyes to adjust as he stared at the curve of carbon-scored metal that arced over his head, illuminated by indirect sunlight that crept from gaps between the walls and floor.

It's a tomb, he thought. *A tomb I still need to escape from.* He felt his belly churn from the crude protein synthetics he had eaten the night before. That and the heaviness of his limbs, courtesy of Chiron's greater-than-Earth gravity, still made him feel out of sorts. He wondered when he would feel whole again.

A face loomed over him, soft and round, with wide blue eyes. A smile followed, and he groaned.

"You look good," said a voice that never failed to torment him with its quiet huskiness.

"Thanks," he said ruefully, glancing down at his chest, which was stronger from his exercises but not quite where he wanted it to be. He still didn't know what to make of Paula and her constant flirtations. "Why do you always arrive at the exact moment I'm waking up, Paula?"

He felt her warm hands on his arms, pulling him up. "You're very predictable, Jahn. You still haven't adjusted to the shortened days on Chiron, and you still wake up every twenty-four hours."

"But you're always here!"

"I've scheduled my shifts around it." She helped

him to a sitting position and checked his pulse and blood pressure, nodding as she did. Jahn took the time to look around his small room. Not a room really, more a curve of carbon-scored metal that the techs had used to form his makeshift recovery area. He wondered when his father would release him from medical care and allow him to work again.

I want to see this world.

When Paula was done he pushed her hands away, wanting to get out of the cryocell under his own power. She stood back respectfully as he leaned on the cold glass edge of the cryocell and heaved himself out onto a low rubber stair, holding his sweaty white bed sheet around his waist.

"Did everyone get this hammered by the cryosleep?" he asked, catching his breath.

"Everyone had to adjust," she said, appraising his movements. "But you were in a cryobay that took some damage during the fighting on the *Unity*, disrupting your life support. You're very lucky to be alive."

"You look like you came through it all right," he said, looking at her tight blue uniform as he lifted his hands to smooth back his long tangle of jet-black hair. At that moment, the sheet slipped from around his waist, leaving him exposed. She stifled a laugh.

"Great," said Jahn, bending over gingerly to pick up the sheet. "Mornings are the worst, I think."

"Do your exercises and get dressed," she said. "I assume I don't have to bathe you anymore."

"You ask me that every morning, Paula."

She laughed again. He looked back at the cryocell with its smooth glass shape. "I'm tired of sleeping in that thing. It smells like death."

"It's been sterilized, Jahn. It doesn't smell like anything."

"It still smells like death to me, and weakness."

"Well, it's about time to move you to the common rooms anyway. You were only staying here because of your father."

He nodded sharply. "Good. I don't want any more special treatment."

She smiled. "Your father will be pleased to hear that. He wants you to join him in the Planet Walk at eight hundred hours."

Jahn looked at her. "He told you that?"

She nodded. "Wear your uniform. I think this is business." She moved closer to him and kissed him on the cheek. He leaned into the kiss, making sure to hold on to his sheet this time.

"Take care of yourself, Jahn," she said. "Chiron is not an easy place to live."

He moved closer to her, and then she turned and pushed through the curtains that served as a door to his crude recovery room.

At least I have a door, he thought, as he threw the sheet in a bundle against the wall and began a series of strengthening exercises his yoga teacher had taught him back on Earth.

Jahn walked with Paula down a narrow, metal-lined hallway. He had washed himself from head to toe with the tepid water in the bathing room, and now had on a clean uniform. He felt good, as fresh as he had felt since arriving on Chiron.

"As you know, your father has done a wonderful job getting this base up and running," Paula said. "When the *Unity* broke apart, the seven pod leaders barely made it down to the surface. In fact, we still don't know where everyone landed, or if they're still alive."

Jahn nodded. He had started to piece all of this together during his recovery, but he appreciated Paula's summary.

"We know that Deirdre Skye is somewhere to the northwest, and Director Morgan is due north, and Zakharov is pretty close by as well. They each had over a thousand people in their landing pods, just like us." She suddenly fell silent as a tall, gangly man in a high-collared white tunic entered the hallway from the other side and walked past them, fixing them both with a cool gaze.

"That was one of Zakharov's citizens," Paula said softly. "Of course the entire crew of the *Unity* is supposed to work together on Chiron, but since we landed far apart there has been a certain degree of self-sufficiency required. Travel on Chiron is hard, and your father fears that the bases may become more like city-states than parts of a larger society. He really wants everyone working together." He felt their shoulders touch briefly.

Coming from Earth, we're used to fighting, he thought. He closed his eyes for a moment and saw the burning rings again, fires that consumed cities.

"Let's go this way." Paula turned a corner into another narrow metal hallway. "I know a shortcut." It was dark, but he could see scorch marks on the metal. They looked as though they'd been caused by close-range weapons fire, and he knitted his eyebrows.

"So it's true," he said. "We really did try to kill each other on the *Unity,* before even reaching the Promised Land."

"If this is the Promised Land, then someone has broken their promise," said Paula, and Jahn glanced at her, startled by the bitterness that sometimes slipped through her warm facade. He ran his hand along the metal of the wall, which felt hot from a sun he could not see.

Three suns, actually, he reminded himself. Alpha Centauri A was the primary star in this system, but Alpha Centauri B would be visible in the skies and have some effect on the tides. The last star, Proxima Centauri, was little more than a hunk of smouldering rock too far away to have much influence at all. Paula picked up her pace and he hurried to catch up to her.

"These hallways are narrower than my cryocell," he said, and she nodded.

"Survival base. Everything you see has been constructed out of pieces of the *Unity*. We've had to become very creative."

As they walked, he noticed how numerous the makeshift innovations were: the spindly wreckage of the *Unity*'s gridded superstructure had apparently been reshaped into hallways, living spaces, and workrooms. Everything was small and crude, but had a certain functional elegance to it.

Up ahead Jahn noticed natural sunlight streaming into the end of the corridor. They reached the end and rounded a corner, and Jahn found himself in a long hallway with glass walls that let sunlight pour in from all sides.

He stopped short at the entrance to the hallway, stunned by the vista that opened up around him. His gaze immediately went to a golden sphere in the sky that looked almost identicle to Earth's sun and then, lower in the horizon, he saw another small nexus of light that burned with a rich orange color.

The new world. And two suns. My God, there are two suns in the sky.

He stared at them, feeling their heat on his face, and knowing it was worthless to look for tiny Proxima Centauri in this bright mid-day light. Finally he let his eyes drift down from the suns to a landscape that stretched on forever, with a far longer horizon than Earth. He felt overwhelmed by the vast emptiness, as flat and rolling land made of a reddish soil rolled on and away from him.

"Chiron," he said in a quiet voice, trying out the name of the new world as he continued to absorb the sight before his eyes. It overwhelmed his memories of crowded, dirty, pre-Apocalypse Earth. He looked up into the sky again, noting its pale blue-white color and tendrils of clouds tinged with brown drifting lazily across it.

"The brown is due to the high nitrogen content of the air," said Paula, following his gaze. "This place is a nitrogen heaven."

"It's incredible," said Jahn. "I haven't really gotten a good look at the landscape until now."

"We can go up to the observation room later. As far as we can tell, the soil everywhere has that reddish brown color. You can see on that hill to the right some of our workers tending a farm, on the slopes leading up to that ridge overlooking the base. The hybrids that we've produced from our emergency stores grow well in Chiron's atmosphere and soil, although the air is too nitrogen heavy for us to breathe for very long without pressure masks. This place is more friendly to Earth's plants than its mammals."

Jahn nodded. The farmers, wearing thick jumpsuits

and light, translucent face masks, tended neat rows of dark green hybrids. They looked quite insignificant against the sweep of Chiron's surface. Coming from an Earth choked with metal and concrete, Jahn could hardly believe the expansiveness of it all.

"Where's the native plant life, this xenofungus I've heard so much about?" he asked.

"Turn around." Paula put her hand on his shoulder as if to steady him.

He turned and felt his spirits dampen a little, as if a shadow had passed across his eyes. The landscape to the right of the hallway differed radically from what he had just seen. The earth still had the same reddish brown soil, but starting at a distance of about ten kilometers from the base, and stretching almost to the horizon, he saw a tangled mass of crimson growths that looked several meters tall. The bright colors and tangle of shapes confused his vision.

"My God," he said. "Why is it so close to the base?"

"This is where we landed. Your father had to decide whether to move the damaged landing pod before setting up a base or hope that nothing bad would come from the xenofungus. So far it hasn't been too bad. The mindworms leave us alone for the most part."

He looked over at her, but her soft face was turned toward the tangled fields. "Can you hear it?" she asked after a moment.

He cocked an eyebrow. "Can I hear what? The fungus?"

She shrugged dismissively. "Some people say they can hear it, although none of our scientists have ever been able to record the sounds." She looked past him to the other end of the hallway and lifted a hand in greeting. "Your father's here. I'd better get moving."

Jahn turned to see his father, Pravin Lal, standing at the far end of the Planet Walk with a woman he didn't recognize.

Pravin waited calmly, his hands clasped behind his back, as Jahn approached. The older Lal wore an elaborate light blue robe pinned with a silver clasp decorated with the United Nations Space Agency seal. The woman next to him was older than Jahn but younger than Pravin, and stood with an almost regal bearing. *That's not my mother,* thought Jahn, and remembered again that his father still hadn't explained what had happened to her. He feared the worst, but the nurses and attendants had told him not to worry, that she was not dead. *Just let her be well,* he thought. *Let me have a chance to talk to her again.*

"Father." Jahn found himself hurrying the last few steps to clasp his father's hand warmly, and then found himself in an embrace.

"Jahn," said Pravin. "It is very, very good to see you alive." They broke the embrace and smiled at each other. "I am very sorry I have not had time to stop by and see you often. Things are very busy here, as you can imagine." He gestured at the woman at his side. "This is my good friend and advisor, Sophia. We are on our way to a council meeting now, and I would like you to accompany us."

Jahn turned to the woman and reached out for her hand. As she touched him, he felt something like an electric shock. Her eyes were bright and green, and her hair, though growing a little wild like that of most of the crew, fell in dark waves around her shoulders. She nodded to him, a nod with all the grace of a queen.

She's a Perfect, Jahn thought, recalling the crew members with near-perfect genetic profiles that had been seeded throughout the *Unity* crew to assure the health of the next generation on the new world.

"Let us go inside, Jahn. The meeting will start shortly."

"Deirdre Skye, Nwabudike Morgan, and Prokhor Zakharov," said Sophia, standing in front of a computer touchpanel salvaged from the *Unity* that displayed everything they now knew of Chiron's terrain, which wasn't much, as far as Jahn could tell. Sophia pointed to locations around the map as she mentioned the three names.

"We know the approximate locations of these three. By chance or design, Deirdre ended up with most of the plant hybrids, Nwabudike ended up with most of the drilling and cutting equipment, and Zakharov, of course, has the finest scientific mind on Chiron, as well as most of the science staff. He also has most of the raw materials for the genetic treatments that our most prominent citizens use to keep young and fit. We've all pledged to work together and share resources as much as possible."

"A pledge and real life are two different things," said a squat man with a reddish face and rough bearing that Jahn already disliked. "Skye would rather piddle around with her plants than help make this planet more habitable for humans, as far as I can tell."

"We're still trying to get ourselves established, Pierson," said Sophia. Jahn studied her eyes discreetly for any hidden feelings about Pierson, good or bad. "We should give them some time."

"Earth was paved with good intentions, that's all

I'm trying to say," said Pierson. "Paved and buried. Just because we're nicknamed the Peacekeepers doesn't mean everyone will listen to whatever we have to say."

"He has a good point," said Pravin. "The sooner we can open permanent commlink channels and establish a mutually beneficial relationship with these three, the sooner we can start knitting the human settlements together again. We have a lot to overcome."

"What about the rest of the command staff?" asked Jahn, unsure of his place in the meeting but deciding a don't-speak-until-spoken-to attitude would get him nowhere. The other advisors, ten of them in all, glanced at him. Some smiled. Most of them seemed well-spoken and intelligent.

"We've pieced together what we could from the *Unity* black box," said Sophia, taking the lead. "As far as we can tell, Miriam Godwinson, the *Unity*'s psych chaplain, made it to a damaged pod and may have landed somewhere to the east of us."

"God help her," said Pierson, and there was some chuckling.

"Executive Officer Yang took command of a pod, but we haven't heard from him. And we believe that Colonel Santiago also took command of a pod and may have landed somewhere to the southwest."

"We need to continue to try to locate these individuals, through any means available to us," said Pravin. "That means scanning and scouting."

A silence fell over the room for a moment, and Jahn could see that the advisors were considering the ramifications.

"An isolationist policy, at least in these early years, might give us a chance to get on our feet," said a thoughtful-looking older woman with long silver-gray hair, whose polished ID badge read Eldridge.

"We have a few working rover vehicles salvaged from the *Unity*," said Pravin. "If we can find the lost crew and help them, we must do it. It is a moral imperative."

"Hard to argue with an imperative," said Pierson quietly.

"Then don't argue with it," Pravin said firmly, looking at the man. "I believe we can better serve ourselves, and all of humanity, by reaching out to the others. It will also help us to explore Chiron's surface. In the meantime we can build a recycling facility here, until Deirdre can help us with some better farming techniques."

"At least let's put a limited crew with the scout patrols," said Sophia. "After all, we might not like what we find out there."

"Agreed," said Pierson. "That singing fungus is bad enough."

In a small room lit only by two salvaged glowlamps, Santiago sat on a cold metal bench and looked into the eyes of each of her advisors. There were only four of them now, most of them good fighters and aggressive crew from the *Unity*, sitting in a circle with her. Diego sat to her immediate right, his broad arms ready to burst out of his tight uniform.

"As far as we can tell, at least some of the other pods landed to our east and northeast," said Messier, a tall and noble-looking warrior with scars running down one side of his jaw. "We need to send a scout patrol to find them."

"Agreed," said Santiago. "We are in dire need of medical technology."

"And more food," said a quiet young man with bright red hair. He looked only at Santiago, refusing to meet the eyes of the other advisors, and he seemed ill at ease.

"Can't your farmers get the hybrids growing fast enough, Brady?" asked Diego in a low voice.

"They're working as best they can. In fact, the atmosphere is very friendly to Earth plants. But without more hybrids, and more citizens to work the farms, our diet will be very sparse."

"Citizens don't work farms. Citizens fight," said Diego. "Besides, the sparse diet will toughen us up." He jabbed a finger at Brady, who brushed a shock of red hair nervously from his face. "Work your people harder, Red. We need our best people to deal with these damn planet worms."

"These worms are unlike anything we could have anticipated," said Messier. "Very few of our troops are able to withstand their attacks."

Santiago nodded, remembering that first terrible attack when the mindworms, hundreds of thousands of the wriggling vermin, boiled out of the xenofungus fields near Sparta Command. She had listened over the comm link as her most disciplined troops had gone down screaming, overwhelmed by visions from their worst nightmares. When the attack was over, dozens of her people were dead, with mindworms still burrowing into their skulls and consuming their flesh.

"We need a harder training regimen," said Santiago. "We have the bulk of the *Unity*'s security force with us. If we can't discipline them to hold their ground against these worms, then no human on this planet has a chance against them."

"I can't create food from air," said Brady, finally looking around at all the men. He lifted his arms, which were well toned and tan but much smaller than those of the toughened fighters in the room. "We should try to make contact with the other pods. If Deirdre Skye is alive, she can help us."

"I can tell you this: all food goes first to our warriors, and then to other Spartans," said Diego. "Everyone has to learn to make do with less. It will make us all stronger."

"You can't build a civilization with warriors alone," said Brady.

"Spoken like a true farmer," said Diego.

"All of our citizens can learn strength and discipline," said Santiago. "In fact, we should give everyone a training regimen."

"And those that fall behind must suffer the consequences," said Diego.

"Spoken like a true fanatic," said Messier. Diego stared at him, but Messier held his gaze coolly.

Santiago continued, heading off the clash of wills. "It's true that most of us here understand the benefits of a strong body and an indomitable spirit. Given what happened on Earth, and the dangers of life on Chiron, we must make sure that the strongest among us have a chance to flourish. We will need strong individuals to work our farms and build walls around our base."

Diego grinned with pleasure. "Any of us here would welcome that hard labor," he said.

"That's why you're here," Santiago said. "Have the technicians continue working on weapons to fight the worms. And send our scout patrols to the east. We need to find better land to farm, and some sign of the others. Dismissed."

Her advisors saluted her and stood up to file out. Santiago dismissed them, ignoring the rumbling in her own belly.

"It's good," Jahn said quietly. He sat with his father on the observation deck, which consisted of a floor welded into the top of a tall cylinder that rose up in the center of the base. In one wall a window had been cut and fitted with glass. Jahn took another sip of liquor from his plastic cup and felt its heat inside of him.

"Do you recognize this place, Jahn?" asked Pravin, gesturing at the space around them.

Jahn stood up and ran his hands along the walls of the room, which were perfectly smooth. "It's part of the fuel injector mechanism from the *Unity*," he said. He looked out the window. Night had fallen, but the two moons of Chiron were both visible, sending a pale wash of light over the landscape.

"Between the shorter days and the lights at night I don't know if I'm sleeping or waking anymore," said Jahn.

"You are finally awake," Pravin informed him lightly. Jahn smiled and looked down over the base. From this height, he could see how the base had been built around the original landing pod. Several tunnels created from salvaged pieces of the *Unity* superstructure radiated out in all directions, creating extra hallways and rooms. Some were covered in metal, while others had been formed by stretching lengths of highly durable colored fabrics over metal grids.

"It's ingenious, what you've done here," said Jahn.

He looked back to see his father smiling, flushed with pride. Jahn frowned. "I wish I could have helped."

"I had to leave you in stasis until we had our medical facilities prepared. But that's behind us now."

Jahn nodded absently. "Will you tell me what happened to Mother now?"

The silence that followed told Jahn more than he needed to know. He took another sip of the liquor in the glass and grimaced. *It really does taste bad.*

Pravin came up behind him to the window. "Is she dead?" asked Jahn, ignoring the shakiness in his own voice. Down below him, he could see tiny lights winking in the farms.

"No," said Pravin. "Pria is in stasis, as you were."

"Then she can still be awakened, like I was!"

"Jahn, your mother was awakened on the *Unity*. She was shot in the back, several times, during the infighting on the ship. She was dying. I had to put her back into cryo." Pravin's voice cracked a little.

Back into cryo. Jahn knew what that meant. He remembered the warnings against putting people back into cryosleep once they had awakened.

He turned and looked at his father, and saw the tears forming in his eyes as he remembered his beloved wife. Jahn felt his father's grief, and his own grief, mingling in the room above the alien surface of Chiron. Jahn gripped his father's shoulder, and then put his arm around him.

"What happened up there?" Jahn asked.

"Human nature," said Pravin quietly. "And we can't ever let it happen again."

chapter two

Six years later

JAHN LAL WENT INTO A CROUCH ON THE PADDED FLOOR OF
the training room, keeping his eyes fixed on his opponent, a young Japanese man named Rankojin
who had trained with some visiting Spartan citizens for over a year. The young man, who called
himself Rank, had removed his shirt and now
flexed muscles that were slick with sweat, keeping
them warm and loose. Jahn still wore a loose-fitting
gi with which he hoped to distract his opponent,
and then use the tightly woven fabric edges for a
choke.

Ever since we found the Spartans I've been on edge,
thought Jahn. He hadn't seen many Spartans, but
when he did meet one he or she was invariably in
top physical condition, and that spurred Jahn on to
greater efforts in his own training.

He straightened up and circled again. Rank
moved warily, keeping on his toes. He danced forward and Jahn lunged for his leg, but Rank danced
back. They circled again.

"Did you take dancing lessons or fighting lessons

from the Spartans?" asked Jahn, taking a moment to wipe the sweat from his eyes.

"Either one would be enough to wear out a Peacekeeper," said Rank with a feral grin. "And if this were a real fight I'd take that hair of yours and jerk you all over this ring."

"Lucky for me you don't think this is a real fight." Jahn shifted his weight, feeling his connection to the floor. He had picked up a pattern in Rank's movements: two jogs forward, one back, two forward, one back.

"Well?" Rank started to say, and at that moment Jahn lunged forward, ducking his head and grabbing his opponent's forward leg. Rank grunted, startled. He was unable to pull away in time, so Jahn pushed forward, shoving his opponent down onto the mat. He felt a hard blow to one shoulder, as if he had been hit with a sharp stone, and he ducked his head again, pushing his face close to Rank's body to minimize the leverage behind any more blows.

Rank breathed heavily and tried to squirm away, but Jahn quickly wrapped his arms and legs around his opponent, keeping close against his center of gravity. Every time his opponent moved an arm, Jahn moved with him, and every time he tried to shift away, Jahn hit him in the kidneys with short punches.

"You know some technique," Rank breathed, trying to get a hand around Jahn's throat, but Jahn knew better and kept his head low. Then he felt a tension in his opponent's hips and knew that Rank was about to make a brute-force attempt to stand and shake Jahn's hold.

Jahn waited, melding himself as closely as possible to Rank's center of gravity, feeling every shift in weight. When Rank shouted and lunged to his feet, Jahn quickly whipped around and grabbed the man's foot in a submission hold. Rank fell with a grunt of pain and Jahn twisted his foot around, grinning with glee and waiting for his opponent to tap out, surrendering the match.

Rank tried to grab Jahn's ankle, but Jahn kept close to his body, putting increasing pressure on his opponent's foot at an angle no human bone was made to turn. He felt Rank thrashing around like a drowning fish, his phenomenal muscle strength nearly lifting Jahn off the mat, but Jahn put every ounce of his weight into twisting the foot.

"Give up!" he said through clenched teeth, but his opponent didn't answer. Jahn kept twisting, and even looked up to see if he was missing Rank's taps of surrender on the mat. But Rank thrashed wildly, his face flushed with anger, and Jahn watched him, mesmerized.

He felt something start to give in the foot and heard a series of light pops. Still Rank had not tapped out, and in fact now stared at him with a burning gaze that looked something like hatred.

He's not tapping out. I'm going to break his ankle!

Jahn felt another pop, and suddenly he let go and rolled away. Rank hopped to his feet with a shout and started running at Jahn with a pronounced limp.

"Stop!" Jahn shouted, jumping to his feet. Rank plowed into him, and the two went down to the mat. "It's over!" Jahn said.

Rank got up again, his face still flushed with exertion. "I didn't tap out, Peacekeeper," he said, jabbing his finger at Jahn.

Jahn stood up, feeling heat flush his own face. "I stopped so you could still walk out of here," he said angrily.

Rank stepped forward, flexing his arms. "Undecided, Jahn. You didn't finish it."

Jahn started to say something, but he felt a fury rising in him and knew it would not bode well for their friendship to express it. He turned away in disgust. "I'm heading for the showers."

He walked toward the padded door to the workout room, and when he reached it he heard his friend grunting and shouting repeatedly. He turned back to see Rank shadowboxing in the middle of the room, making furious jabs at a phantom opponent.

Jahn left the room and closed the door.

He entered the closest shower room, which was empty at this hour except for a stocky young woman just finishing a tepid shower. He stripped off his *gi* and stepped under another shower nozzle, feeling the cool water wash over him. He rinsed off and dried himself with a thin towel, half hoping his friend would show up so they could talk about . . . whatever had happened in there.

A beeping sound came from his uniform, piled on a low bench. He picked it up, checking the small, flexible "quicklink" computer that was built into the sleeve and that linked him with other citizens around the base.

The council meeting was convening. He put on his uniform and was about to rush out the door, but he stopped at a small mirror and adjusted his hair, combing it as well as he could.

* * *

"I hear your father has done a little remodeling in the meeting room," said Pierson as he came up next to Jahn in the Planet Walk outside the conference room. "I guess we've all learned to humor him about his little projects that don't help humans survive on Chiron."

"What kind of little projects do you mean, Pierson?" asked Jahn, annoyed, although he knew exactly what the man was talking about.

"This hallway, for example," said Pierson, gesturing to the glass walls around them. "Do you know how many rooms went without windows in this base so that Pravin could build this hallway right after planetfall?"

"This is a monument to the beauty of Chiron, and it inspires our citizens."

"But it does nothing to help us survive," said Pierson, and Jahn could see the man puffing up, enjoying the verbal sparring.

"It lifts our spirits, and my father is most interested in reconnecting us with our humanity. If we're all going to live in dark boxes and eat gruel, we may as well have reverted back to protoplasm," said Jahn.

"Well stated," came a voice that played down Jahn's back like a musical scale. He turned to see Sophia, dressed in a clean blue uniform and walking with two other council members. "I love this place."

"And I would love a nice thick steak for dinner and a hot tub in my quarters, but a clean place for the children to live is more important," said Pierson, but the heat had gone out of his argument. "Anyway, let's get inside."

He turned and pushed his way through the doorway into the council room. Jahn swept his hand forward, indicating that he would follow Sophia, and then walked in after her.

The Peacekeeper base that Pravin had founded was named United Nations Headquarters, to remind people of the United Nations charter that set forth the goals of the Alpha Centauri mission. Like most of the other citizens living in the base, Jahn had taken to calling the base UNHQ for short.

The council room of UNHQ occupied the bottom portion of the tall cylinder that used to be part of the fuel injector mechanism for the *Unity* and that now served as the heart of the base. The cylinder had several floors, created by welding sheets of thick metal into place at various heights, including the observation deck on the top floor. Pravin had chosen to give the council room an unusually high ceiling—about 10 meters high, by Jahn's estimation—to create a feeling of spaciousness. Another one of his "little projects."

In the center of the floor rested a semicircular conference table made of black metal sheared cleanly from the outer shell of a landing pod. Around the table sat several chairs, also from *Unity*, stuffed and comfortable but many torn and scorched from the explosion that had rocked the *Unity*'s command center during the descent.

Jahn and the other advisors took seats around the table. After a moment Pravin entered and walked briskly to the center seat.

"Greetings, everyone. I hope you're having a good day here in the new world," he said. There were murmurs of assent.

"Let's begin. Many of our citizens have been hard at work, in more ways than one, I see: I notice that our children's quarters are almost full." There were some appreciative chuckles. "It's very heartening to see that life continues even around this new star. But we must continue to advance the ideals of the mission. How are the food supplies?"

"They're holding up," said Pierson. "We have surplus that we store away. It's been good having some contact with Deirdre Skye's citizens. They eat, breathe, and shit plant life."

Don't we all, thought Jahn, momentarily craving a good piece of meat.

"Very good," said Pravin. "It is unfortunate that our scout patrols must spend so much time exploring and so little time establishing better contact with Deirdre Skye and her people."

"I agree," said Pierson, "but perhaps for different reasons. I'd like to know what Skye is up to, and Morgan and Santiago as well. They're very far from central command." Jahn noticed how everyone on the council of advisors assumed that UNHQ was the center command for all of the settlements. "I propose that we use our resources to build another fleet of rovers. I think our technicians are up to the challenge."

"I have a counterproposal," said Pravin. "I suggest that we start to assemble a group of people to colonize a new base. Our scouts have found a marvelous piece of land to the southwest. There is good rainfall there, and sunlight on the upper elevations, and our surveyors believe that good minerals exist in abundance. A colony there could double our overall production, and in turn help us expand our headquarters into something very special, an inspiration for all the citizens on Chiron."

There was some stirring as people considered this proposal.

"I don't object in principle," said Eldridge. "In fact, I think our citizens have earned the right to live in a habitat that inspires them. But I think we're looking too far ahead. I share Pierson's concern about the other pod leaders. Santiago worries me in particular. I find it psychologically telling that she named her base Sparta Command, and I would like to send a team to investigate her."

"We have the authority to investigate any of the settlements, of course," said Pravin.

"Do we?" asked Pierson. "We take it for granted that Captain Garland passed control of the mission to us before the *Unity* blew up . . ."

To my father, not to you, Jahn corrected him mentally.

". . . But Santiago or any of these people could make the case that command passed to Executive Officer Yang, who is nowhere to be found," Pierson finished.

"Control passed to me, by word of Captain Garland himself," Pravin said firmly.

"Father, I have one more consideration," said Jahn. "Santiago may know that command of the settlements lies with you, but what if she doesn't care?"

No one spoke for a moment.

"What you are suggesting, Jahn, is mutiny," said Pravin.

"We know it happened up there," said Jahn, gesturing skyward. "And I hope to Chiron it never happens again. But there is no planetary police force that will go to Sparta for us and order Santiago to do our bidding."

"Well said!" interjected Pierson. "In fact, if there is a planetary police force, it's probably run by Santiago herself."

"Which returns me to my proposal," said Pravin. "Let's send out a small group of colonists to lay the groundwork for a new base. There doesn't need to be any major building for now. They will only explore and begin another set of farms. The location I have selected is closer to Santiago, so we can assist her with additional food supplies as well as keep a better eye on her. It will be good for all of us."

"I would prefer that we build faster scouts and construct some sensors along our perimeter," said Pierson. "You never know what could be out there."

"No sensors," said Pravin. "New rooms for the children and some solar collectors on the high ridge are more important. We still have our regular armed patrols to warn us of any attacks."

"I'd like a vote," responded Pierson. Pravin nodded his agreement, and all ten advisors bowed their heads and typed a vote into the touchscreens by their seats.

"Six to four in favor of the sensors," said Pravin. He lapsed into thought for a moment. "This is a narrow majority. I am exercising my veto power. We will build the sensors in due time, but not now. I am working on a plan that will increase our mineral production dramatically, after which we can address the sensor issue again." He looked them all in the eye, reinforcing his authority. "Meeting adjourned."

Jahn stood in the Planet Walk, talking quietly to Sophia about some of the issues raised during the council meeting. As they talked his eyes kept drifting to the rich orange light of the Centauri sunset, and then back to her face to watch how the light rested there.

"Your father is a good man," said Sophia. "I hope the others can see that. He doesn't seek power for power's sake."

"Yes, but his dreams of peace and prosperity tend to make them a little nervous. The trouble with idealists is that they tend not to be realists."

"Someone has to aim high, though." Sophia reached out and casually touched his arm. He felt that electric thrill go through him again, and he reflected how happy he was to be back in shape.

"I haven't felt this good in years," he said. "Decades, if you count the cryosleep." He looked at her, hypnotized by her eyes, and then he started to lean in. She drew away slightly, and her expression became apologetic.

"Your father is our leader," she said. "And even after six years, I really don't know you that well."

"Does that matter?" Jahn's mood crashed with disappointment. He reached out to touch her hand, hoping she wouldn't pull away again.

"Jahn," said a voice, quiet but edgy. Jahn looked up to see Rankojin standing in the hallway about ten meters away. His friend stood stiffly, his hands folded across his chest, but Jahn thought he could see vulnerability in Rank's face.

Jahn looked back at Sophia, inwardly shaking his head as the moment slipped away. "Please excuse me," he said. "I hope you understand."

Sophia nodded with a regal tilt of her head, her face already composed into a perfect mask. "That's all right." She turned, nodded politely at Rankojin, then headed down the hallway.

As soon as Sophia was gone Rank dropped his guard, and his face seemed to collapse into an expression of deep regret. "I'm sorry for what happened in the training room," he said. "There's no excuse."

"Accepted. . . . But I can't say I understand. You became a different person in there."

"You *know* what I became," said Rank.

"I don't know what you mean."

"I became a Spartan," Rank said bluntly, looking at Jahn through dark eyes. "Their training has gotten under my skin."

Jahn stared at his friend. "A Spartan would rather lose an ankle than lose a fight?"

"I didn't lose either, Jahn. I didn't yield; you stopped. The Spartans have incredible tolerance for pain, and they don't surrender. If you had broken my foot and stood up to leave, I would have kept on fighting."

Jahn shook his head, still trying to fathom this new side to his friend. "So because I refused to break your ankle you think you won the fight?"

"I know I didn't lose the fight. And because of your concern for me, you don't really know if you won."

"You learned this from training with them for a year?"

"What I learned is nothing. They're starting to train their young at an early age. I hear these kids have to be chained to the floor sometimes, to stop them from fighting after they've lost a match. The best of them, their elite troops, won't admit defeat."

"Who are they fighting against?" asked Jahn, thinking of the council meeting that had just passed, and Pierson's statement that Santiago's people might be the closest thing to a planetary police.

"Just each other, and the mindworms. But I hope it never goes beyond that." He clapped Jahn on the shoulder and turned away.

"Would you like to go for a drink?" Jahn asked, mostly hoping his friend would turn him down so he could have time to absorb all of this.

Rank shook his head. "I've asked for fungus patrol tonight. Maybe later we'll spar again."

"Not if I can help it," said Jahn, and smiled. Rank walked away, flashing the old Earth sign for peace as he left.

All Jahn could think about was the cracking sounds in his friend's foot, and how little he understood the Spartan mind.

Santiago pushed open a narrow wooden door somewhere in the center of Sparta Command and entered a small viewing room with windows on three sides. She closed the door and stepped to the opposite window.

Below her she could see the Birthing Room. Spartan women, some citizens but many simple workers and noncombatants, lay in hard beds around a large square room, with almost no privacy. The food supplies were still low and so the birthrate was even lower, but six of the beds were still occupied, each with a metal bucket of water at the foot. A nurse in a white tunic sat on a stool at the foot of one of the beds, where a brunette with a flushed and sweaty face gasped against the pain.

"Push now, Citizen," said the nurse. "Once more and this should be over."

The woman gave no indication that she had heard the nurse, but gasped in pain and contorted her body again. A bloody rag lay at the foot of the bed, under the nurse's feet.

Santiago watched to see if the woman would demand drugs, but she did not, and Santiago nodded approvingly. *Her offspring will be strong,* she thought.

The door to the viewing room opened behind her and a man walked in, wearing the simple white tunic of a Spartan medic. She turned and accepted his salute.

"Colonel Santiago," said the man.

"Captain Kimura," Santiago said. The captain went directly to one of the other windows, and Santiago joined him.

Below them lay the children's quarters. The long, wide room was scattered with all kinds of toys and equipment, from small stuffed fighting dummies to rings and ropes to hanging targets. Wooden swords, poles, and small shields lay in neat piles around the floor.

There were about fifty children in the room, ranging in age from two to seven, watched by five adults in brown tunics. Infants wore diapers and ran about the room in energetic play, while the other children, male and female, wore only loincloths and engaged in more structured play to develop their bodies.

"There are many good fighters down there," said Captain Kimura. "See that black-haired one. He has a good hand with the sword."

"Yes," Santiago agreed. "And that girl with the blond hair. She attacks the heavy bags like a banshee."

The captain nodded and took out a touchpanel. He looked at each child in turn, making notes about their development.

"The green-eyed boy. I think it is time," said Kimura. Santiago looked down. In one corner, two older boys sat in a pile of straw, practicing a basic parry-and-riposte sword movement with agonizing slowness. One of them had soft features and green eyes, while the other sat in a slightly hunched posture and had a perfectly shaved head.

As Santiago watched, one of the attendants came over and began to beat the green-eyed boy about the head and shoulders with her fist. He began sobbing almost immediately, which infuriated the attendant even more.

Captain Kimura watched for a few moments, then shouted down through the window, "That won't be necessary. The lad's time has come."

Several of the children looked up, unusually quiet. Santiago watched as the attendant grabbed the boy and pulled him across the room and through a narrow wooden door. Santiago closed her eyes and imagined the scene behind the door . . . the drawing of the blade, then the quick cut across the throat.

A scream sounded from behind the door, high and afraid, like a baby's cry. It ended quickly. *Food supplies are short,* Santiago reminded herself.

"Unfortunately, your son will now have to find another playmate," said the captain calmly, and turned to walk out the door.

"Paula," Jahn whispered. The sleeping form next to him grunted and stirred, but did not awaken.

He slipped out of the narrow bed and felt around in the pitch darkness for his clothes. He finally found his uniform and felt his way to the quicklink on the sleeve, which had a small light built in. He turned it on, and a soft white glow illuminated the tiny room.

He stood over Paula, looking at her pleasantly rounded form underneath the sheets. After sleeping in the common quarters for years, he had decided that using his father's influence wasn't such a bad idea, and put in for a small room built during the last base expansion. Since then Paula had approached him often, wanting companionship and relief from the crowded sleeping quarters.

That's not completely fair, he told himself. *She feels genuine affection for me.*

He looked at her body again, and again he began to imagine the long, slender form of Sophia stretched out on his bed, and her lush black hair and this soft light on her face. He reached out and touched Paula on the shoulder, filled with a deep remorse that he could no longer look at her without thinking of another woman.

I have to forget about her, he thought, testing the thought, letting it sink into his mind.

His mind churned. Knowing he wouldn't get back to sleep, he put on his uniform and slipped out into the dark hallway.

He found himself in the Planet Walk, and from there he went up the narrow metal staircase to the observation deck, where he found his father. Two other citizens slept curled together on a couch in the far corner of the room, but Pravin ignored them, staring out over the dark landscape. The two moons, Nessus and Pholus, floated in the sky. Alpha Centauri B was not currently visible in the night sky.

"Father," said Jahn softly, and sat next to him.

Neither seemed surprised to find the other there in the middle of the night. "What did you think of the council meeting today?"

"It seemed to go well," said Pravin.

"There was some tension."

"Indeed. I know you are not an official part of the council of advisors, Jahn, but I do value your input. You have managed to earn their respect." He paused. "I am proud of you."

"Thank you."

"You also seem to get along particularly well with one of them," Pravin said, looking at him.

"Pierson? We get along all right." Jahn couldn't stop the smile from breaking across his face. *Sophia.*

"Marriage did go out of style on Earth, of course, but there are those of us who still shoot the moon," Pravin said, referring to Pria. "The rewards are great if you choose the correct person. And on this new world, the tighter social structure of having a Chosen can benefit a child, as well as the society as a whole."

"We'll have to see. Right now she doesn't really even know me." Jahn felt a little stab of pain in his gut.

Pravin nodded. "And do you wonder if she is a Perfect?"

"She appears that way to me." Jahn knew that his father would have full access to the records that detailed the genetic profiles of everyone on the crew. He thought a moment. "I really don't care if she is or not."

Pravin nodded as if in approval. "Jahn, I want you to know my intentions for the future, so you can understand and perhaps support me in council. I have been talking frequently to Deirdre Skye and Nwabudike Morgan. As you know, they have specialized heavily, Deirdre in plant genetics and Nwabudike in mining and production."

"I hear he has beautiful living quarters, and that he seduces his citizens with luxuries," said Jahn.

"Rumors have a tendency to grow away from the truth, but there is a basis to what you say. I feel that we can forge an alliance with these two and get food and raw materials to expand this base into something worth living in, something far beyond the survival facilities that characterize the settlements now."

Jahn nodded, seeing the wisdom of his plan. Pravin continued, "If we focus our citizens too much on threats that haven't materialized, we will antagonize the other leaders and hurt our ability to create a solid foundation for future prosperity."

"Still, violence is always a possibility. In fact, I wanted to tell you about this Spartan training."

Pravin nodded and touched Jahn's arm to regain his attention. "I know the Spartans could be valuable as allies, Jahn, but right now Skye and Morgan are the most important. I want this base to be for all of us, as a symbol of hope for everyone on Chiron, all human citizens. I want to make it large and open, a real city with monuments and whatever culture our citizens can produce. Art and music and history. Can you see that?"

Jahn could see the fire of idealism shining in his father's eyes, an idealism that inspired others to follow him and that assured him his position on the *Unity*. Jahn felt for a moment like a small child again, staring at his father, the orator for peace, and he nodded.

"We need this vision, Jahn. I want to make it happen. And I do not think the others can see yet how important it is. It will knit the settlements back together again."

"It's a good dream."

"And when we build it, it will become a center for engineering and science as well. The science of healing, Jahn." Pravin grabbed his son's wrist and held it firmly. "We can save your mother. I know we can bring her back from the sleep."

Jahn did not look at his father this time, but kept his eyes on the night sky outside, where two alien moons floated impassively.

chapter three

One month later

JAHN STOOD OUTSIDE, FEELING THE WARMTH OF ALPHA Centauri A on his shoulders. He wore his regular uniform, but over his face he wore a lightweight pressure mask made of translucent plastic, which connected to a compact oxygen unit on his back. His breath fogged the faceplate every time he exhaled, but humans could not breathe the thick, nitrogen-rich air of Chiron for very long without some unpleasant side effects.

Although, I hear some of the side effects are pretty pleasant for a while, he thought. He had read security reports about some of the younger, more adventurous crew going outside and taking off their masks for a while, letting the high concentration of nitrogen in the air give them a "natural" high.

Jahn walked around several large water tanks that stood on platforms just outside the base, looking for the two technicians that were working on the broken water filtration system. He found them laboring beside a large metal box. Inside Jahn could see metal filters and smaller pressurized tanks, plus a large pipe driven into Chiron's red soil.

"How's it coming?" Jahn asked.

"One of the valves has stuck closed, sir," said a technician. "It could be a computer malfunction."

"Is the facilities manager sure the water's unsafe?" asked the second technician, a thin, high-strung man.

"Yes," said Jahn. "The nitrogen isn't being filtered from the water. We've had to go to our backup water supply."

"Well, everything looks all right in here," said the first technician. "I'll call the code guys and see what's put a bug up the system's ass."

Jahn reached down to slap the man on the back when a loud explosion hit his ears like a thunderclap and rattled the metal tanks.

"What was that?" shouted the second technician, looking around the purifier tanks frantically.

"It came from over there," said Jahn, breathing deeply to calm his racing heart. He looked past the edge of UNHQ to where some of the new farms pushed lush green Earth hybrids into the pale blue sky. He could see a thick cloud of smoke rising slowly from the long storage building beyond the fields.

"What's happening?" asked the first technician.

Jahn had already started running toward the farms, even though they were at least a half kilometer away. As he ran he activated his quicklink and located the link address of the head farm worker on duty.

"Foreman Takai, are you there? This is Jahn Lal from UNHQ."

There was no answer except static. Jahn quickly

dialed the second-in-command, and a frantic voice came on almost immediately.

"Help us!" came the ragged voice.

"Stay calm. Help is on the way," said Jahn. *Of course, that's only me for the time being.* "What's happening over there?"

"Attack," said the woman, her breath coming in gasps. "There are people here with guns. We're trying to shut the main doors—" Suddenly, an uneven burst of staccato gunfire crackled through the connection, and the woman broke the link.

"Can you still hear me?" he shouted. He continued to run, his legs burning from the effort, but he felt as if he were approaching the farms at a crawl.

I wonder how much oxygen my tank really holds, he thought, dialing a connection to the security advisor inside the base. He had grabbed a small tank today, thinking he would be out for only a half hour or so.

"Goorman, this is Jahn Lal. I'm outside the base and headed for the farms. We have citizens under attack by an unknown force, armed with guns and possibly explosives."

There was a pause before a deep male voice replied, sounding as if the man had just awakened from a nap. "What? Are you certain that this is a deliberate attack?"

"Affirmative. I have no visual contact yet, but shots were fired and there are citizens down. I need you to tell the maintenance crew to stand down. Don't let them approach the farm buildings. Commandeer their vehicles and approach carefully from the flanks. And put someone up in the observation tower."

"Of course," said Goorman, but Jahn could hear

some confusion in his voice. *It's like he never believed something could really happen.*

"Do you have all of that?"

"Yes, of course. I have to locate the armory key."

"Then do it!" shouted Jahn. "There are at least fifty citizens working these farms. I'll report again when I get there."

He broke the link and looked up to find himself only a few steps from the edge of the nearest fields. He saw the thick smoke beyond pushing slowly up into the heavy atmosphere, and he heard another explosion, followed by more gunfire. Then he plunged into the fields.

Corn. Centauri hybrid corn, he realized as the tall green stalks rose up around him. He felt cooler immediately, but had to slow his pace as he pushed through the massive stalks. Growing like wildfire in the nitrogen-rich soil, these hybrids rose three meters above him, closing off the sky.

He stopped for a moment, listening for any other movements. The gunshots seemed to be coming from the main storage shed. He began to angle off, wanting to approach from the flank, and started running again. The thick green stalks crashed around him, and the rich plant smell filled his lungs even through the filters on his pressure mask.

I have no weapon. The thought finally occurred to him. He glanced around helplessly as if one of the corn stalks would be growing shredder pistols. *Have to improvise . . .*

He saw light ahead and slowed his pace, finally parting stalks of corn to look out from the edge of the fields. About ten meters away stood the large metal storage building. He could near nothing but the wind, and he wondered if he had somehow imagined the attack, when suddenly he heard another burst of gunfire inside the building. Thick smoke rose on the other side, where the main doors were located.

He looked back toward UNHQ. He heard no sound of rovers or any activity. *Looks like the cavalry isn't coming.*

In the corner of the storage building closest to him he could see a large, glass-paned window. He got into a crouch and crossed to the window, then stood up and peered in.

The inside of the building consisted of one large, shadowy room filled with crates and various pieces of mechanized farm equipment. On the wall opposite him he could see two large metal doors on tracks, one of them open and letting sunlight stream into the interior in a broad wedge, the only source of light. Scattered around the floor he could see the dark, crumpled forms of bodies, some obviously dead, some still moving weakly.

In the center of the building stood a group of white-robed people, men and women, most of them tall and rangy. They pointed around at the farm equipment and chattered loudly, ignoring the wounded.

He glanced down. Just beneath him, crouched behind some large plastic barrels, about eight Peacekeeper citizens were huddled in a small group.

Jahn suddenly heard guttural speech coming from around the corner of the building and footsteps approaching his position. He looked around quickly for a weapon and saw something glinting in the dirt.

It was the broken-off end of some kind of cutting implement, about a meter long. He hefted it, feeling its weight, and quietly jogged to the corner of the building.

He reached the corner just as two men came around it, almost running into him. He had a fleeting impression of matted, dirty hair and two tan but haggard faces behind dusty pressure masks. Both men grunted as Jahn jumped back, and then he saw one of them pull a rusty shredder pistol.

Got to keep this quiet . . .

He lunged forward and hooked the legs of the nearest man, throwing him onto his back, then turned and swung the metal blade hard into the other man. He felt the blade bite deep into skin and then bone, and saw a look of shock come over eyes that were bright blue beneath the pressure mask. Jahn grabbed for the shredder pistol, but the man fell backwards, a red stain blooming on dirty white cloth.

The smell of these people!

The second man rolled to his feet and came up with another pistol from somewhere in his robes, his eyes burning with some kind of intense battle fanaticism. He drew a breath to yell and Jahn lunged forward, wrapping himself around the man's body.

His opponent's muscles felt thin but as strong as bands of steel. The two rolled on the ground, and Jahn stayed close against the man's body, conscious of the pistol banging into the side of his head as the man tried to position it for a shot.

He's too strong, Jahn realized. *Time to fight dirty.*

His hand found the man's pressure mask and he tore it off. The man grinned savagely and spat at Jahn, obviously knowing that breathing the air did not mean immediate death. Jahn grabbed a handful of red Centauri earth and threw it hard into the man's face. His opponent blinked furiously and spit out what sounded like a cross between a curse and a prayer. Suddenly Jahn felt a sharp pain in his throat as his opponent jabbed him with a hand that felt like leather-wrapped iron.

Jahn put his hand into the man's hair and jerked his head around, throwing him off balance. Next he wrapped his hands in the man's tangled white robes and found a seam near the collar.

Rolling over, Jahn wrapped himself around the man's back and pulled the seam around his throat, cutting deeply into the carotid artery. He leaned back and continued to apply pressure with all his strength. The man lurched to his feet and then fell over on his stomach, but Jahn did not let go. He heard the shredder pistol discharge, the sound oddly muffled.

Something's wrong. But he didn't release the choke until the man slackened underneath him.

He stood up and turned the man's body over. The shredder pistol had discharged underneath him, and blood stained the robes near his belly. Jahn picked up the pistol, which was old and in desperate need of maintenance. Then something on the body caught his eye, and he bent over for a closer look.

Around the man's neck hung a silver cross. He flipped it over and on the back he saw the word *Believer.*

Jahn took up a position, crouched along the side of the building, with his attacker's shredder pistol in hand. He had left the two dead men behind him, both in their bloody robes, thankful that the fight had taken place in relative silence. Now he looked toward the front of the building, where three of the

"Believers" stood next to a poorly maintained scout rover and one of the farm's mechanized threshers, talking and pointing at the equipment.

"Jahn Lal to command," he whispered into his quicklink, and the military advisor's voice responded after a moment.

"Yes, this is Goorman."

"I'm at the side of the storage building. Are you in the observation tower?"

"I'm here, with your father and some of the other advisors." *Sophia?* Jahn wanted to ask, but didn't. "We have rovers outfitted and on the way."

"I don't hear them yet," said Jahn.

"They're at the main gate," came the voice of Sophia, sending a warm rush through him. "The soldiers are checking their equipment and then they're all coming out, Jahn."

"Good. Tell them to approach quietly." Jahn filled them in quickly on what he had learned of the attack. "Park the rovers at the rear of the building, one on each side. There are some citizens inside the rear window; put two soldiers there, and send the rest around to each side of the building. I'm at the northwest corner."

There was a pause, and he could imagine the squabbling as the military advisor engaged in a turf war. Finally Pravin's voice came on. "It will be done, Jahn. I'd like you to fall back and stay with the rover, Son."

"For efficiency's sake, I'll coordinate the attack," Jahn said, leaving it open as to whether he had heard his father. "On my mark, we'll close in from both sides. And send medical help quickly. Lots of it." *For them or for us.*

He finally heard a rover approach the back of the building, moving slowly to minimize the noise of its engine. He heard the hatches open and looked back to see Peacekeepers in thick work suits running toward him, holding shredder pistols. Four headed in his direction, and he thought he saw five head to the other side.

The four crouched behind him. The first citizen to reach him touched his shoulder and handed him a well-oiled weapon. Inside the pressure helmet, Jahn could see the calm face of Rank.

"What's the plan?" Rank asked, his finger twitching on a modified shredder semiautomatic.

"The enemy is in two groups, one outside the shed by a rover and a thresher, the other inside," said Jahn. "There are friendlies hidden in the southwest corner. We don't have time for subtlety, so we'll go in on my mark from both sides. Deadly force is authorized."

"Basic tactics," said Rank, and Jahn wasn't sure if Rank was congratulating him or berating him for not coming up with something better. He thought back to his hand-to-hand training, and how his instructor had emphasized angles of attack.

Angles of attack, Jahn thought, and then looked up. *Would they expect an attack from above?*

"I'm going up to the roof," said Jahn. "You lead the attack on this side."

Rank nodded. Jahn ran back to the southwest corner and used the rover parked there to boost himself up to the edge of the roof. He hurried across the hot metal in a crouch.

"Go," he said into his quicklink.

The Peacekeepers exploded from both sides of

the storage building, spreading out and raking gunfire into the scruffy white figures standing around
the rover. The Believers turned and, instead of running for cover, pulled out their weapons and
opened fire, strangely silent. Jahn came over the lip
of the roof to see a tall Believer wrapped in white
jerk back repeatedly, fire raking his belly, but the
man still fired back, cutting two Peacekeepers
down at the knees. The two fell, howling in pain.

Jahn pulled out the shredder pistol and took aim.
He opened fire, shifting his aim from the chest to
the head as he saw the Believers crouch and continue to fire, in spite of bloody patches spreading on
their shoulders, chests, and legs. He took down two
of them, their heads jerking back from the impact,
but even those two kept their fingers locked on their
triggers, sending a stream of rounds into the sky.

In a moment, all of the Believers outside were
down.

"Go inside!" Jahn ordered through his quicklink.
Several of the Peacekeepers hesitated, bewildered
by the violence erupting around them, but Rank
ran for the doors with a shout. He performed a
smooth commando roll into the entrance and Jahn
heard the gunfire echo harshly inside the metal
walls of the storage building.

Jahn looked around, seeing a hatch in the roof.
He ran to it and threw it open, then dropped down
into a low-ceilinged attic filled with piles of shred-
ded vegetable matter and bags of fertilizer. The air
was hot and a thick dust filled the air. A line of gunfire exploded through the metal floor from the
fighting below.

He took a breath and found himself sucking on

nothing. His oxygen had run out, and in the heat of battle he had neglected to ask for a fresh tank. He tore the mask from his face and threw it and the tank to the floor.

Jahn ran to a square hole in the attic floor and jumped down into the melee. Rank had charged the Believers in the center of the room, where they had put their backs to a bladed thresher. One of them shot at Rank point-blank, hitting him in the chest and throwing him back, but then the Believer's weapon misfired. Jahn felt his heart leap into his throat.

Rank climbed to his feet and lunged into the Believer with a howl of fury. The Believer staggered back under the assault, his back crunching into a thresher blade. Rank pressed his advantage and swung his shredder savagely, splitting the man's skull.

Jahn had only a moment to register his shock at the violence of Rank's attack. The remaining Believers started to scatter toward the back of the building, where two Peacekeepers had come through the back window. Jahn could imagine the hidden farm workers getting caught in the crossfire.

He grabbed a release cord for the attic storage area and pulled it with all his strength. A large trapdoor in the ceiling opened, spilling tons of vegetable matter onto the floor below. Bags of fertilizer burst open, filling the air with clouds of white dust. Jahn ran through the clouds, feeling as if his mind were departing his body. He fired into the Believers, suddenly sure he looked like an apparition, emerging from the churning clouds.

A Believer turned on him with some kind of crude rocket canister and Jahn shot the man in the chest and legs. Suddenly the swirling fertilizer in the air ignited, rocking the shed with an explosive impact. Jahn felt himself lifted on a cushion of hot air and thrown forward, toward the doors of the shed and toward the light coming through them.

I think it's over, thought Jahn, and let himself close his eyes for a moment.

He opened his eyes and found himself in the aftermath of the battle, lying in a far corner of the shed. Everything was quiet, and no one seemed to know where he had gone. He got to his feet and staggered outside, the soupy Chiron air filling his lungs and making him feel lightheaded.

He saw a Peacekeeper rover pull up to the front of the building. He looked at it with relief as the hatch opened and several high-ranking people stepped out. Even with their translucent pressure masks in place, he could tell that one of them was his father, one was the stocky form of Pierson, and one was Sophia.

Jahn staggered toward them, his muscles barely able to support his body, and lifted an arm to wave. The sky seemed to get brighter as giddiness washed over him. The sky engulfed the figures, which turned to bright blurs.

He started to laugh uncontrollably and felt the world shift under him, or was that his legs giving out? He saw one of the blurry figures heading for him at a run, and then a sweet smell filled his nose as hands touched him on the shoulders and chest.

His lips opened to say something and he saw, through a haze, Sophia removing her pressure mask and bending over him, touching him, and

then he felt her wet mouth on his for a moment.
Or so he thought.

He felt the rigid surface of a pressure mask enclose
his face, and then a burst of clean oxygenated air.

"Just lie here," he heard her say. "You'll be all
right."

He breathed in the air and let himself float.

"You're fine," said the medic, nodding. Jahn
nodded too, and felt his chest gingerly. He had lots
of bruises but no major injuries.

He got up slowly, swinging his feet off the bed.
He was in one of the medlabs, a large, sterile room
with several dozen monitored beds and a bank of
cool white lights overhead. It was the most modern
room in all of UNHQ, he realized.

On a nearby bed lay Rank, his face a calm mask
and his eyes open. A large pressure bandage encir-
cled his midsection, but his eyes looked clear, and
Jahn was suddenly sure that Rank had refused pain
medication.

"I told you I'd keep fighting," said Rank. He
looked at Jahn. "But why I am I telling you? You
fought with a Spartan's spirit, all the way until the
end." He smiled. "At least I still had oxygen."

Jahn smiled back weakly, his thoughts elsewhere.

"Your father is over there." Rank nodded to the
other side of the medlab.

"Thanks." Jahn gripped his friend's hand. On the
beds to either side of Rank, Peacekeepers lay unconscious, red monitor lights measuring out what
might be their last hours. One of them had been
hit in the throat, and Jahn could hear a gurgling
sound with each breath.

It always comes back to this, he suddenly realized, and remembered the feeling of the blade in his hand sinking into the body of the first Believer.

Jahn made his way over to a corner of the medlab where his father, Sophia, and some of the other advisors were holding an impromptu meeting. He still wore his torn and dusty uniform, and knew that scratches still covered his face and arms, but he didn't think anyone would stand on ceremony.

"Jahn," said his father quietly, gripping his hand. Sophia looked at him briefly, then quickly looked away, as if embarrassed. *Now what's happening?*

"I'm all right," said Jahn.

"You did well, Jahn," said Pierson. He nodded his head. "It was a good fight. You saved lives."

"And maybe cost some," said Jahn, looking around the medlab.

"The attackers all had those silver crosses," said Pravin. "Most of the attackers are dead, but two are just wounded. They won't talk much, but we gather they report to Miriam Godwinson."

"Where is she?" asked Jahn, startled.

"She landed far to the east. Her people are a long way from home. Apparently they've been plagued by mindworm attacks since they landed, and they're surrounded by xenofungus. They have almost no equipment from the *Unity,* and they've come to rely on a deep faith in God to help them through this time of crisis."

"So they came here to steal our food?" asked Sophia. She still hadn't looked in Jahn's direction. *Is she angry that I risked my life? Did I imagine our kiss?*

"I need to contact Miriam somehow, but she

sounds very far away," said Pravin. "I can't imagine she authorized these attacks. Still, we'll have to strengthen our defenses." Pravin glanced at Pierson, who nodded tersely.

"We'll have a council tomorrow and talk further," said Pravin. He turned to Jahn. "Jahn, you'll have to be debriefed by our security advisor, I think. You might as well do it now, while the memories are still fresh."

"All right."

Pravin, Pierson, and Sophia walked away, and Jahn could see the weight of command on his father's shoulders.

It was well past nightfall when Jahn finally walked down the hallway to the shower rooms. Every part of him ached, and he still wore his torn and bloody uniform. The base felt dark and silent around him, as if no one dared to disturb the peace that they had once taken for granted.

The shower room was dark, lit only by a single glowlamp, but he didn't bother turning on any more lights. Everyone else from the battle had long since retired, and he liked the quiet peace.

"Peace," he said aloud, as if testing the word.

He pulled off his uniform gingerly, thinking of Paula and how nice it would be to have her caring for him now. *Too late for that,* he thought ruefully.

He stood under the water and let it run over his face and body. All of the hot water from the solar tanks was long gone, but even cold it was better than nothing.

The door to the shower room opened and closed again. He ignored it, leaving his eyes closed, until he realized that he had not heard a sound for over three minutes.

He opened his eyes to see Sophia standing outside of the showers, staring at him. She wore a comfortable white shift, the kind she might wear in her quarters, and her body emerged from the shadows in a series of soft curves. Her long dark hair, which usually fell around her shoulders, was pinned up with an elegant golden hair clip.

"Um," was all he could think to say. He stood facing her, his heart pounding, and she continued to watch him. Finally she stepped forward.

She reached out with her long, slender fingers to touch his face, and her eyes opened as wide as moons, and he became lost in all the shades of her irises, which were green and gray and gold. He finally reached out to brush the graceful curve of her neck, revealed to him beneath the piled sweeps of her hair.

The water from the shower bounced into her, soaking the front of her shift and molding it to her skin.

She stepped close to him, and he felt her clothes brush against his skin. She pulled her shift down around her shoulders and shrugged out of it, her body emerging from the wet cloth.

Jahn's heart pounded in his ears as he moved against her. Her eyes were wide as she began to kiss him. She touched his face every time he tried to speak, and it occurred to him she was living out some richly imagined fantasy.

Let her, he thought, and he embraced her fully, without speaking.

The next morning Jahn awoke to the golden light of twin suns falling across a bed as wide as any he had seen since landing on Chiron. He blinked against the light and sat up, feeling cool white sheets around him. Every muscle ached, yet somehow he felt better than he had felt since planetfall.

He was in Sophia's room, of course. As an advisor she had her pick of the best Chiron had to offer, which in UNHQ included a room that was larger than most—about eight meters square—and a large glass window.

And a double bed, he reflected, considering why she had chosen that luxury. Then he shrugged to himself. *Forget it. She's a grown woman.*

She was nowhere in the room. He lay back for a moment and closed his eyes against the sun, sinking into a reverie that included memories of their lovemaking in the shower, then a heart-pounding run through the back halls of the base, holding scraps of clothing against their naked bodies. *Which clearly excited her,* Jahn thought. *She appreciates danger.* And then her glorious bed, a world as wide and deep as any among the stars.

The door to her room clicked open, and he looked up to see her peering around the doorjamb at him. She smiled brightly as she entered the room and closed the door behind her.

"Good morning," he said, feeling that the heat of his own smile rivaled the sunlight coming in through the window.

"Good morning." She sat on the edge of the bed and ran her fingers along his arm. He noticed that her hair was pinned up again, behind the golden clip. He sat up.

"This is very nice," he said, touching the clip and letting his fingers brush through her hair.

"It was my grandmother's," she said. "It's my one item, the one personal item I chose to bring on board." She removed it from her hair, and he felt a tiny flicker of disappointment as her dark hair cascaded back down around her shoulders.

Was this a one-night stand or something more? came the first dark thoughts. *She's probably a Perfect. Her genes are a great asset to the mission, to be passed on carefully.*

He studied her face. "I'm not a Perfect," he said finally, and her eyes snapped to his. Her hand stopped moving against his skin.

"Why did you say that?"

"I'm not sure." Jahn looked at her eyes, which had hardened. He hesitated. "I meant that you're a beautiful woman."

"That's not what you meant," she stated firmly. She stared at him. "Are we prisoners to our bodies, Jahn?" He shook his head in confusion, praying for some heavenly force to tell him what to say. "Is it just a beautiful woman you want?"

"But you *are* a beautiful woman."

She stood up, walked across the room, and dropped the hair clip into a small metal tin on a table by the window. He flinched at the clattering sound.

"We'll be having the council meeting in fifteen minutes," she said. "It's about the fighting, of course. I'll see you there."

She left the room, her back straight and head high.

Jahn watched her, confused. Part of him felt as if he had destroyed something good through his own stupidity.

He looked around the sunny room and realized just how empty it felt without her.

Jahn got dressed and headed for the council room. He arrived late and had to slip into his seat quietly. He glanced first at Sophia, who looked fixedly at Pravin, her face a mask. Then he looked at his father.

Pravin stood before the council with a pale face, his shoulders stooped.

"Let me tell you more about yesterday's attack," he said. "Fourteen Peacekeepers died, all citizens working on the farms. Eight more are seriously wounded. We will have a mass funeral for the dead tomorrow."

"Why tomorrow?" asked Pierson, his voice breaking into Pravin's soft rhythm of speech. "Why not now?"

Pravin looked directly at him. "Some of the eight are barely hanging on," he said. "A few may not make it to morning. I want to let everyone absorb the impact of this attack today, and avoid the pain of two mass funerals. This decision is not open to debate."

Jahn shook his head inwardly. *There was no need to add that,* he reflected. *No logical person would have challenged his reasoning on the funerals.*

Pravin nodded to all of them. "Of course we have to reassess our security force. We will be taking measures to make sure the base is better protected. And we cannot let this incident divert us from our primary goal, which is a thriving, peaceful, and prosperous society on Chiron."

"I'd settle for just peaceful," murmured Pierson, and watched Pravin as the meeting continued.

*   *   *

After the meeting adjourned, Jahn spent the rest of the day walking the base, talking to citizens and trying to set their mind at rest. As the son of Pravin Lal, but with no official council position, it was a job that suited him.

His father did not contact him, and Jahn imagined the flurry of meetings that probably threatened to overwhelm him. Sophia did not contact him either, and finally he put on gear and went out to the farms, losing himself in the physical labor of repairing the damaged storage building.

Nightfall did not stop him, nor did he stop for food, until finally he looked up to see a sky beyond the repair lights as black as pitch but glittering with the thousands of stars visible from Chiron.

No pollution to ruin the view, he marveled, and stopped to look at the display of celestial majesty above and around him. He closed his eyes for a moment and prayed for a bit of that universal harmony in his own small life.

Looking up at the observation tower rising above the growing sprawl of the base, he could see its soft light, and on a hunch he decided to go there. He checked out with the foreman and walked back to base in the cool night air.

"You're here," he said, and she turned to face him. She, Sophia, was silhouetted against the glittering night sky, and the soft light in the room revealed her to him in stages. "I felt you might be here."

"Don't be dramatic," she said. "You sent me a link message asking me to meet you here." She looked at him sternly. "I'm not a child, Jahn. I'm passionate, but I'm a mature woman, not some airy-headed romantic. I don't believe we're star-crossed lovers, or that the turning of the heavens has brought us together."

"I know." He hesitated. "About my behavior earlier. I don't care who you are, or where you came from. I never asked my father about your . . . origins. I just wanted you to know who I am."

"So your body determines who you are?" She shook her head. "Your statements this morning reflected poorly on you. Why do you feel that I would care where you came from, or what your genetic profile was? I know what's important in a companion, and I saw it in you."

He looked at her, nodding slowly. *She doesn't care. And why should she?* He crossed the room to her, and touched her again, then pulled her into a slow embrace. She didn't resist. He thought of her family, and the painful and expensive genetic treatments her mother must have endured.

"Do you miss your grandmother?" he asked suddenly, thinking about her treasured hair clip as they held each other by the window.

"I miss her more than anyone," said Sophia. "And, just like you, she wasn't a Perfect."

Jahn opened his eyes from a doze to see his father standing over him, his face haggard in the night shadows. Jahn shook his head to get his bearings: he was sprawled on the couch in the observation room, Sophia's warm body lying peacefully against him.

"Jahn, we should speak now," said his father softly. Jahn carefully untangled himself from Sophia and left her sleeping comfortably. He left the room with Pravin, and they began walking the quiet hallways.

"I cannot tell you how proud I am of your performance during the battle," Pravin said. "I am afraid we were caught off guard."

"I was in the right place, at the right time."

Pravin shook his head. "You rose to the occasion. I am not much of a tactician, so I tend not to see those traits in you. But you have them. I am trying to work with Miriam politically, but we must be better prepared now." He put his hand on Jahn's shoulder. "I am putting you in charge of the military. That means you become one of my advisors, with all the authority and responsibilities of that position."

Jahn tried to absorb the implications of what his father had just offered. "Does that mean there is now a council of eleven?"

"No," said Pravin firmly. "I want to keep the council's power in balance with my own. I have been loath to put you, my own son, on the council, but with your performance against the Believers, no one will object."

"Who will step down, then?" Jahn thought of some of the quieter members of the council who seemed to rubber-stamp the decisions of the more vocal members.

"I believe it will be Pierson."

"But he's been in favor of increasing the military all along, Father!" Jahn protested.

"You fulfill that role now, Jahn. But don't worry; I have great respect for Pierson. He will be in charge of construction and defense at our second base, and he will still serve the council in an advisory capacity. When Base Two is complete, perhaps he can

rejoin us. Until then, I am entering into new nego-
tiations with Morgan, Skye, and Santiago, and I'm
afraid he would only antagonize them."

Jahn nodded slowly but didn't answer.

"It's my decision, Jahn. Please trust me."

"Trust." Jahn nodded, but he knew they had
reached the end of the time when trust was enough
to assure their survival on Chiron.

They stopped and Pravin gestured to the door in
front of them. "Do you know where we are?"

"The medlabs," said Jahn.

"I visit your mother sometimes, when I can." He
hesitated. "You are welcome to join me."

Jahn nodded and they entered the medlabs, where
interior lights still winked in the darkness. Pravin
went to a side door and opened it slowly, revealing a
small room with clean walls and soft lighting. In the
center of the room rested a single cryocell on a black
platform, elevating the glass coffin-like shape. The
glass capsule of the cryocell was still sealed, and Jahn
could see the blue-tinted cryogel inside glowing
softly in the shadowed room.

His father stood before the cryocell and stared
down into it, one hand on its smooth surface. Jahn
stepped up next to him and looked down as well.

Pria.

Jahn could see down through the bluish gel to an
indistinct form encased within, a soft brown body
etched with shadows. He watched the liquid pulse
and move around his mother's still form. He remembered his last thoughts as the cryogenic solu-
tions slipped up his nose and down the back of his
throat in the suspension facility back on Earth, be-

fore his forty-year imprisonment began. He remembered praying that he wouldn't dream. He remembered how the blue liquid tasted like death.

Looking down at his mother encased in the cryogel, Jahn hoped that she hadn't tasted it before the lights faded around her, that her thoughts as she surrendered were happier ones.

"She was dying, right in my arms," Pravin said quietly. "I had no time to save her. I had to refreeze her."

"I know," said Jahn quietly. A human taken from cryosleep and then refrozen would either die or reawaken to a life not worth living. Jahn had seen images of test subjects on Earth; massive swaths of blackened skin covered them, their fingers or even entire limbs eaten by decay.

Pria had been a beautiful woman, a pure woman, and the center of Pravin's existence. And now . . . Jahn could see his father's fingers trembling with grief.

"Will you ever try to awaken her?" Jahn asked.

"It's a race between technology and death. I keep praying we will make some kind of breakthrough that could bring her out alive—and whole."

"Is that another reason for expanding our facilities?"

Pravin turned to look at Jahn. "One of them. If I did not love her, if I did not try, I may as well have not survived the journey."

Jahn finally reached out to touch the cryocell. It occurred to him, looking down at his mother, that as a result of their journey across the stars he was now older than she had been at the time the sleep began. He looked at his father, realizing that if it weren't for the genetic treatments that helped keep

Pravin's body from decay, he would probably be dead by now, with his beloved wife still suspended between life and death.

How long can he last? Will she finally awaken to find him a husk of the man he once was?

"I want her back," said Pravin quietly. "She is my Chosen. She is your mother."

Jahn remembered. He closed his eyes and remembered her, holding him, soothing him as the explosions rocked the streets outside, smiling softly when his anger at the world threatened to overwhelm him.

And he looked at his father, staring down at the cryocell. Alone, in this room, Jahn saw the masks fall aside that his father wore before the others. Here he wasn't Pravin the leader, Pravin the rational thinker, Pravin the visionary. He was just Pravin, a powerless man on a faraway world, trying to make sense of his life.

chapter four

five years later

SANTIAGO GAVE THE METAL TRAINING DUMMY A FINAL three kicks to the side of the head, feeling the burn in the muscles of her thighs and abdomen. She relished the sound of the impact and could see the seams on the side of the dummy's head weakening. Soon she would have the pleasure of sending its head skittering across the hard stone floor. Again.

She turned and jumped up to seize a bar set into the ceiling, and began counting off quick pull-ups. All around her, in the long stone room, men and women worked out under dim lighting, sweat pouring off them. Spartans sparred and did a variety of calisthenics everywhere in the room, but they always gave Santiago her space.

"Twenty. Twenty-one," she grunted, and then she noticed someone at the low, wide entrance to the training hall. An unusually thin person for a Spartan, with a shock of red hair.

She crunched out fifteen more pull-ups, wondering if he would have the courage to enter the hall. He seemed to hesitate, then finally started toward her.

She dropped to the ground and bent over a low basin of water, pouring a scoop of the liquid over her naked back to cool herself down. She straightened just as he arrived. He quickly averted his eyes from her bare breasts, a show of weakness she mostly despised. He, of course, was fully clothed, and stuck out like a sore thumb in the Spartan training environment.

"Sir," Brady said, saluting her.

"What do you want?" she asked.

"I want to tell you, before the council meeting later today, that I feel we are spending too much of our resources on the military and the development of new weapons. I felt I had to tell you here, outside of the antagonistic environment of the council."

"Has council been difficult for you, Brady?" She never called him "Red," the nickname almost everyone else called him. "Look at this," she said abruptly, pointing.

On the other side of the room a fight had broken out between two burly men who had been sparring with wooden swords. Each man gripped the other hard around the throat, their massive legs bent low to the ground. One of them released a hand and began striking the other in the chest and belly, and other Spartans began to gather, shouting their encouragement.

"Technique!" Santiago yelled from across the room. The fight grew more heated, and both men began striking each other in the face, scattering blood. Finally one of the men dumped the other on the ground and crashed down on top of him, then reached down and pushed his thumb hard into the other man's left eye socket. There was a bellow of pain, and Brady looked away as something bloody came out of the man's eye socket.

"Enough!" shouted Santiago. "It's a draw. Let the medic through!" She turned to Brady. "We're violent people, Brady. That kind of fury exists in anyone who survived the final days on Earth. It's a part of us. It ensures that we're strong, and that we'll survive."

"But to minimize our food and humanitarian research initiatives can only mean our eventual death. Fighting spirit is not enough to sustain us."

She took a step closer to him, her hands on her hips. He held his ground. "You talk like a Peacekeeper, Brady. Are you sure you got the right pod?" It was a standard Spartan taunt used on those who didn't seem tough enough to hold their own, but it had ceased to have an effect on him. He shook his head in disappointment.

"I just thought you would understand my position better than the others. Some balance is necessary. There's only so much food we can live without."

"If we need food, we can take it from someone."

"We've talked about this before, sir. I know you were once friends with Pravin Lal. He patched you up when . . ."

She struck him across the face, and his head snapped back. She continued to clench the fingers of her right fist together, watching him, and a part of her wondered why she had lashed out so quickly. "That is the nature of our lives, Brady. Injuries happen, and medics come to assist us, as Pravin assisted me. But that was a long time ago, and relationships between people change."

"The Spartans are out of balance." Brady had not backed away from her. "You command these people because you have a broader vision than they do, and you know more than they do about what it takes to survive as a human being in a harsh environment." As she watched him, blood began leaking from his nose. "It takes balance. Without balance comes pain."

"Pain is something we can take."

"Not this kind of pain. It's a pain that will eat us up inside, until there's nothing human left in us." He closed his mouth, apparently finished.

"You're brave to speak to me so directly, I'll give you that. But you and I can no longer talk as freely as we once did. Those times have passed." She nodded to him. "I'll take what you've said under advisement. You're dismissed."

He saluted her and turned away. He walked out of the training hall, not bothering to staunch the bleeding from his nose until he reached the door.

Jahn entered the spacious new council room after Sophia as he always did, looking around at the new arched ceiling and the comfortable chairs his father had installed. He took a seat next to Sophia and waited for the meeting to start.

The other advisors filed in and took their seats, and Jahn glanced at them while his father stood up to make his customary opening remarks. The citizens of UNHQ looked clean and content in their crisp new uniforms, sewn of machine-made fabric in a new production facility. Even Pierson, visiting from the Base Two construction site to advise on Spartan troop movements, looked almost presentable in crisp Peacekeeper blue. *It's starting to feel like home here,* Jahn thought, and tuned back in to his father's speech.

"As you know, we've managed to forge the various arms of the settlements into a loose whole. Transportation and commerce are on the rise, and the Believers have given us no more trouble. Does anyone disagree?"

"For all her emphasis on organization, Colonel Santiago has been less than a team player," Pierson said. "She refuses to let our citizens into Sparta Command for intensive training, and she seems to run hot and cold about this new base we're founding."

"Why would she object to our new base?" asked Pravin. "It will be close to her, and it can assist her against the mindworm attacks."

"It's very close to her," said Pierson. "In fact, when we sent the colonists there we hadn't fully mapped out the surrounding territory. Our new base exists on a stretch of land between Santiago and the rest of us."

"And she's told you it makes her unhappy?" asked Pravin.

"I'm not sure of the ramifications of what you're saying," interjected Goorman. "Are you suggesting that this base has a military significance, such as for an invasion force?"

"I'm saying Santiago is a fighter, and she sees the world with a fighter's mind. The mere act of putting a base in this location could really be . . . pissing her off."

"She has lodged no formal complaint," said Pravin.

"Maybe she's waiting for us to finish the base and then she'll try to move her citizens into it," said Jahn. Several heads swiveled in his direction.

"Maybe," said Pierson, touching his chin.

"That would be an act of war," said Pravin. "It's unthinkable."

"The attacks by Miriam seemed unthinkable, until citizens full of rusty shredder bolts made us think about them," said Pierson.

"Miriam needed food," said Sophia. "And those people operated without her blessing."

"The Spartans need food, and Miriam *said* those people operated without her blessing," said Pierson. "I work closer to the Spartans than any of you, constructing this new base. They spend almost all of their resources making new weapons, supposedly to fight off the mindworms. Eventually they're going to get hungry."

"Are you suggesting we move the location of this base?" asked Sophia.

"We will not do that," said Pravin firmly. "We have laid too much foundation, and the land is ideal. There is food, and good sunlight, and we have begun digging mines . . ."

"Oh, I don't suggest moving the base, for all of those reasons," said Pierson. "Plus it really is a good strategic location, and I don't want Santiago to have it. I *am* suggesting that we start defending our bases, by building walls around them."

"Walls? You mean like a walled city?" asked Pravin.

Pierson nodded. "Yes. Sparta Command has walls, supposedly to protect against mindworm attacks. Besides, walls will add to the symmetry of the base, making it look more like a unified whole than a collection of buildings. It will protect against natural disasters, and against Believers."

"I'm not sure if we have the resources," said Sophia.

"If we build walls around any base, naturally it will be UNHQ first," Pravin said, and Jahn could see his mind working, visualizing the great city rising from the plain.

"Base Two is closer to Santiago," said Pierson.

"UNHQ is the center of our government," said Pravin. "This base will be our model of human achievement on Chiron, and it's worth protecting."

"Fine by me," said Pierson, shaking his head. "Between the Spartans and the Believers, I say build the walls. But I'm going to arm every colonist that works under me until Base Two gets the protection it needs."

"Base Two is so far just some farms and pressure tents," said Eldridge. "And I'm still worried about resources."

"I'll talk to Nwabudike Morgan," Pravin said. "I believe he'll be excited about providing us with some of the resources to build these walls around UNHQ. And I want our architects to take a look at the design. I like the idea of a unified city, of symmetry."

"I'd like a vote," said Sophia. "I don't want to send the wrong message to Santiago."

"Why should we ask Santiago's permission to protect the center of Chiron's government?" asked Jahn.

"We're still not sure how much she believes we *are* the center of Chiron's government," said Sophia. "But let's vote."

The vote returned, six in favor and four against.

"Very well," said Pravin. "The vote stands. Walls it is."

Jahn stood at the edge of the training grounds and watched his people run through their calis-

thenics. Sophia approached him, putting her hand
lightly on his back. "Hungry?"

He looked at her and smiled. *Hard to resist those
eyes.* He turned back to the troops, who had broken
into smaller groups for daily sparring. He blew a
whistle to get their attention.

"You citizens have done very well today. You can
continue with your training, or knock off a little
early as a reward for a job well done. Dismissed."

There was some cheering from the crowd, and
soldiers began collecting their gear and walking or
jogging for the locker rooms. Jahn continued to
watch them, noting who stayed to train a little
longer. Rank was in one of those groups, forcing
out another round of push-ups.

"The benevolent dictator," Sophia said, teasing
him. "Let's go eat."

They went to the training mess hall, which was
closer than any of the other UNHQ eating facilities.
They piled their plates from trays set along a clean,
well-maintained line and sat down at a small table
by a window. Above them sturdy wooden beams
held up the ceiling. The hall could seat hundreds at
its thick, clean wooden tables, courtesy of the forests
that now flourished on the hillsides around UNHQ.

"I usually don't eat here," said Sophia. "The
food's quite good. Have you been training chefs instead of soldiers? Or are you skimming the best off
Deirdre Skye's shipments?"

He smiled. "A little. My father has a very close
relationship with her, and I've made sure our security forces benefit from some of her food shipments."

"I hear the Spartans aren't so lucky." Sophia took a large spoonful of steaming, fragrant vegetables from her plate. "Deirdre doesn't like them because they hunt the mindworms, and your father has to be careful that Deirdre doesn't get angry at him for helping Santiago."

"It's awkward," agreed Jahn. "Santiago remains so aloof that it's hard for anyone to work with her. And she makes no secret that she likes her people to suffer."

"It doesn't sound like part of the United Nations Charter for the new world."

"Perhaps this new city design will bring us closer together."

"Did you vote for the walls, Jahn?" she asked abruptly. Jahn remained silent for a moment, and then nodded.

"I did. I have great respect for anything you say in council, Sophia, but the wars on Earth are still too close for me to drop my guard. And then there's the fighting with the Believers."

"But this could be a chance to move away from Earth's mistakes, to get away from the constant offensive and defensive buildup."

"It could, you're right. But our citizens trust us to protect them and look out for their interests. When I think of my mother, lying in that cryocell—" He stopped, realizing he had to recollect his thoughts. "I'm a builder at heart," he continued after a moment. "I look at my task as head of the security forces as a constructive one . . . forging a worthy defensive force, rather than forging a human weapon designed to kill. Even this food matters . . . I want my people to be strong. I consider the city walls an extension of that. I want to build them high, so that we can be safe inside."

Sophia nodded, looking down at her food. "I voted for the walls as well." She looked up to meet Jahn's surprised look. "I wasn't going to, of course, but at the last minute, I felt I had to. Maybe it's the things you say, about the wars on Earth, or about human nature. It just seems inevitable that we'll need them."

Jahn reached out and squeezed her hand. "Listen," he said. "Deirdre Skye will be visiting later this month. It'll be a time of celebration. I'd like one more thing to celebrate. Will you . . ." He shook his head, suddenly realizing he was doing this all wrong. He slipped out of his chair and knelt on the ground in front of her.

"Sophia, will you become my Chosen, and live with me here on Chiron?"

She looked down at him, her dark hair falling around her shoulders. She smiled, and he saw her eyes mist over with emotion.

"I suppose I will," she said finally, and leaned down to kiss him. And then from around them came the booming of a hundred soldiers pounding on a hundred wooden tables, followed by cheers.

Santiago sat on a hard metal bench in her command room and looked at her top advisors gathered around her. They stared back, the scars and marks of battle and hard training on their faces, and on their bare arms and hands. She suppressed a smile at the success of her training regimes.

"Any concerns?"

"Pravin Lal has created a strong alliance with Deirdre Skye," said Messier. "Our patrols have seen large supply trains heading for the UNHQ, and her botanists are assisting him with new hybrids. I'm sure he's getting more than his fair share of her food."

"We have enough to live on," said Diego. "Why is this our concern? We could take one of those supply trains in an instant."

"It's the power dynamic that concerns me," said Messier. "With more food there will be more Peacekeepers. We're increasingly isolated here."

"All of us are supposed to be working together for the greater good," said Brady, brushing his shock of red hair from his face. "The Peacekeepers are still sending us some supply trains."

"But they're unhappy about our powerful army," said Messier. "And Deirdre Skye has two bases now, while the best of her food is going to feed her own people. And her own army, I might add."

"An army of bean sprouts," said Diego, and the others laughed.

"I agree," said Santiago. "Deirdre Skye couldn't challenge us. But look at the bigger picture. We were all supposed to work together on this mission, but the *Unity* malfunction spread us too far apart. Because of the distance between us, we've all become increasingly independent and self-reliant."

The others nodded in agreement, except for Brady.

"What of the Conventions?" he asked. "Governor Lal might agree to unconditionally guarantee our food supply if we guarantee defenses against the native life-forms. Then we could put some of our free workers into expanding our base facilities."

"Governor Lal has his own security force as well," said Messier. "What's the implication of that?"

"Our warriors are strong," said Santiago. "But we have a different way of life here. The others don't sacrifice their weakest members or train their citizens to survive in a difficult world. Likewise, Nwabudike Morgan puts the lion's share of his production resources into building for his own citizens, forcing us to develop our own supplementary production facilities. What holds the settlements together is not the Conventions, but a loose network of alliances. Alliances that can be broken."

"To break an alliance would threaten the existence of the human race on Chiron," said Brady. "We have much more to gain from working together. And so far the Peacekeepers have been honorable."

"Perhaps," said Santiago, not looking at him. "But we believe in our way of life. Why should the Spartans endure such hardships to protect the others, and then be denied our fair share of the food supply? And if we are ever put under siege, our supplies will run out quickly. We should pressure Pravin Lal for more."

"Agreed," said Diego. "If the others won't send us the food we need, we'll start hitting their supply trains."

"That's a military action," said Brady. "By Spartan bylaws, Colonel Santiago can overrule it."

"Unless the council is unanimously in favor," said Diego, staring at Brady.

"There is no need to argue," said Santiago. "I will authorize sporadic raiding of the supply trains, to send a message to the others. We Spartans will not go hungry."

Three of her four council members nodded in agreement.

* * * *

Jahn adjusted his pressure mask and waited for Deidre Skye's rovers to reach UNHQ. He stood on a brand-new platform that had been built outside of the north gates for the purpose of holding parked rovers; it was constructed of white stone and shone brilliantly under the clear sky. He enjoyed the feeling of solidity beneath his feet.

"Look at that," said Sophia, pointing to a glint of sun between two hills to the northwest. She stood next to him, her arm looped casually in his while they waited. He lifted a pair of high-powered binoculars and zeroed in on the glint.

"It looks like three rovers, headed our way." He paused, making some adjustments to the optics. "The lead rover is flying a flag with Deirdre's seal," he said, referring to the green diamond enclosing an abstract rose that Deirdre Skye used to mark her food shipments. "Apparently she's calling herself a Gaian, to remind us of the importance of our connection to the planet."

"It's got a nice ring to it," said Sophia, watching the rovers' course toward UNHQ. "It looks like they're angling for the xenofields."

"Deirdre loves native planet life. It wouldn't surprise me if she hopped out to take some samples for home." He spoke into his quicklink, notifying Pravin and the other advisors that Deirdre Skye was coming.

Pravin, Jahn, and the other advisors waited under the Centauri sky as the rovers approached. Citizen workers helped to guide the rovers to a stop, where they parked side by side on the platform behind the northern gates. A hatch on the side of the lead rover opened, and two men in green pressure suits and helmets jumped down, holding shredder rifles salvaged from the *Unity*. Soon after came Deirdre Skye, wearing a shiny green dress and no pressure mask. She smiled and came toward Pravin, and as she walked her legs flashed through slits in the long tunic. Jahn noticed how tan her body was and how her dark hair framed her face. She radiated a healthy glow, as if she spent a lot of time outdoors.

"Pravin, hello," said Deirdre, grasping Pravin's hand lightly.

"Deirdre, welcome. I wish that you would wear a pressure mask outside like the rest of us."

She shook her head lightly. "I do if I'm out for longer than five minutes, but there's no harm in short-term exposure. So why don't we skip the formalities and get inside the base?" She smiled again.

"Of course." Pravin motioned her toward the open gates and the pressure hatch beyond. Jahn looked after Deirdre, watching her body move underneath her dress, until he felt an elbow in the ribs.

"She's not perfect," came a sharp whisper from Sophia that he heard even through his pressure mask.

He smiled weakly and headed for the gates. Behind him more Gaians descended from the three rovers, and he noticed that his father had stopped to study the vehicles with a concerned look on his face, as if missing a piece to a puzzle.

"What's wrong, Father?" Jahn asked.

"She was supposed to bring more food supplies with her," said Pravin. "But we'll clear it up. Perhaps we can expect them later today."

Jahn looked back at the rovers, and the thin but tough-looking men and women who dismounted.

None of them looked as if they expected much of anything.

"Delicious," said Deirdre, sitting at ease in a stuffed chair in the observation room. She drank fresh-squeezed juice from a wide glass, and closed her eyes as if savoring the finest wine.

"We made it from the apple and pear hybrids you helped develop," said Pravin. "We also added lemon, which we managed to grow ourselves."

"Very good." She nodded, and then her eyes drifted to the landscape outside. Pravin had remodeled the room before Deirdre's visit, and now floor-to-ceiling windows opened in every direction, revealing Chiron in all its glory. "This is a wonderful space, Pravin."

Around Deirdre her advisors nodded in agreement. They were mostly wiry blond men and women with wide, ethereal eyes, all dressed in loose-fitting robes held by pieces of *Unity* pressure suits. The uniforms seemed odd and tossed-together, except for their pressure masks, which Jahn had noticed fit snugly. Their eyes shifted left and right, wide blue and green moons.

Pravin and his advisors sat in an assortment of chairs that had been assembled in the observation room under Pravin's direction. "Deirdre, now that you have taken the grand tour and seen the plan for the new base, I wonder if we can talk business."

"Of course." She nodded to Pravin, waiting for him to take the lead.

"First of all, I notice that there were no supply transports with you. I wonder if you remembered that you had promised a shipment of vegetables and protein hybrids."

"Promised," Deirdre repeated. She took another sip from her glass.

"We're concerned that you're taking food supplies and redistributing them to Colonel Santiago," spoke up an old man with a strong, weathered face and long gray hair.

Pravin nodded. "There is a kernel of truth in that. We have sent Santiago food, and she has helped to train some of our soldiers. But we are only sending her food that we have raised ourselves, right here on our own farms."

"If you take our food and then give her your food, there's no difference," said the old man. "Either way we're helping to feed Santiago."

"Is this a problem?" asked Jahn. "She needs to eat."

Deirdre set down her glass on a low table. "The problem is that she has taken an unhealthy interest in destroying native life-forms."

"She has suffered some mindworm attacks, but we all know that these are deadly creatures that kill humans and bore holes into their brains," said Jahn. "You can't blame her for attacking them."

"But she's started hunting these worms, to train her troops. And she's using her flame guns to wipe out the xenofields near her base."

The Peacekeeper council fell silent for a moment, reading each others' thoughts. They had all talked about destroying the xenofields near their own bases. The thick, alien fields of crimson tubules hampered their scout patrols and took up valuable farming space.

Deirdre cleared her throat. "I have a strong belief

that destroying and altering the planetary ecosystem causes a response from the ecosystem itself, in the form of these mindworm attacks. If we would stop upsetting the ecosystem, we might find ways to live in harmony with the mindworms."

"Are you suggesting that we stop farming and drilling?" asked Jahn.

Deirdre nodded. "Perhaps." She shifted, and Jahn noticed again how lean and tight her body was. "Will we be contacting Morgan later?"

"Yes," said Pravin. "I wanted to talk about my plans for the base."

"Then we can discuss it more at that time." Deirdre smiled. "I've prepared a presentation for you both."

Santiago sat in a small, windowless room connected to her quarters. There was a knock on the door, and then it opened. An attendant stood in the shadows of the doorway, holding the shoulder of a young boy.

"Leave him," said Santiago. The attendant pushed the boy inside and closed the door. The boy stood awkwardly.

"How is your training?" Santiago finally asked.

"Good," said the boy, which was all he ever said. Santiago picked up the small glowlamp next to her stool and raised it. The boy's face and torso were covered with scars and angry black bruises. His right eye was so swollen he could barely see out of it; the eye behind the bruise shifted like an animal hiding in a deep cave.

"If you keep at it, you'll become strong. I want you to pay attention to every lesson in tactics. Use your mind when your body fails you. Never admit defeat."

"They're going to kill me," said the boy.

"Nonsense!" Santiago found her voice cracking. "Besides, that's not your decision. Your decision is to continue to live, until the decision to live is taken away from you by something beyond your power." She reached out and pinched his arm, feeling the muscle tone. "How's your back?"

"Hurts," said the boy, which was all he ever said. Santiago motioned him to turn and sit in front of her.

She picked up a razor and looked at the stubble growing on his head. After a moment she started to shave it with long, careful strokes.

The image on the touchpanel in the council room flickered and then resolved itself into a crystal-clear image of Nwabudike Morgan, from his base that he called Morgan Industries. He broke into a wide smile.

"Wonderful!" he said with delight.

Jahn smiled in spite of himself. Director Morgan had an infectious ability to take things as they came, and usually turn them to his advantage.

"Welcome, Nwabudike," said Pravin. "We're all here."

"Ah, yes. There you are, Pravin. And your son as well, and the lovely Deirdre Skye and your advisors. Are you enjoying your visit, Deirdre?"

"Of course."

"You'll have to come to my world headquarters sometime," he said. "We'll keep you in the lap of luxury. You must get tired of sleeping in those pressure tents and scraping the dirt from your fingernails every evening."

"Actually, we're building our new facilities above

---

the ground, on some interesting rock formations we've located. But thank you for your concern, Nwabudike."

He smiled again. Jahn noticed that his rich, dark face still retained a youthful smoothness, and his clothes were immaculate, the finest that Jahn had seen on Chiron. "Well, what shall we talk about today?"

"The new development for this base," said Pravin. "As you know, my advisors have approved the plans for the expansion of UNHQ."

"The one with the beautiful walls," said Morgan.

"Yes," said Pravin. "I want both you and Deirdre to be involved in this project. We intend to make UNHQ a monument to human achievement on Chiron, and an inspiration for all human citizens. It will be a real city, not just a colony base."

"I've already spoken to your advisor, Eldridge, in some detail about all the construction. It sounds expensive, but expensive never bothers me. I'll help you build it for the appropriate amount of supplies and labor."

Pravin smiled a tight smile. "I must ask you one more time, Nwabudike. Is it so important that you be compensated? This project is a noble undertaking."

"I'm trying to instill in my citizens the knowledge that a strong economic base is the key to future prosperity on Chiron. You may not agree, but economics is my unique area of expertise."

"That and the mining equipment you possess," said Jahn, a little peeved.

"That, too," agreed Morgan. "We're all friends here. If you want my expertise on mineral collec-

tion, I'll exchange it for raw labor and goods produced at your base, as well as access to some of your
best scientists. I've been unable to duplicate your
recycling facilities to my satisfaction."

"What about the vision of a real city on Chiron?"
asked Eldridge.

"I look forward to visiting your city, to be sure,"
said Morgan. "But I need to expand my own facilities into a second location as well. There's excellent
mining to be had at a spot to my east."

Deirdre shifted in her chair as if she could contain herself no more. "I want to protest all of this
mining activity," she said. "I have reason to believe
that our activities are causing the mindworm attacks, which have grown more frequent."

"Nonsense," said Morgan flatly.

"You've been so busy digging into Chiron's crust
that you haven't had an opportunity to notice simple cause and effect," said Deirdre. "How many
mindworm attacks have you endured?"

"Several," said Morgan. "But we're near large expanses of xenofields."

"It's not coincidence." Deirdre let out a deep
breath. "Let me show you both something before
this argument goes any further." She took out a
small memory card and handed it to Pravin. He
slipped it into the touchpanel and configured it to
broadcast to Morgan as well.

Jahn watched the footage that appeared on the
screen. Deirdre had obviously edited together
scenes from the ship's datalinks into a montage of
the last days of Earth, before the launch of the
Unity. Before the end of everything.

* * *

Earth, 2059. Cities had grown faster and faster, covering the world with a cancer of metal and cement. These cities had become dominated by corporations and military dictators, or combined into massive governments that rose and then collapsed into smaller, more stable but more violent city-nations.

People lived everywhere, in every conceivable space and climate, in every kind of horrid living condition. "An indomitable will to live coupled with a life not worth living," as one philosopher had described the existence of 99 percent of the human race.

People died from disease. They died from starvation. They died from being gunned down in lawless, smog-filled, vermin-infested streets. They died from cuts on rusty metal. The poor died at the walls of sleek, hi-tech hospitals that had become fortresses.

And the cycle of hate eventually culminated in a series of attacks by terrorists and by rogue nations using biological and nuclear devices.

Jahn watched, his expression hardening as the footage continued.

Footage of the first Flash War, a series of coordinated attacks launched in major Chinese cities by rogue guerrilla fighters known as the Fallen. Footage of biological attacks in the network of underground tunnels that crisscrossed the United States' East Coast metropolitan sprawl, their effects magnified beyond anyone's estimation when the pathogen spread to the urban rat population and got carried from Boston down to Atlanta.

Political instability tearing across the globe like wildfire. Fallout coming down like rain. The Seven-

Minute War, turning India and Pakistan into blackened wastelands.

Jahn tightened his jaw against these images . . .
he remembered the polluted, burning streets of
New Delhi where he and his father had both
served in the medical corps. He remembered his father assigning himself to border duty in order to
tend to children and mothers who were beyond
saving—blind and burned.

"The Middle East had long since gone up in
flames by this time," said Deirdre softly. "We had
already seen the truth—that ancient hatreds could
destroy civilizations—yet we couldn't stop it. And
we watched it happen again and again."

Children with black holes for eyes and bloody
membranes for skin. Men with metal and plastic
armor melted into their flesh, fused into their
bone. Newborns with missing limbs, extra thumbs;
stillborns with eyes in their chests.

And Jahn remembered the heat. Almost all of Earth
had grown unbearably hot, from climate changes,
and chemicals, and power plants, and fallout. Cool
areas had become hot and dry, and hot areas like
India had become furnaces, all but unlivable except
for special "ice box" cold shelters. There were no trees
and no birds, only insects that crawled the baking
streets. Death shadowed the Earth, through every
turn, through every orbit, all under an impassive sun.

Pravin reached over and turned off the video.
Morgan's face reappeared. He paused to collect
himself for a moment.

"Well," he said. "A trip down memory lane. But
that didn't look like Chiron to me."

"It could," said Deirdre. "And that's my point. The decisions we make now will stay with us for a long time. Are we striving for an ecological paradise, or a factory world that will end as Earth did?"

"Your goals are admirable, but we're just a handful of life on a large world," said Morgan. "And you certainly have no authority to curtail my mining efforts when we barely have the resources to stay alive." He looked at Pravin. "Well, Pravin. You have the terms of my deal. I wish you well in the construction of your new city." He nodded to them all and then broke the connection.

Pravin looked at Deirdre. "Your goals are admirable, but he does have a point," he said. "We need good homes, and better schools, and museums to help us remember."

"Such as in your new city?" she asked, then nodded before he could answer. "I understand your position. But I'll continue to remind you that we came here to escape the horrors of Earth, not to transplant them."

She looked around the council room, and then at the UN symbol that shone from the high ceiling.

Jahn Lal took the last step up into the new observation room, his spirit lifting. The wide, rolling landscape of Chiron was visible outside the glass on all sides, and the warm light of the sunset washed the landscape in rich colors. To the northeast the xenofields had their own alien beauty as they waited silently under the emerging moons.

His father waited for him, smiling gently from a low platform in front of the southern window, framed by the twin moons. Simple white candles glowed all around the room, and cascades of exotic flowers, brought by Deirdre Skye in one of her rovers, tumbled from glass vases in every corner of the room.

Jahn crossed the room, brushing past a Peacekeeper media specialist, who would capture the ceremony and link it out to all citizens in the base. The man looked at Jahn with a cool efficiency, obviously more concerned about camera angles and making his father look good than about the ceremony itself.

Forget it, Jahn thought. *It's the cost of being a leader's son.*

Jahn shook his father's hand and took his place on the platform. He glanced at Deirdre Skye, who sat in a nearby chair with several other prominent citizens. She was dressed in a sleeveless yellow shift and smiled quietly at Pravin and Jahn, though Jahn knew she was upset about the base expansion, which would involve burning out a portion of the xenofungus fields.

Then Jahn's attention was captured by a movement at the door.

Sophia stepped into the room, wearing a simple shift of white homespun silk that fell around her body like the moonlight. Her hair was piled in dark waves around her face, held by her golden hair clip, and she was barefoot, a small touch that Jahn found mildly erotic. She carried herself with the grace of a queen.

She really is perfect, thought Jahn.

She smiled at him as she approached, and he felt his spirit soaring. She stepped lightly onto the platform and took his hand, and he turned to her and let himself get lost in her eyes.

"This is a formal ceremony, but a small one, with

none of the pomp and circumstance befitting two citizens as noble as the ones before us," said Pravin. "Here on Chiron, we all have to make do with less, at least where material goods are concerned. Yet where love is concerned, and human connection, these two before us have abundance enough to fill this new world, and we can be thankful that they have seen fit to share it with us."

Pravin turned to Sophia and smiled at her. "We'll keep this simple. Do you take Jahn to be your Chosen, your partner in love and companionship for the rest of your living days?"

"I do," said Sophia.

"And do you, Jahn, take Sophia to be your Chosen, your partner in love and companionship for the rest of your living days?"

"I do, Father," said Jahn.

"Then I recognize the two of you as Chosen and partners for life, with all of the privileges and responsibilities that accompany it." He took a deep breath, drinking in the sight of the two of them against the sweep of Chiron, illuminated by candlelight. "You may kiss."

Jahn stared at her, at her eyes and the candlelight flickering on her face. "Thank you," he said, and fell into her kiss.

Behind them Pravin watched their embrace, and the ghost of his sleeping wife settled in his eyes and watched them too.

chapter five

five years later

DIEGO PRESSED HIS BELLY INTO THE RED EARTH AND LOOKED over a low rise. The dust of Chiron covered his armor and his pressure mask, dulling the sun's glare so that he would not be seen. He looked around at the positions of his other warriors, and noted that he could not see any of them.

Except one, near an odd columnar rock formation two hundred meters to his east.

"Hurry and move into your position, Victor," he said into his quicklink. "If you expose us I'll shoot you before the enemy does."

"Affirmative," came the high-pitched voice, with no further argument.

"At least he knows the protocol, sir," said Lansing, Diego's second-in-command for this mission.

"Learning the protocol is the only thing he does well," said Diego.

Lansing laughed. "I thought the colonel wanted him to experience a raid from a command position."

"A good commander will take on any task, no matter how lowly or dangerous. That's his lesson for

the day," said Diego. "If he's shot on recon, at least
he dies honorably, and my squad is stronger for it."

"If he dies, Santiago will eat your balls."

Diego only grinned and tightened the muscles in
his arms. "Sounds very pleasant. I'd like her to try."

Diego surveyed the land again. He was in his element now, every nerve ready for a fight. Over the
last several years he had gotten the supply train attacks down to a science: not too frequent, never
dangerous, and knowing Santiago would respond
to the outrage of the settlements by blaming the attack on a rogue commander who needed food for
his troops on patrol.

*And so far, no killing. But Sparta help them if they re-
sist.*

His finger twitched on the trigger of his autoshredder.

"Five beetles approaching," came Victor's voice
over the link, using the code word for food transports.

"Roger," said Diego. He pulled out his binoculars.
"Sure enough. They never learn."

They waited in utter silence until the transports,
which basically looked like large metal boxes on
thick wheels, had rounded the rock pillar and were
ranged out in front of them. Diego noted that the
Gaians had taken to spreading the transports out
more, to discourage a concentrated attack.

It won't help.

"Alpha go," said Diego. The Spartans jumped up
from several positions along the low ridge overlooking the transports and commenced their attack. Concussion grenades arced toward the rear
transport and exploded underneath, sending the

transport jolting at an odd angle, the entire front axle torn off its mounting. Diego and his fellow warriors followed up with concussion grenades on the front vehicle and then a barrage of automatic shredder fire, riddling the sides of the transports and shattering their broad glass windows.

"Gaians and their glass," Diego laughed, as fragments exploded back into the transport, hitting the pilots.

"Stop your transports and step out!" said Lansing through a voice broadcaster. "You will not be harmed."

A hatch on the top of the middle transport opened, and from it emerged the bald head and then the torso of a burly man in a thick green uniform. He waved to the Spartans.

"What is he waving at?" said Diego, annoyed.

Suddenly the man pulled a crude handheld rocket launcher from inside the transport and fired it. The rocket streaked into a hillside and exploded in front of a Spartan, sending gouts of flame and chunks of earth into the man's face and torso. Diego saw the man fly into the air like a tattered rag doll.

"Open fire!" shouted Diego, as hatches opened on the Gaian transports and gun barrels emerged, firing into the Spartans. Diego raked the side of the number two transport with shredder fire, tearing broad gashes into the metal and filling the inside with ricocheting bullets. His weapon, a massive automatic with a constant feed belt, trembled in his hands as it unloaded its ammo. The transport ground to a halt, and he imagined the carnage inside. He grinned.

I've been waiting for this.

The two remaining functional transports turned

around, knocking the disabled rear transport aside as they fled the scene. The bald Gaian let another rocket fly. It sailed past Diego and exploded behind him.

"Laser speeder into position," ordered Diego. He fired at the bald Gaian, but the man ducked back into his vehicle.

From over a nearby rise came a small, fast speeder, mounted with a laser turret and driven by an experienced Spartan crew. As the transports fled, the small speeder released its energy charge, and a burst of concentrated blue-white light engulfed one of the transports. When the light cleared it left only a chunk of smoking slag on melted wheels that rolled slowly into a hillside and stopped.

"Four down, one to go," said Diego, as the laser speeder swiveled its weapon to fire at the last Gaian transport, which now kicked up red dust, heading at top speed back toward the rock pillar.

From the melting wreck of the burned transport the bald Gaian pushed his way out, his face blackened and armor melted on his skin like green soup. He collapsed across the top of the smoking transport and let one more rocket fly.

The rocket streaked in a yellow-white line toward the laser speeder and hit the turret dead on, shattering it. An energy cell inside the speeder suddenly discharged with a deep blue flash, splitting open the top of the scout.

"The speeder is hit!" shouted Diego. "Go and get the last transport!"

He opened heavy fire on the last transport, watching as the barrel of his automatic shredder went from black to glowing red, but his target receded into the distance, vanishing around the tall stone formation. In frustration he turned his weapon on the bald, dying Gaian, turning the man's charred skull into ash.

"After it," he said angrily, when from behind the rock pillar the sound of a concussion grenade echoed back to them.

"What the hell was that?" asked Diego.

"The kid is there. Victor," said Lansing.

Diego and Lansing sprinted to the position of the last transport. As they rounded the rock formation, they found three Gaian soldiers, the typical tall and thin variety, standing over the body of Victor.

"Stand back," shouted Lansing. The Gaians turned, weapons swiveling into position. Diego opened fire without hesitation, drawing lines in red across their bellies, and then he turned his fire toward the back of the transport, puncturing its hull. Finally something in the engine exploded, showering the area with flame and hot debris. Chunks of metal fell and sizzled on the red earth, one of them burning into the chest of a dying Gaian, who opened his mouth but did not cry out.

When the air had cleared, Lansing stepped forward and kicked Victor in the side.

"Is he dead?" asked Diego.

Victor stirred. "No, sir," said Lansing. "Looks like his own concussion grenade knocked him right off his recon perch."

Diego opened the hatch on the transport and looked inside. Gaians in torn and bloody clothing lay sprawled in the transport's interior, and the explosion had shattered crates of vegetables and other foods. Some kind of thick protein concentrate had burst from a wooden crate, bubbling from the heat of the explosion.

"This food's no good," said Diego. He turned back and looked at Victor, who lay as still as a corpse.

"Looks like you missed your chance to be a hero, Baldy," said Diego. He looked at Lansing. "Let's get back to the others and see if there are any live ones left."

"What about him?" asked Lansing "Should we call the medic?"

"No. Leave him there. He got caught in the blast radius of his own concussion grenade." Diego walked over and brought his heavy black boot down hard on Victor's quicklink. "Looks like it knocked out his transmitter as well. We'll mark him as KIA."

"What if he makes it back, sir?" asked Lansing.

"Then I was wrong," said Diego, and headed back to the other transports.

Late afternoon

Victor stirred and waited for the red-and-blue blurs to resolve into the ground and the sky as he knew them. His head ached, and his chest and stomach felt like one large bruise, a result of his fall from the lookout perch. He didn't think he had any life-threatening injuries.

He shook his head against the sting of failure, knowing his own concussion grenade had knocked him down. *I'm not meant to be a Spartan.*

After a while he climbed slowly to his feet. He found himself next to the remains of the Gaian transport, which no longer smoldered, but that wasn't unusual. Nothing burned for long in the thick Chiron atmosphere.

He checked his oxygen mixer and saw that it was over halfway depleted. He pushed his way into the transport, staring dully at the twisted, bloody bodies of the Gaians, feeling no twang of sympathy. He felt as though he had experienced a thousand deaths worse than these in the Spartan training rooms.

In a storage locker underneath the hardened goop of spilled protein concentrate he found some Gaian exploration supplies, including more oxygen tanks. They resembled the Spartan design but weren't identical. He took off his pressure mask and put on a Gaian model, finding it much lighter and more comfortable than the Spartan mask.

He attached a mixer tank to his belt and started the flow, then packed two more tanks and rations into a backpack, which he shouldered. He was weak by Spartan standards, but his training had still made him strong by any other measure. He knew he could probably outwalk and outcarry most of these adult Gaians.

Especially since they're dead.

He climbed back out of the transport and looked around. Centauri A was receding toward the horizon, but Centauri B was just rising, making for easy night walking. He got out a compass and checked his orientation. He knew that Diego's patrol was headed back to Sparta Command to the southeast, but he also knew Diego would take a roundabout route to try to "accidentally" encounter more Gaian supply trains.

He checked his quicklink transmitter. It looked

broken, the screen flickering dimly. He couldn't raise anyone. He was on his own.

He knew that he could be self-sufficient and head directly for Sparta Command. He had enough oxygen. But he also thought that if he went due east for a while, and didn't pay a lot of attention to his distances, he just might run into the small new Peacekeeper settlement instead.

Are you sure you got the right pod? How many times had he heard that?

Maybe they were right. But then he thought of Sparta Command, its imposing structure rising out of the red earth, and thought of the sweat and blood he had shed inside. He lived in a different world from that of any Peacekeeper, a world of pain and honor.

He set off at a fast clip to the southeast, his shadow stretching out before him.

Night had fallen, and a torrential storm lashed Victor, driving him haphazardly across the landscape. The winds gusted behind him, blowing his small body eastward, and rain lashed at his pressure mask. Still he kept walking, continuing for hours, letting the water soak him.

Finally the rain lessened, and he stopped to rest on a big rock, watching the storm clouds roll on eastward. The sky cleared and Centauri B, low on the horizon, sent a pale wash of light over the wet red earth. Victor wondered how far off course he had strayed.

Maybe I'm in Peacekeeper territory, he thought, and considered idly what he would do if a blue Peacekeeper scout crested a nearby ridge. *Go down fighting?*

He pulled out some Gaian supply biscuits and

started eating them. He thought they tasted very good, with a flavor that made them superior to even regular Spartan dinner fare. He began to understand why the Spartans felt so morally superior to the rest of the human settlements, with their self-discipline and sacrifice. But he also thought the biscuits tasted pretty good.

As he ate he fiddled with another device from the Gaian supply kit. It was a land sensor, of a type that the Spartans also used to survey the surrounding terrain, but it seemed more refined than the Spartan model. He turned it on and played with it, sweeping it around and watching the display fill in terrain features for him, as if building a world right before his eyes.

He stopped. Something flashed on the display, indicating a mark to the north, just over a nearby hill.

That usually means a Unity *supply pod,* he realized, his heart pounding. *Unity* supply pods had been scattered from the ship across Chiron's surface during planetfall. They often contained valuable supplies and could bring great honor to a citizen who found one.

He packed up the supply kit and headed over the ridge. He walked for about two hundred meters, homing in on the mark.

Great Sparta.

A chill went down his spine. There, in the center of a large crater, was not an oval *Unity* supply pod but a huge chunk of metal from the *Unity* itself, about six meters high, bristling with jagged lengths of metal where it had torn free from the superstructure.

He approached it slowly, not sure what to make of its size and shape, and a sense of awe crept over him as he realized that this deformed hunk of metal had fallen from the sky, and originated on Earth, a planet he had never seen. He walked around it, looking at tongues of blackened, jagged metal that seemed to claw the sky above.

On the far side of the wreckage he found a metal cover of some kind, still intact, about one meter square.

He took out his shredder pistol and fired a burst at the hinges of the cover. Shredder bolts ricocheted off the surface, but he kept firing until the cover sprang open. Behind it he found another door, made of an unusual white metal, which he pulled open with his fingers. And behind that door he found three glorious sheets of multifaceted crystal that shimmered in the pale light of Centauri B as he moved them.

Datalinks.

Even with his limited knowledge of history and science he knew the extraordinary value of his find. These were optical datalinks from the *Unity*, potentially full of valuable information that had been lost on the journey from Earth.

He packed the datalinks carefully and continued on toward Sparta Command, somewhere to the southeast.

Morning

Pierson steadied a support beam as one of his engineers welded it into place. As he worked he looked down across the new base, marveling how beams of metal became grid-like structures, and how those structures became hallways and rooms. They were creating a world out of nothing but bits of metal and plastics.

He released the beam and massaged his neck. Sweat poured off his forehead, but with the pressure mask in place it was difficult to wipe the stinging drops from his eyes.

"I'll be happy when we get this area pressurized," he said, and MacLean, his engineer, nodded profusely while finishing her weld. He had just picked up the next beam when an urgent communication flashed in from UNHQ.

"Do you have to take that?" asked the petite blonde, tapping her foot with mock impatience.

He frowned as he checked his quicklink display. "Actually, I do. It's coming over the security channel." He took a few steps away and read the communication.

"Another Gaian supply train attacked," he said suddenly. MacLean stopped working, her welding gun sputtering flames in her hand. "Several deaths this time. The last transmission came . . . west of here, about seven kilometers."

"That's close!"

He got on an open line of communication. "Everyone, there's been an attack on a supply train at a position near here. Anyone who can shoot a weapon, drive a rover, or dress a wound, get to the speeders. I'll lead in Colony One."

From around the construction site figures hurried, and transmissions crossed the quicklinks. Pierson ran for the lead rover, MacLean right behind him. Both had produced shredder pistols from their belts.

"I told you this day would come," said Pierson.

"If we can't beat them with skill, we'll overwhelm them with numbers."

"And raw stupidity," she said.

"Jahn Lal is en route from UNHQ. I want to take these people before he shows up and says something sensible."

"It's going to be messy." MacLean looked worried, but she also relished the adrenaline rush.

"If you wanted it clean, you should have stayed at UNHQ. I like it messy."

They climbed into a clean speeder marked Colony One.

"Go," Pierson said to the driver, and the rover took off across the red soil.

Victor walked steadily, a white rag tied over his head to keep off the sun, and as he walked he fiddled with his quicklink transmitter absently, trying to get it to work again.

He was on his last oxygen tank, and he thought about what would happen when it ran out. He knew he could breathe Chiron's air for a while, but that he would start acting strange, perhaps laughing uncontrollably. Eventually he would die. Some Spartans took long, grueling runs without their pressure masks, however. It was a matter of will.

Suddenly his transmitter flickered back to life, and his heart leaped.

Back on line!

"Thresher Fourteen to Command," he said, using his code name from Diego's squad.

"Command to Thresher Fourteen, over," came the efficient voice of a Spartan radioman. "What's your status, T-14? We have you marked as KIA."

"Negative," said Victor, mentally cursing Diego. "I'm good. But I have something here. I have datalinks from the *Unity.*"

"One moment," the radioman said coolly, but Victor knew that he had shaken the man. There was a long pause, and then Santiago's voice came on-line.

"Victor, this is Colonel Santiago. You have datalinks?"

"Yes, sir." He described their appearance.

"Yes, those are datalinks. Now, look carefully. There should be a code number etched on the edge of each of them. Read me the codes."

He stopped and pulled the translucent sheets from his backpack and read the tiny numbered codes from the side. There was a long pause while she cross-referenced the numbers with records from the *Unity.* Her voice came back on, and he could hear her excitement.

"Victor, you have found datalinks detailing the uses of high-energy chemistry, of the kind used in making powerful armor and deadly chemical weapons." There was exultation in her voice. "This information will be invaluable to us as warriors. Do you understand?"

"Yes, sir." Suddenly he felt his chest swell with pride.

"We need this information, but your locator puts you nearer to the Peacekeeper bases than to us. We want to make sure we get these datalinks back to Sparta Command. Do you understand?"

"Yes, sir."

"Good. I'm ordering Diego to come and get you. You must find a hiding place near your current location and remain there. Do not let anyone see you. Hide your pack, or bury it in case someone does find you. Understand?"

"Yes, sir."

"How do you feel?"

"Good." This time he meant it, a little.

"Santiago out."

The link closed. He looked around. To his east was an open plain, but to his west were some low hills. He thought there might be a small valley there that he could hide in.

He packed the datalinks carefully back in his pack. *Deadly chemical weapons.* Maybe now the Spartans would honor him.

He shouldered the pack and headed into the hills.

Pierson walked along the line of shattered Gaian transports, his face turning deep red with anger. Around him almost twenty Peacekeeper rovers idled, most of them not designed for combat.

"Look at this," he hissed. Gaians lay scattered everywhere, dry blood staining the ground beneath them. The transports sat under the Centauri sun, inert, their hatches torn open.

"There is no sign it was a Spartan attack, sir," said MacLean. "But of course we know it was," she added before he could launch into a tirade.

"Yes. This is most certainly the handiwork of the so-called rogue Spartan patrol. No one else could be so damn brutal."

"It looks like the Gaians fought back this time, sir," said another engineer, looking at a burned corpse lying on the ground. The man had thick armor melted into his skin, and he had no head.

"Good for them," said Pierson. He looked at the

transports, torn open by firepower that he could hardly imagine existed on this virgin world. But when he looked at it he didn't feel frightened, he felt angrier than ever.

"Sir, I have something," said one of his young engineers, running up to him with excitement. He showed Pierson the display on a long-range scanner. "Three vehicles, coming back from the west and heading to our east in a hurry."

"Spartans," Pierson said. "Looks like they're coming back." He hefted his shredder pistol and looked at his workers again. "We're going to clean up this mess, one way or the other. Follow my lead!" He jumped back into Colony One, leaving the Gaian dead burning underneath the Centauri sky.

Three speeders appeared at the mouth of Victor's small valley, all of them with Spartan insignia. He waited until they got closer and stepped out from behind a small rock, waving to them.

The speeders angled toward him and accelerated to full speed, coming to a noisy stop only a few meters away. The laser speeder still had a damaged turret; it hung in pieces off the top.

The hatch flew open on the laser speeder and Diego jumped out, landing hard on the ground. He grabbed Victor by the shoulder, and Victor winced as the big man's fingers dug in.

"Where are the datalinks?" he asked with no fanfare.

"I buried them behind that rock, just in case. Sir." Victor pointed to a pyramid-shaped rock on the other side of the narrow valley.

"There are Peacekeeper scouts rolling toward this

location." Diego pulled Victor toward the pointy rock. "A lot of them. We don't know what they're doing, but they could be looking for us."

Lansing popped his head out of the speeder, holding a long automatic shredder pistol. "They're coming!" he said.

Diego cursed and accelerated toward the hiding place, then glanced back toward the mouth of the valley and stopped. Victor looked back as well, but he kept moving toward the objective.

That's no scouting party, he thought.

In the mouth of the valley had appeared not one or two Peacekeeper rovers but five, and then ten, and then more. And they didn't stop to hail the Spartans, but came at them full speed, like charging animals.

"They know we attacked the supply train," shouted Diego. He pulled out his weapon and fell to one knee. "Shoot to kill, and prepare to make a run for the mouth of the valley when we have the datalinks."

Spartans jumped out of their speeders and opened fire on the approaching Peacekeepers, who hadn't slowed their pace.

"Those rovers have no mounted weapons," said Diego. "They're going to have to stop and fight us."

"I don't really think they're going to stop," said Victor.

Diego opened fire, throwing shots into the face of the approaching vehicles. Flames burst across the front of one rover. It flipped, rolling over and over like a landlocked comet, kicking up dirt and debris. Two rovers behind it swerved wildly to avoid it.

Lansing shouted orders at two Spartans on the ground, who lobbed concussion grenades at the enemy. But the Peacekeeper rovers, instead of slowing or maintaining their speed, accelerated, heading right toward the dismounted Spartans.

"Look out!" shouted Diego. He began to run for the pointy boulder behind Victor, but the rovers were on them like a wall of moving steel. One rover rocked up on two wheels as it cut sideways to ram Diego, and he tensed every muscle in his body to do a seemingly impossible leap backwards. A hatch on the top of the rover banged open and an older Peacekeeper man, his face flushed red, popped up and opened fire.

Shredder bolts riddled the ground around Victor. He saw a Peacekeeper rover heading right for him, its grille filling his vision, and he threw himself into the dirt. He was aware of a flash of darkness above him, the scream of metal, and a red-hot engine smell, and then the vehicle had passed over him.

I'm intact. I think.

Diego rolled to his feet, but the old Peacekeeper had turned and opened fire. With incredible speed and calm, Diego aimed his gun and squeezed off some shots. The Peacekeeper's head snapped back, and he fell halfway out of the rover from the impact of a hit. The vehicle jammed on its brakes and squealed to a halt, sending a cloud of dust into the air.

Diego grinned as more enemy vehicles screeched to a halt, rocking on their suspensions and sending dust into the air. He began firing at any exposed Peacekeeper. Victor had scrambled to his feet when he saw two more Peacekeeper rovers bearing down, masked by the sounds and the dust of the others stopping. But these weren't stopping.

"Commander!" he yelled, but it was too late. One of them accelerated right into Diego. Diego heard it at the last second and turned, putting down one hand and trying to push off the edge of the rover and leap out of the way, but the front grille caught him hard and sent him spinning into the air. Incredibly, even as he twisted in flight he managed to turn his gun back on the rover that had hit him and open fire, sending sparks dancing along its front.

The other rover must have been damaged, or perhaps the driver intended to end his life as a Peacekeeper legend, because that rover headed straight into the two Spartan vehicles and gunned its engines, striking both of them and sending them spinning away in opposite directions. The Peacekeeper rover went up on its two front wheels and a blue figure smashed halfway through the windshield, jagged shards of glass cutting into him or her, and then the vehicle flipped forward and landed upside down.

Diego lay twisted on the ground, then slowly he started to push himself to his feet.

"Regroup!" shouted Lansing, and then three more Peacekeepers roared into the valley, cleaner and newer than the first wave. Trained Peacekeeper security forces popped up out of the rovers like rabbits, and a cloud of shredder bolts filled the air. Lansing made a loud gurgling sound as a shredder bolt nicked him in the throat. He slumped down over the mouth of the speeder hatch.

Victor lunged forward toward the hidden datalinks, and then felt a stinging pain in his thigh, which didn't bother him as much as he thought it would. His body seemed wired to push on toward whatever goal he had programmed into his nervous system, which in this case was the datalinks.

Another shot hit him in the shin, shattering bone, and then one in the hip, but he still pushed forward. *If they cut off my head, my body would still fight its way to the datalinks and carry them back to Sparta Command*, he marveled.

"That's it. Spartans fall back!" shouted a new voice, a young blond man with cropped hair and a prominent brow. He aimed a small rocket launcher at the biggest grouping of Peacekeeper speeders and let it loose. A streak of fire crossed the tiny valley and a column of flame flashed into the sky.

Victor looked down and noted to his surprise that he was now crawling, dragging a shattered leg behind him. He stared at the leg and at the white chips of bone, but he felt no pain.

In front of him three Peacekeepers ran, not really noticing him as they tried to anchor a line at the pointy rock. He let himself fall to the ground as he pulled out his pistol.

A boot clamped down on his pistol hand, hard. He looked up to see a tower of blue above him—a Peacekeeper, obviously a leader by his bearing. The man aimed a pistol at Victor's head but looked in no hurry to use it.

Victor jabbed at the Peacekeeper's knee but the man quickly danced aside and kicked the pistol away. Victor then grabbed for the man's foot but missed. He tried to get to his feet but then a column of pain shot down his spine and into his foot, filling his broken leg with fire.

The Peacekeeper gave him a simple push, sending him back to the ground. Victor looked up, humiliated. The Keeper's face was deep brown behind the pressure mask, and calm even in the battle. It even looked as if he was concerned about Victor's damaged leg.

Suddenly the man tensed and then dove backward as a burst of gunfire raked across the space where he had just stood. Victor saw him dive behind the rock, and saw rock fragments exploding into the air as if in slow motion, more and more of them as the barrage continued. A concussion grenade exploding behind Victor buffeted him.

The Peacekeeper had dived right toward the datalinks' hiding place. *I should never have let go of them,* he thought with regret.

Suddenly hands grabbed him from behind and yanked him to his feet. He felt himself lifted up and thrown like a sack through the hatch of a Spartan speeder. Then another form came down on top of him . . . Diego, still holding his gun but gritting his teeth against pain.

The hatch clanged shut, cutting off the sun and the sounds of battle. The speeder churned the dust and took off for the mouth of the valley, leaving the datalinks behind, and Victor's last thought was that he would rather be lying on the ground with a Peacekeeper bullet in his skull.

Jahn Lal took one more look at the blue-suited bodies stretched out in the golden sunlight. He motioned to one of the citizens from his crew, and they both started grabbing white sheets from the med rover and draping them over the bodies.

Two medics went by, carrying a stretcher with the still-living body of Pierson on it. Jahn motioned them to stop and took a quick look at the man's injuries.

"A bullet right through the cheek," said Jahn. "Somehow it ricocheted off of that thick skull of his."

"Thick skulls save lives," said a weak voice, and Jahn looked down to see Pierson's eyes open. He grabbed the man's hand with genuine affection.

"You're a brave man, my friend. Foolish but brave. This was the most uncoordinated operation in Peacekeeper history."

"I'll leave it to you to top me," wheezed Pierson. He looked at Jahn. "I figure I'll live."

"You'll live. You'll be back on your feet in no time, unfortunately."

Pierson smiled weakly, and the medics carried him toward the med rover. Jahn shook his head and spoke angrily to no one in particular.

"This was a lot of foolish waste for nothing more than his own anger. Five of our people dead, four wounded, a former council member almost killed, and we achieved very little."

"We showed them we can hurt them," said the medic helping him with the bodies. Jahn looked at the set of the man's jaw and realized that Pierson's take-no-prisoners attitude was trickling down through the ranks.

"Think before you speak," said Jahn firmly. "We were unorganized and had no real tactics or weapons. We outnumbered them twenty to one, and still suffered casualties. And we took almost nothing away—no Spartan weapons or technology, and no prisoners."

"Sir!" shouted a citizen from behind the pointy rock. Jahn looked over to see a pretty blond woman holding up what looked like a dusty Gaian exploration pack. "Looks like they were hiding something."

"What's in there?" Jahn asked, heading her way.

"Datalinks, sir."

Jahn looked as the woman pulled out three unmistakable crystal panels and turned them in the sunlight.

The three speeders pulled into Sparta Command. As soon as the outside pressure hatch closed Santiago and her other advisors surrounded the first speeder. Its hatch opened and a citizen climbed out, helping Diego out with him.

Diego dropped down to the ground and tried to regain his feet, then collapsed. The next out was Victor, whose face looked white as a ghost. Blood soaked through the leg of his uniform, and bone fragments showed through. The Spartan that helped him down released him carelessly, and Victor lay down, gasping in pain.

"Explain yourself," said Santiago to Diego.

"Ambushed, sir," breathed Diego. The other advisors on council stood over him like watchtowers. "Peacekeepers came after us because of the attack on the supply train."

"I told you to step down your assaults on the supply trains. Pravin will cut off food shipments to us for certain."

"It wasn't planned," Diego said through teeth clenched against pain. "They came upon us. No choice."

"I choose not to believe you, Lieutenant. But what about the datalinks? How did you lose those?"

Diego pointed at her son. "He buried them. Toc-chet pulled us out of the battle when I fell." He grimaced, and then shouted, mostly to release his pain. "I have no excuse, sir!"

"I know you don't, Diego. Now the Peacekeepers have those datalinks, and I want them back." She stared down at him. "Look at you. You allowed the Peacekeepers to get access to advanced military technologies. Do you think your life was worth those datalinks?"

"No sir," said Diego angrily. "But God help the Peacekeepers because I lived, sir."

"Get medics to them both," said Santiago to a citizen. "We'll have council, and then I'll contact Pravin Lal. Those datalinks belong at Sparta Command."

Corazon Santiago looked at Pravin Lal steadily from the flat gray of his touchpanel. Her face betrayed no emotion other than a quiet intensity.

"Pravin, I must ask you to return the datalinks that were taken from my citizens, or give me full access to your research network. I must also ask that you break off your trade agreement with Nwabudike Morgan so that he can redirect some of his production resources to me. My people need some basic food and medical facilities more than you need a new art museum."

"Let's talk about the attack on the supply train first," said Pravin. "Gaian citizens were brutally murdered by your Spartans."

"The Gaians fired on us first." Santiago's face darkened. "The patrol commander was only defending himself."

"I believe that your commander destroyed several transports, and a firefight erupted."

"I have disciplined the man severely, and I assure you he will be attacking no one for a long time. But this brings us back to the issue at hand. We need Morgan's resources to build farms and hospitals, so my troops won't behave so erratically. And we want those datalinks that you took from us."

Pravin's eyes flickered away as he considered her proposal. "What you are asking of me is unreasonable, Corazon. I have carefully nurtured a relationship with Director Morgan to make sure that our new headquarters, the symbol of everything we humans have hoped to build on Chiron, gets constructed in good time. As for the datalinks, they contain information on potent weapons that have no place in the new world order."

Santiago nodded as if she had expected his reply.

"I must speak frankly, Pravin. I am finding your speeches about the future of humanity oppressive. You, Morgan, Skye, we Spartans, all of us want the best future for humanity. But we Spartans are warriors. We're the army of Chiron. It makes sense for us to have those datalinks."

"Because of the mindworms?"

"Yes," said Santiago. "And anything else that threatens us."

"Let us leave aside the issue right now that the datalinks contain information on chemical weapons that affect the *human* nervous system, and the distaste we all share for the use of such weapons. The datalinks were found on Peacekeeper soil, and I have determined that the information they contain is too dangerous to disseminate. I am determined to build our new world on a foundation of peace."

Santiago stared at him. "You hold yourself out as a shining example of new world politics, but you push your agenda as ruthlessly as any, Pravin. Talk to your advisors, and make sure you have consensus on your decision."

"I will do that, but I am sure they share my view, Corazon. We will not turn the datalinks over to you."

"Think carefully, Pravin. Santiago out."

She broke the link.

Pravin faced his advisors in council, skipping his opening remarks. All the men and women there sensed the gravity of this particular meeting.

"I believe that all of you have reviewed the communication from our friend Corazon Santiago," Pravin said. "I think her request is clear. But it is not clear what she will do if we refuse her."

"I know what she'll do," rasped Pierson. He sat propped up in a sleek black hospital chair that had been wheeled in for this council. "I am no longer on council, but I'm a witness to what her fighters can do. Those bastards fight with rage and skill. And the last thing she needs is more ways to kill us." He stopped for a rasping breath. "One of the Gaian transports had a hole melted into its side. Melted!"

"We can certainly refuse her the datalinks, but can we refuse her humanitarian relief?" asked Sophia. "She has made no direct threat against us."

"She has attacked Gaian supply trains. She has gunned down our soldiers!" said Pierson.

"She assures us that she disciplined the commander responsible," said Eldridge, brushing her long gray hair back from her face. There was a pause. "I guess we don't really believe her."

"Her people don't shit without permission from a superior officer," said Pierson.

"Yet she still seems to want peace," said Eldridge. "Perhaps we should give her what she asks."

"She wants the rest of us to give her food and resources so she can build up her army," Pierson spat.

"Consider this," said Jahn, turning to face the council and meeting their eyes one by one as he spoke. "Santiago is a warrior. She and her people live for combat, and they're trained to fight. If they don't fight, they'll become like rusty swords."

"But she wouldn't want her people to die," said Eldridge. "What good is that?"

"No, she wouldn't. But while the Spartans rest they don't serve their purpose. And though we may give her this concession now, and maintain peace, she will demand more concessions in the future, and more, while her army grows stronger and stronger."

"We have a good security force as well," said Pravin. "We have not been idle."

"We'll never be idle," said Jahn. "But we want to build new bases, and homes and parks and peacetime endeavors. She wants to build weapons. And I find it telling that she wants the datalinks. Even if Santiago sees the ways of reason, her own advisors will put pressure on her to fight. Having built this grand army, how long can she resist the temptation to use it?"

Jahn took a deep breath and released it. "As much as it pains me, I say we should draw a line in the sand now, while we're strong enough to fight her. Before she becomes too deadly to handle."

The council members fell silent, and Pravin stared at his son. Finally, Eldridge spoke. "There's something to what you say. But this is a very serious step. None of us want bloodshed."

"We will not declare war on Santiago, of course," said Pravin, lifting one slender hand. "We will only turn down her request to break our trade agreement with Director Morgan and to give her the datalinks."

Several heads nodded. Pravin looked at each advisor carefully.

"If we take this step, we are committed to whatever follows," he said. "We really don't know what she will do. But there could be war."

"There'll be more bloodshed if we wait," said Pierson. "The concept of a military coup is one we're all familiar with. Skye and Morgan couldn't stand up to her army."

"There is no need to vote on the issue of turning over the datalinks. I cannot ever allow that," Pravin said. "But on the issue of breaking our agreement with Director Morgan, let us vote. And I want to remind you what the Peacekeepers stand for."

Every advisor bowed to his or her touchscreen.

"Eight in favor of refusing Santiago's request." He nodded. "I will tell Santiago what we have decided. I hope I will have your support if any ill comes of this," he said, looking each of them in the eye. Last of all, as the meeting broke up, he looked at his son.

Jahn opened the door to the quarters he now shared with Sophia. Soft light slipped through the windows on the far side, and everything in the room looked clean and white: painted white walls, white sheets on the bed, and white planetcloth robes laid out for both of them. Discreetly placed glowlamps sent warm orange light around the bed, and on a small table a hybrid orchid grew in a ceramic dish, its blooms curving down in a delicate arc.

Jahn walked to the orchid and touched the soil, feeling for dryness. He knew this flower, obtained from Deirdre, would be difficult to keep alive, but so far he had risen to the challenge. Next to the orchid rested a pitcher and two glasses. He poured himself some water and looked out one of the windows.

The door opened behind him and he heard light footsteps.

"I'm home," came Sophia's voice.

"At last." Jahn smiled, still looking out the window. *Home.* They had indeed managed to build a home here, in this small room in this faraway place. They had few luxuries, but still managed to create a space they both cherished.

He listened for the rustle of her uniform slipping off her body and turned at the appropriate moment. His wife, his Chosen, stood naked in the soft light of the glowlamps, and he enjoyed the sight of her body for a moment, her long limbs and the health she radiated, even after an exhausting day. She looked up and saw him watching, and turned a little to give him a nice profile before wrapping her robe around her.

"Did you enjoy the show?" she asked, walking to him and slipping her arm around him.

"Always."

She took the glass of water from his hand and

drank from it. They looked out their small window over the base.

"Your father has done a good job," said Sophia. Their quarters were in a tall white building that rose up in the eastern part of UNHQ. Its walls were solid and strong, and the roof was tinted a pleasant gold. From their windows, about twenty meters up, they could see the network of hallways and pressure domes that crisscrossed the city below them. Farther west they could see the tall central tower and the glass of the observation room on top, and beyond that, in every direction, they could see the nearly finished new walls of UNHQ.

"It's amazing that a handful of metal and some pressure domes could turn into a small city so quickly," said Jahn. They watched it glow and hum for a few moments.

"What do you think of Santiago?" Sophia asked finally, and Jahn felt a subtle tension creep into his muscles at the mention of her name.

"She feels wronged. She wants the datalinks, and she may even want the infrastructure that we've built. But I hope that she'll stop short of civil war."

"I think she'll attack." Jahn looked at her, but she continued to look out the window. "Your father has this vision of Chiron that we all admire, but in this vision he's the benevolent philosopher king. Not everyone sees it that way. Santiago is a fighter, and she's been involved in more civil strife than any of us."

Jahn disengaged from her and paced the room. "But would she really go to war with us? She'll have to back down when she realizes the enormity of it."

"It was you who pointed out that an unused sword becomes rusty."

He shook his head in annoyance and turned down the sheets on his side of the bed. *But of course I think she's right. That's why I'm so angry.*

"Jahn," said Sophia, and he looked up at her. She stood facing him, wrapped in her white robe. "You know that I don't want this to happen. I want peace. We all want peace."

"We all want peace and power. If we all just wanted peace, there would be no conflict. And I'm no different."

Sophia nodded and walked toward him. She pushed him down on the bed and lay next to him, stroking his arm. "We're building something here, and Santiago threatens to tear it down. That's why we have to fight."

He nodded. She took one of his hands and slipped it under her robe. She guided his hand to the warm flesh of her belly and held it there. He felt the flesh for a moment, and then it dawned on him. He looked up into her eyes, which watched him with amused anticipation.

"Something else to take care of, Jahn," she said.

chapter six

Three years later

SANTIAGO SLIPPED INTO A SLEEVELESS VEST AND LEFT HER sparse quarters. She walked through halls that had no windows and little light except for glowlamps and the periodic flash of sun from a cannon port. She went downstairs and turned into a hallway that led her deeper into the center of Sparta Command.

Finally she came to a metal door marked "R & D." Two guards came to attention as she approached, and one of them pounded on the door. After a moment it opened.

A wiry man with hungry, gray eyes stood in the doorway and saluted her. His name was Malachai.

"Thank you for coming, Colonel," Malachai said. Santiago returned his salute, and they walked together into the labs. The metal door clanged shut behind them.

"It sounds like you have something very unusual to show me, Major," she said. Her eyes slid over to him. He didn't have the physical conditioning of a typical Spartan, but there was a devil-may-care psychosis about him that indicated he could hold his own in a fight.

His mind makes him a Spartan, Santiago reminded herself. *His mind relishes victory, enjoys violence, and would rather bleed than submit.*

Not to mention that he spent most hours of every day thinking about new ways to kill.

He led her to a long, low-ceilinged room, bolting the door behind them. On a nearby table rested several shredder pistols, along with some curious pieces of metal. At the other end of the room stood a Spartan soldier in thick armor, standing at attention.

"Here's the material that we obtained from Nwabudike Morgan," said Malachai, picking up one of the pieces of the metal and handing it to her. "It's very strong, but we were able to improve it with our new research into high-energy chemistry. Unfortunately, we haven't been able to re-create the nerve gas formulas that Pravin now holds, but you'll see that this material is quite useful."

She held the metal, which had a peculiar black sheen that seemed to repel light from its surface. It felt very light and even somewhat flexible.

"Impressive," she said. "But what can it do?"

He picked up a shredder pistol and motioned to the Spartan standing at attention on the other side of the long room, about twenty meters away. Santiago noticed that the soldier wore a suit of the black material.

"Shredder fire at this distance the armor will deflect," he said. He fired and hit the soldier in the armored shoulder. The soldier staggered back a half step but did not fall and quickly returned to position. "That will leave a bruise, but he can still fight."

Santiago nodded. Malachai motioned the soldier forward, and the man moved to a position about fifteen meters away. "Against automatic shredder fire it's still effective," he said, and opened fire. Shredder bolts hit the soldier full on the chest and pounded him backwards. The soldier fell down, and Malachai swept the stream of shredder bolts around his hips and legs. "You have to be careful of the feet," he said over the fire. "We haven't molded the boots yet." He stopped firing. The Spartan rolled on the floor for a few moments, and then slowly stood up again.

"Very good," said Santiago. "Can the armor fail?"

Malachai motioned the man forward, and he limped to within eight meters. "At close range the seams will come apart." He opened fire into the chest again, and as the soldier staggered back Malachai followed him. As Santiago watched, the chest plate began to split open, revealing a gray membrane at the core of the armor, and then that too pulled apart. Malachai stopped firing as the Spartan shouted something.

"How soon can you make more?" asked Santiago.

"We can construct it fairly quickly, but we need the material from Morgan as a base. We won't be able to manufacture the base material for several years, and it's very expensive."

"I want it for my personal guard, and quickly. By the time the entire army gets it, Pravin will have unlocked the secrets of the datalinks and have the nerve gas and superior armor in his possession."

Malachai nodded. "We have enough raw materials for your personal guard, and something special for you, Colonel. I guess you want me to keep all this a secret for now?"

"Of course."

"So I shouldn't tell anyone outside of my personal staff?" He studied her face with his feral gray eyes.

"Yes. I'll send my Myrmidons down for outfitting. No one else needs to know." She turned and left the room, the metal door banging shut behind her.

Malachai watched her leave and then walked over to stand above the Spartan soldier groaning on the floor.

"One more test," he said. He aimed the shredder pistol and started firing again, watching the armor split open like a rose in bloom.

"Is that them?" Pravin asked his lead scientist, staring at several rubbery globes that rested under a glass display.

"Yes," said Ella, walking over to him. She had a creamy brown complexion from her African/Indian roots, and long dark hair that she had tied back from her face with what looked like a shiny length of bundled optical fibers. "Don't look so dangerous now, do they?"

"I'm not sure," said Pravin. In fact the globes seemed to change shape slowly as he watched them, as if some kind of slow but sinister life force animated them.

"Well, there they are," she said. "Ready for . . . whatever it is you want to do with them."

He looked at her. She held a portable touchpanel and was apparently checking some numbers, absently tapping her stylus against the glass case. Trained first in Zakharov's University Base, she seemed to have taken on the old Russian's complete lack of moral concern about the uses of her creations.

"Let me see the video again," he said, and she looked at him, taking a moment to process his request.

"The video feed? Of the experiments?"

"Yes," said Pravin. She shrugged and led him to a monitor, where she dialed up a reference code from UNHQ's digital archives. Pravin sat down to watch, and as she moved away, intent on other business, he grabbed her wrist and stopped her.

"Watch with me," he said.

On the monitor appeared a simple title screen, identifying the video source as the datalinks found near the second Peacekeeper base some three years earlier. Then the video appeared, starting with a young woman's smooth, expressionless face, her black hair tied back in a tight bun.

"Our research into high-energy chemistry has created near limitless potential for armor and weaponry, assisting us in reaching the greater goals of the state. By controlling molecules down to their most fundamental level, we have unleashed the marvelous ability to split, combine, merge, and blend the most powerful forces of nature.

"The uses of this research are many, but the most effective is a blend of acidic chemicals that can be deployed over large urban areas. Observe now . . ."

The woman continued speaking as the camera cut to a wide city street outside a vast building, one of the hospital-fortresses of pre-launch Earth. A riot had developed outside the hospital, and a sea of citizens, poor, ragged, and hungry, surged against the sides of the massive complex again and again. From the roof of the hospital hundreds of police in riot gear and gas masks fired tear gas into the crowds.

The camera, obviously mounted on a helicopter, swept over the rioting population, which pounded the massive stone walls of the hospital from all sides.

"We will deploy the gas now on this experimental population," said the woman, and into the frame dropped a single flexible capsule, looking very much like the ones Pravin had seen under the glass. The capsule lengthened as it fell, as if reaching out for the chaotic streets below, and then it vanished into the masses.

A moment passed, and Pravin found himself clenching his hands in anticipation. Suddenly a strange jittering motion started in the crowd and spread out in a wave.

The camera zoomed in on ragged rioters as they jerked uncontrollably, twisting and thrashing spasmodically. The wave of thrashing rioters rippled out—although Pravin couldn't even see the gas itself—until the entire broad street, hundreds of thousands of people, had turned into a shuddering mass of dying humanity. The camera swept over to the hospital walls, where people in ragged clothing slammed repeatedly into the great walls, leaving streaks of blood on the stone.

"This is spectacular, but nothing special when modern weaponry is considered," continued the narrator. "The effect of this gas goes far beyond a localized massacre. In fact the pod contains a concentrated acid and nerve gas mixture that will burn through clothing, plastic, and porous materials such as stone and wood."

Pravin saw police in gas masks starting to jerk as well, tearing at their own faces and arms. The camera pulled back, and Pravin could see the adjoining streets erupt into chaos, and then people crashing through glass windows above the streets, their bodies slamming into the metal bars on their windows.

The helicopter pulled up, and the chaos and death went on, through walls, down streets . . . even underground, Pravin imagined.

"This was once the city of our enemy," said the voice. "Now it is ours for the taking, if we want it."

"Who would want that?" broke in Ella, looking at the streets choked with death.

Pravin shook his head. "We cannot use these gas pods. They are an utter atrocity, too brutal to imagine. Put them in a vault, lock them far away, and never let me see them again."

"Yes, sir," said the scientist, switching off the video. "I'll do it right away."

Santiago marched down the broad central hallway of Sparta Command, staring up at the narrow bands of sunlight that came down through the cannon ports. Ahead of her the main gates opened onto a rocky expanse of land, far beyond which lay the bases of the Peacekeepers.

She heard footsteps behind her and turned as Diego and Messier came up on her flanks. She stared at them coolly as they saluted her.

"Colonel, the last of the new laser speeders has come off the production line," said Diego. "We now have a full complement."

"Very good," said Santiago.

"That means it's time. We're ready to march on the Peacekeepers and take back what they took from Sparta."

She nodded. "I'll contact Pravin first, as we discussed. Maybe he'll have a change of heart."

"Doubtful," said Messier. "He's taken his stand. I think all of us know this is a prelude to war."

The touchscreen flickered and Santiago's face appeared. Her features were smooth and impassive, and Pravin felt his heart start pounding. Behind him his closest advisors waited, including his son, their faces expressionless.

"Greetings, Corazon. How are things at Sparta Command?"

"They are well, Pravin. But you know I prefer to skip the formalities. I wanted to ask you one last time whether you would turn over the information in the datalinks."

Pravin lifted his hands. "You have our terms, Colonel."

She nodded. "Then I have one more request that may satisfy us both. Turn over to me your new base, the one you call Base Two, that you have located so close to Sparta Command. I'm tired of being watched by your security forces, and I could make use of the farms and mines you have installed there."

"You are part of the settlements like any other, Corazon. That base belongs to all of humanity. But if you want us to turn control of the base's operations over to you, then the answer is no."

"You didn't consult with your advisors, Pravin."

"I don't need to consult with my advisors on that question, Corazon."

She nodded. Her eyes had darkened in color throughout the transmission, until now they burned like black coals. "Very well. Unfortunately, my own

council feels that your unwillingness to give Sparta
Command access to your datalinks amounts to an
act of aggression counter to the spirit of the UN Conventions. Therefore I have no choice but to send my
representatives to discuss this matter face-to-face."

"Are we talking about civil war, Corazon?"

"Our people are as different as night and day,
Pravin. But I want you to remember that you, the
great democrat, could have prevented all of this."
She paused as if acknowledging an inner voice.
"Colonel Santiago out."

The touchscreen flickered back to darkness. No
one spoke for several moments.

"We knew it would come to this," said Pierson,
breaking the silence. Pravin nodded.

"Pierson, you'll have to alert your citizens that
they're in danger," said Sophia. "And we have to let
Morgan and Skye know as well."

"Yes," said Pravin. He looked up at the UN seal
on the ceiling.

"Base Two won't stand up to a full-fledged Spartan attack," said Sophia.

"I'll take my citizens into the hills," said Pierson.
"The colonists there are tough, or they would have
remained here at UNHQ, where life is easy." He
grinned ruefully. "Let Santiago have the base for
now. It has no defenses and few facilities. We can
return from the hills and make her feel our pain."

"What if she comes here?" asked Jahn. All eyes
turned to him. "There's no other prize worth having."

"We are too strong for her," said Pravin. "As long
as we stay behind the walls, she would be foolish to
attack." He paused, then looked at Jahn. "But pre-

pare the security forces. We must be ready for anything."

"Anything," Jahn said, nodding.

Corazon sat on a cold metal bench and faced her advisors. Diego waited in silence, as he usually did now. Though he had long since recovered from his injuries three years ago, the bitter defeat seemed to have permanently darkened his mood.

"The last meeting with Pravin Lal had the intended effect," she said. "We gave him two requests he would never agree to, and now we have the excuse we need to march on his second base."

"Base Two doesn't interest me as a target," said Diego. "It's barely functioning. We could overrun it in a moment. UNHQ is the heart of their power, and the place where they hold the datalinks and most of their technology. We should strike at their heart."

"So you want to hurt them," said Santiago. "We don't risk thousands of Spartan soldiers for revenge, Diego."

"Then for what?" asked Diego. "Revenge is just another word for honor. The Peacekeepers have toyed with our food supplies, taken what rightfully belongs to us, and refused our requests. They've diminished our ability to survive, and for that we must strike back at them."

"But this is a military campaign," said Messier. "UNHQ has walls and well-developed defenses. Base Two is an excellent first target."

"I know what you say is out of caution and not cowardice," said Diego, and Messier's face flushed red with anger. "But the Peacekeepers are not foolish. They know the intention of Colonel Santiago's transmission. They know we want to fight. They'll pour all of their resources into their military now, to prepare for the inevitable. We'll never be stronger, relative to UNHQ, than we are now."

Messier nodded. "There may be truth in that."

"Taking the new base is like taking a pawn in a chess match," continued Diego. "It's a small and symbolic victory that will likely turn the rest of the settlements against us and doom our way of life. If we're going to attack, it must be full force, against the seat of government itself. This must be a coup."

"Many lives will be lost if we march against UNHQ," said Santiago. "All of us know the ramifications. I won't support this attack."

"By Spartan bylaws the commander can be overruled in a military matter if the council votes unanimously against her," said Diego. "And I vote for an attack on their headquarters. Who will support me?"

"I will," said the third advisor, Halleck.

"I will," said Messier after a moment. "Perhaps the threat of force alone will get us what we want."

"I will not support it," said Brady.

Santiago nodded. "All four of you must overrule me to alter our strategy, and you did not. We march on Peacekeeper Base Two. Draw up your plans. Dismissed."

She nodded to them and left the room. Diego remained, a dark mood overtaking him.

Brady sat at a large table in Sparta Command's library, straining his eyes to read under the flickering orange light. Like most rooms in the base, there were no windows, and it wasn't deemed important to outfit the room with powerful banks of new glowlamps.

The only touchpanel at the table was broken, so he took a piece of black charcoal and sketched out his plans for a new recreation commons, carefully drawing in the various areas inside the complex. A new library, a comfortable room for viewing digital movies from the datalinks, a play room, and a good eating facility were all drawn in.

He stopped sketching and looked at the plans. *Pathetic.* He had heard stories of the new facilities at UNHQ, with good food, and the museum of artifacts from Earth, and the glass-lined observation room that showed the sweep of Chiron. Not to mention Morgan's bases, where citizens had clean, private bathrooms, several sets of fashionable clothes, and their own video network.

He stood up and left the empty library, going down a dark stone hallway toward a halo of light at the end, where one of the few glass windows afforded a view of Chiron. He entered a small round alcove and stopped, looking out over the landscape, where the Spartan troops drilled in perfect formation.

It's so wide, and so full of potential. There are a thousand ways our lives could go. Why this way?

He squinted, staring as far out as he could. Somewhere out there to the east was the new Peacekeeper base, that Santiago would march on in due time. Somewhere to the southeast was the ocean, calm and vast, like Earth's oceans had been.

He thought about the Peacekeeper base again. He could take a speeder and go due east, arriving there in a few days. They would welcome him if he brought news of Santiago's plans. Maybe they needed another architect.

No. I'm not a traitor. If he had wanted to kill Spartans, he would have voted to let them march on UNHQ, with its great walls and thick defenses.

He heard a sound behind him and turned to see what it was. He saw a blur of movement and something slammed into his face, something broad and wet that stung his eyes and his skin. He shouted and clutched his eyes, doubling over.

A hand grabbed the back of his neck and he felt a series of small slaps into his belly. He still couldn't see, and his unseen assailant pushed him hard into the stone wall.

He blinked furiously, trying to clear his eyes, and as he did his hand went down to his stomach. He felt a warm smear of liquid there, turning his fingers slick, and then he felt the soft coil of something that belonged inside him.

"No," he said quietly, no longer bothering to shout. He was a Spartan, after all. He guessed he would be remembered for how he went out.

He thought about going down the hall for help, but decided his attacker had done the job well. He slumped against the wall and slid down to a sitting position, feeling the blood pool around him.

Red.

He turned his face to the window. He still couldn't see, but at least he could feel the bright light on his face while he died.

"There will be a full investigation into this matter," said Santiago, fury crackling in her voice. "The assassination of a ranking advisor is unacceptable in Sparta Command."

The other advisors nodded, their faces grim.

"If I find the bastard I'll kill him myself," said Diego. Santiago looked at him coldly.

"Everyone on the council will account for their whereabouts as well," she said. "This could be a politically motivated attack."

"Is there any particular council member you have in mind, Colonel?" asked Diego. Santiago was on her feet in less than an instant, her cat-like reflexes propelling her forward faster than Diego could have anticipated. He leaned back as she moved her face very close to his, as if studying every pore on his skin.

"I don't like your tone, Commander."

"I only asked the Colonel's mind," he said sullenly.

"If I want to say more to you I will. If I want to say less, you will accept it and smile." She continued to stare at him. "Let me see you smile."

He stared back at her, his eyes cold and hard. Finally the corners of his lips curled up into a tight smile.

"Yes, sir."

"This bickering is getting us nowhere," said Messier. Santiago resumed her seat. She gestured to a new advisor, sitting in the chair Brady used to occupy, a stocky woman with short, jet-black hair.

"What does our new facilities advisor have to say, Gruber?"

"I've looked over Brady's plans," she said, lifting a stack of sketched papers and his touchpanel computer. "He appeared very concerned with increasing our farming and basic support, and also about rounding out the Spartan spirit by building various new social and recreational facilities, many of them resource intensive."

"And he was regularly voted down," said Diego. "Though he made a worthy effort."

"He did," she said. "Frankly, I think many of the facilities he proposed would be a worthy addition to Sparta, of more benefit than we perhaps imagine."

"Then I assume that you will present your own plans about how we should distribute our critical resources?" asked Messier.

She cleared her throat. "Actually, I have a counterproposal. The Peacekeeper main base, UNHQ, has many of the facilities we need. I've read the transcripts of previous councils, and I concur with the vote to march against UNHQ."

"That issue is closed," said Santiago.

"Then I reopen it for debate," said Diego. "As is my right."

"It hardly matters, Lieutenant," said Santiago. "We'll have the troops stand down until the matter of this murder is settled."

Messier spoke. "With all due respect, Colonel, the troops are ready to march into battle, to risk their lives. It would be unfortunate to demonstrate any confusion at the command level at this time."

"I'm afraid I have to agree," said Halleck.

"What of the confusion when we change objectives from the new base to the Peacekeeper headquarters?" asked Santiago.

"The citizens already know there was talk of vendetta," said Diego. "They are mentally and physically prepared for the challenge. They want it."

"We must reopen this issue, as Diego says," said Messier. "After all, Colonel, the bylaws were created to assure our citizens that no one individual could make a costly strategic mistake for Sparta."

Diego nodded. "Peacekeeper Base Two is too much risk for too little gain, and it will align all of the other settlement citizens against us. There will never be a better time to take UNHQ. They have walls but few weapons, and they'll only get more powerful with time. This is what we've prepared for all these years, whether we admit it or not. Who will support me?"

Santiago watched as the council voted unanimously in support. Finally she nodded.

"Very well. I've been overruled. We'll march to UNHQ and take back what was taken from us."

"As the bylaws state, in a contested decision the council will assign one of the commanders for the attack, and you assign the other, Colonel," said Messier. "I believe Diego has the shrewdest tactical mind, as well as the will to succeed. He should command one battalion." The other advisors nodded in the affirmative. Diego nodded and settled back in his chair.

Messier looked at Santiago. "I assume you will assign yourself as the other battalion commander. No one has a better tactical mind, and it would be most fitting."

Santiago shook her head. "Nothing is fitting about this attack. As the second commander, I select my son."

Santiago stepped into the long tunnel that led to broad wooden gates. Beyond the gates lay Valhalla, the large open area in Sparta Command where the funeral pyres of citizens waited for the final death rites. Torches burned along the walls of the tunnel, and on a platform in the middle of the hall rested the body of Brady.

She went to the body and looked down at it. A Spartan military chaplain adjusted the clothes on the body and smoothed the bright red hair into place.

"He's not really a citizen, you know," said the chaplain as Santiago stared at the body. His uniform covered the ugly wounds in his belly, but his face looked pale and cold. She could see no serenity there.

"He is an advisor who gave his life to Sparta," said Santiago. "He deserves this rite of passage."

The chaplain nodded. "Of course. As a prelude to launching the invasion, a funeral with full honors will stir the citizens' hearts and prepare them for a good campaign. It's a wise choice."

Santiago looked at him. "Is that why you believe he's getting full honors?"

The chaplain paused, weighing his next words carefully. "Of course not," he finally said, then shifted uneasily. "We'll be taking him to the pyre in five minutes." The chaplain moved away from her.

Someone else stepped up next to the platform, and Santiago looked over. Victor stood there, looking down at the body without expression. Her son had grown into a slender but much stronger man, and his face seemed hardened by physical and emotional pain.

"Why did you choose me to lead the invasion force, sir?" he asked.

"Because you will follow orders, and you have a tactical mind. And because you know suffering, and that may help you to choose wisely, when others would choose to sacrifice our citizens in a fruitless blaze of glory." She looked down at the body of Brady.

Victor took a deep breath and looked around to make sure no one was nearby. "Why are you here,

Mother?" he asked. She looked at him, and he held her gaze. Finally she shrugged.

"I'm not quite sure." She studied her son's face, and then noticed his normally shaved head, where a row of stubble now grew. "You've stopped shaving your head," she said.

"It's time," he said simply.

She nodded, and lifted her hand to run it through the stubble.

Red.

Six Spartan warriors carried the body of Brady out the tunnel and into the open courtyard, where a pyre of precious wood harvested from the struggling Spartan forests awaited them. In uniforms and pressure masks, hundreds of Spartan citizens stood at attention in the courtyard. They were organized into battalions and companies, in perfect square formations. The Spartan honor guard placed his body on top of the pyre.

Santiago stepped up next to the pyre with the chaplain and removed her pressure mask to address the crowd more clearly.

"We hold this funeral outside, in the open air of Chiron, to honor the world we fight and die on. And we stand here at full attention, with our weapons at our side, ready to march on behalf of our fellow citizens."

She motioned to the pyre. "This man, Brady, served all of Sparta with his wisdom and discretion on my council. We should remember that." She took a deep breath and looked at his body on the pyre. "We came from a world of fire, and to fire we must return."

With that she took a long torch from the chaplain and pushed it into the pyre. Flames licked around the edges, struggling to catch hold in the low-oxygen Chiron atmosphere. Two of the honor guard stepped forward in red masks, holding blowers that directed jets of oxygenated air across the pyre.

The flames roared to life, sending dark smoke into the thick atmosphere. Santiago replaced her pressure mask and watched the flames engulf the body of Brady. When the body had started its journey to ashes, she turned and signaled the two battalion commanders in full Spartan battle armor.

"Attention!" said Diego into his quicklink. "Prepare to march!" He issued a string of orders, and over half of the assembled citizens presented their weapons and turned with precise movements, then began marching toward the huge front gates of Sparta. Diego marched in front of them.

When the citizens had assembled at the gates, Santiago looked to Victor, who stood near the smaller division of Spartan soldiers. He called them to attention, his voice firm but not overly loud. They obeyed his orders with perfect military precision as he directed them to the gates.

And then only a small division was left staring at the pyre, a small group of elite soldiers under Santiago's personal command. Her Myrmidons. She would not relinquish the command of these troops to anyone.

She ordered the Myrmidons toward the massive gates, which now swung open, revealing the vast landscape of Chiron outside. A hundred speeders and rovers waited, also in formation, each assigned to a particular squad. Santiago had her own speeders waiting, ready to take her and her deadliest fighters toward UNHQ.

They won't join the fight, she thought, looking at her Myrmidons in the shredder-resistant armor that Malachai had built for them. *I will not watch Sparta Command be torn down by the vengeful hands of every human in the settlements.*

Outside Sparta Command, two thousand soldiers gathered to march toward the horizon.

chapter seven

One week later

PRAVIN LAL STOOD WITH HIS SON IN THE BATTLEMENTS OF UNHQ. They looked south of their base, over the towering new south gates, past their farms and mines and out to the horizon.

From that horizon a long shadow appeared and advanced toward their position. As they watched the shadow resolved into marching troops and armored rovers, all advancing at a perfect, measured pace.

"I never thought I would see this day," said Pravin. Jahn looked at him; his father looked tired, and a little pale. "How did this happen?"

"We couldn't give what Santiago wanted to take," said Jahn. He picked up a pair of binoculars and looked over the approaching force carefully. "What could we do? Not build walls, give Santiago access to all of our technology, let her become the most deadly force on Chiron?"

"Perhaps. At least there would be no deaths."

"There would be deaths. It seems inevitable."

Pravin nodded. "Pierson will be disappointed they didn't come for him, I think."

"The Spartans will take Base Two at their leisure, after they attack here. Pierson didn't have a chance."

"He took his citizens into the hills," Pravin mused. "Is there a way we can still use them to our advantage?"

"Perhaps. Pierson has standing orders to make life difficult for the Spartans as soon as they attack. I intend for him to hit the Spartan line from behind at his discretion, forcing them to spend the extra effort worrying about him. He's crazy anyway; it's the perfect task for him."

Jahn continued to watch as the Spartans began spreading out on the plain, still far from the walls of the base. "It looks like they're going to form a half circle around us, probably anchored on either end by their best troops. They'll have difficulty getting around us to the east side because of the xenofungus. On the west side they'll have to go uphill, up to Sol Ridge, where our solar collectors catch the suns. It's a perfect position to shell the city from, and we can't let them take it. But they won't camp there. It's too steep and rocky."

He fell silent for a moment. The Spartan shadow hadn't stopped rolling forward.

"How many do they have?" asked Pravin.

"It looks like at least fifteen hundred soldiers, plus maybe fifty armed speeders."

"And how many do we have?"

"We have seven hundred citizens ready to fight, but only half of them have been trained extensively. We have very fast rovers if we want to meet them on the plain and disrupt their attacks. And we have our walls, thank Chiron."

"I'm going to contact the other leaders and let

them see the magnitude of what is happening here," said Pravin. "I hope the information in the datalinks was worth all this."

"We had no choice," said Jahn, and he looked at his father.

He doesn't know that I have already built the nerve gas pods, thought Pravin. *Not that it matters anyway. Both of us know they can never be used.*

Jahn continued his analysis. "As for Santiago, I suspect her people will fight to the death, but if we disable their speeders they'll be unable to do good repair work in the field. They've spent too much of their time on building weapons. Damaging them quickly and decisively is more important than a kill."

"What about diplomacy?" asked Pravin.

"Of course, diplomacy is best."

They heard footsteps behind them and turned to see Sophia approaching in her uniform of rank. She walked up and stood close to Jahn. When she saw the Spartans on the field, she sighed deeply.

"This seems unreal, like a dream," she said.

"The dream was peace," said Jahn. Sophia turned to Pravin.

"All the workers are in from the farms, mines, and solar facilities," she told him. "We did an accelerated harvest of everything we could, although there are still forests above the farms, near Sol Ridge. There's food piled to the ceiling in the storage rooms and kitchens. It should last for a year, with rationing."

"Do you think that Santiago would remain here a year?" asked Pravin.

"She might, if we have a standoff," said Jahn. "She could set up a supply line from Sparta Command."

"She could also take our farms at Base Two," said Sophia, and Jahn nodded.

"We'll order Pierson to come down from the hills and burn those farms," he said.

Pravin and Sophia looked at Jahn quietly. He knew what they were thinking, that he was ordering their own citizens to destroy precious resources that they had coaxed from this alien soil.

"I am going to contact Deirdre and Morgan. And even Zakharov," said Pravin. "Surely no one wants this."

"Good luck," said Jahn quietly. Pravin turned and left the battlements, and Jahn slipped his arm around Sophia's waist. Alpha Centauri A sat low in the sky, burning like Earth's yellow sun. Far away, but still within sight, the tiny figures of the Spartans set up their camp.

"Things are so different here on Chiron, and yet very much the same," said Sophia.

"I know what you mean." The rich colors of the sun, the touch of his hand on her back, the feeling of stone beneath his feet, all were no different on Earth.

He picked up his binoculars and scanned the Spartan force again. They had spread out into a semicircle, as he had anticipated, and were setting up row after row of translucent pressurized tents, a design straight from the *Unity*.

"They've left themselves a lot of distance," said Jahn. "They have no intention of letting their soldiers get picked off by a shot from our walls." In fact he could see more speeders heading into a range of small hills south of the farms, hidden from view and anchoring the west end of the Spartan line.

"Look at that," said Sophia. On the east end of

the line, three speeders flying Spartan battle flags set up near a cluster of tents. "There must be a commander in there."

"Probably," said Jahn. "Or it could be a trick. You never can tell, and you don't want to risk your life for something you can't see with your own eyes."

"Do you think Santiago is down there in person?" Sophia asked.

Jahn considered. "She could be. She would want to see her war machine in action. I remember her from training back on Earth. There's a part of her that doesn't care if she lives or dies."

He lapsed into silence, remembering his fight with Rank, so long ago. *But I care,* he realized. *I care that I come home, to my wife and my son. Will that work for me or against me?*

He pulled Sophia closer and watched the sunset.

Santiago pushed through the pressure door and into the command tent. It was relatively small, not much larger than the barracks tents and mess tents, so that it would not become a target for the enemy. A metal table and several chairs were set up in the center of the tent. Along one side another long table was set up, covered with computer equipment, communication links, and some charts and papers.

Diego and Victor, and several of their subordinate officers, came to their feet as Santiago entered. At the long table along the wall, two citizens, a communications officer and the operations director, continued to work, monitoring every aspect of their surroundings.

"Report," said Santiago.

"We have made camp and established our

perimeter, sir," said Diego. "All weapons have been checked, and orders have been distributed for the attack. We've all agreed that the first attack should be a quick strike to the left side followed by a rush forward to shatter the gates. Laser speeders will take care of any Peacekeepers on the wall, along with our infantry using handheld rockets. Our objective is to drive a speeder full of explosives directly into the gates."

"Do we know how strong the gates are?" asked Santiago, knowing full well that it was she, through diplomacy, who had been able to acquire that information.

"Of course, Colonel," said Diego stiffly. "Nwabudike Morgan gave us a rough idea of the strength of the gates. One explosive charge set against the hinges should be enough. Also, once we get close enough to their walls, we'll hit their city with mortars."

"We'll be firing blind, but we can still hurt them. Good," said Santiago. "They're not fighters; they'll probably stop the battle for a funeral procession at every Peacekeeper casualty."

"Exactly, sir," said Diego.

Victor stepped forward. "Sir, we will coordinate with First Battalion on a morning assault on the ridge to the west of the city. We'll destroy the solar arrays and then use the superior position to fire directly down on the city."

"Over the walls," said Santiago with a tight smile. "Good. That ridge is a key position. It will be hard to take but easy to defend."

"After that we'll send a scouting party north to make sure that Deirdre Skye doesn't come from the north to assist them."

"Let her," said Diego. He flexed his arms. Santiago could tell he held the Gaians partially responsible for the injuries he suffered after the supply train attack. He paused. "As long as we're laying out the battle plans, Colonel, where will your personal Myrmidon force be when the attack commences?"

"Most of them will be back at Sparta Command, guarding against a sneak attack," said Santiago. "I'm sending them back tonight. Do you have any further tactical questions?" She stared at him with dark eyes until he shook his head.

"No, sir."

"Dismissed," said Santiago.

"Nwabudike," said Pravin.

Nwabudike Morgan's face appeared on the touchscreen. Jahn waited behind his father, watching the interchange. He could see a new gravity on Morgan's face.

"Pravin Lal. I hear you're having some difficulty in your little slice of Chiron."

"I am, Nwabudike. Did you look at the video feed of the Spartan troops outside of my base?"

"I did. I hope my walls do well by you."

"I hope you can lend me more support than that, Nwabudike. It is starting to look like Earth out there."

Nwabudike shifted and averted his eyes. "We're not even close to looking like Earth."

"Don't you care that Santiago has built up a military force and that she's now turning it against me? Against other members of the settlements?"

"If you're asking me to send my own troops, Pravin, I have few troops to spare. I pride myself on a strong defense, and my charm. Corazon Santiago and I get along very well. It helps that we're far apart, of course."

"Will you care when she tries to take control of the planetary government, Nwabudike? What happens when she finally appears outside your gate?"

"You're both strong, Pravin. Either you'll settle your differences, or there will be too little left of anyone to threaten my rocky holdings. Either way there's little I can do. Building an army wasn't my top priority here."

Pravin stared at Nwabudike, trying to read something in his implacable face. "So you have given me walls, and that is enough?"

"When you build walls, someone will test them, my friend. That's the lesson I learned from Earth: it is far better to seduce your enemies, and make them depend on you."

Jahn stepped forward. "Is that supposed to be some kind of advice?"

"It's too late to follow that particular advice. But I suggest you give Santiago what she wants, or sell it to her. I'd hate to see bloodshed so soon on this world." He bowed to Pravin and Jahn. "You have my sympathy." The link ended.

"Something's wrong," said Jahn. "I've heard from citizens who visited Morgan's bases. He has more problems with mindworms than any of us. I know he has soldiers to fight them."

"We can not force him to give us anything," said Pravin, and Jahn saw how tired he looked. "Perhaps Santiago has bought his support with weaponry."

He turned back to the touchpanel.

"Deirdre Skye."

* * *

Messier found his way through the camp to the tightly closed ring of tents that served as Santiago's command. He noticed that a few of the tents glowed with light from the inside, but most of them were empty.

He found Santiago's personal tent and headed for it. Outside the tent stood two of her Myrmidons, wearing the strange jet-black armor forged in the Spartan research labs. They stood at attention, utterly impassive, and their pressure masks were tinted dark gray as well. They looked like some kind of living dead.

He nodded to the one on the left and pushed his way into the tent. He kept his pace measured, but every instinct screamed against a blade in the back. He had seen a Myrmidon throw a small knife into a man's eye from twenty meters.

"Colonel," he said, when he had pushed his way inside. Her tent was large, and unlike most of the others the surface was not translucent like the standard *Unity* issue tents. The tent contained a cot, a chest for her armor, a metal table with equipment on it, and a training dummy standing in one corner.

She nodded to him. He saw that her battle chest was open and that she was polishing a shin guard rhythmically. Her armor resembled the Myrmidons', but it was a striking deep red. It could turn back shredder bolts at all but point-blank range, and the sight of it, with its color, finish and unusual headpiece, tended to startle the enemy and inspire the loyal troops. There was nothing like it on Chiron.

"You look as if you're preparing to fight, Colonel," said Messier.

"If the need comes, I'll fight. Until then, the

armor stays in its chest. After all, there's no reason for a commander to risk her life on the front line, is there?"

"No, sir," said Messier, bowing his head. "But I did want to speak to you. The council is concerned about the Myrmidons."

"The Myrmidons can take care of themselves, Messier. Try and cross one if you feel otherwise."

"Never," said Messier. He let out a breath. "Permission to speak freely, sir."

"Granted."

"The council feels that you're withholding your Myrmidons from the battle because you disagree with the wisdom of this assault."

"Whether or not that's true, Messier, the Myrmidons are but a handful of troops in a very large army. And I won't put them under someone else's command. Since I've chosen my son to lead the second battalion, the Myrmidons will serve as reinforcements only."

"And why did you choose your son to lead in your place, Colonel? He's failed at almost everything, from his training to bringing back the datalinks."

"Because I'm the commander, Messier. I see things the rest of you don't."

"What you see in him is your own flesh and blood, sir. We all know he should have been dispatched long ago."

Santiago banged the shin guard down and came around the table toward Messier, her entire musculature as tight as a cat's. "Messier, when this battle is over I will see you and Diego and the rest of you in the training tent, and I will teach you the meaning of hardship and suffering. This whole faction, and all it endures, is but a shadow of what I endured as a child, and every day since. That's why *I* lead the Spartans, and decide who will lead my armies." He backed up a step and she stared at him, breathing deeply.

"Your permission to speak freely is rescinded for the evening, Messier. Dismissed."

Santiago turned her back on him and went back to the table.

Pravin stood and stretched.

Jahn shook his head and counted failed alliances on his fingers. "Morgan won't send assistance. Deirdre Skye insists she's nearly defenseless, and sees all of the fighting as a war against the planet. Zakharov says he'll speak with us later." He looked at Pravin. "What now?"

"They're waiting, I think. I'm certain that Morgan and Zakharov have spoken to Santiago in secret, trying to buy their safety. I wish them well. At any rate I'll make one more call, without the council present."

Jahn nodded as Pravin tapped in a secret transmitter code, and after a moment the smooth, cold face of Santiago appeared on the touchscreen. It appeared that she sat in her quarters, alone. Like his father, she had access to the precious genetic treatments from Zakharov's labs, and it had forestalled the specter of age. Unlike his father, she looked as strong and powerful as a young warrior, vitality humming through her muscles and tendons, and Jahn felt a twinge of fear as he looked at her.

"Pravin Lal," she said. "We're so close, you really could have stopped by for a face-to-face meeting. As you can see, my tent is very private."

"Perhaps, Corazon, but I am getting too old now.

You could certainly come to UNHQ for a tour, though. We can talk on the battlements, and you can keep an eye on your army the whole time."

"Is that your son behind you?" asked Santiago. Pravin nodded. "Let me see him."

Jahn stepped forward, keeping his face impassive. He nodded to her.

"Hard to believe that we would have lived so long that our children could become enemies," said Santiago.

"We are not enemies yet, Corazon," said Pravin. "Nor are our children."

"It's only a matter of time, Pravin. Have you forgotten Earth already?"

"Of course I have not forgotten. I remember every burning city, and every blind child. So many people lost their sight during the Flash Wars, I grew tired of counting. And so few could be saved."

Santiago stared at him, her own eyes unblinking. "The strong could be saved, Pravin. They had to be saved. Because the strong could impose their will on the new world order."

Jahn stared at Corazon Santiago. Her face remained as cool and aloof as ever, but he felt it masked some deep turmoil inside her, a violence done to her a lifetime ago and a star away. Pravin spoke again.

"Corazon, I can tell that this is not just a negotiation. I ask you this one last time: What do you want?"

"An end to the violence, of course, and the threat of violence," she said.

"That is what I want," Pravin said. "Turn around and leave this place, and the violence will end."

Santiago shook her head. "It will only end when all of my enemies are vanquished, and none can rise up to do me injustice. It will end when only the strongest is left, Pravin. Because until the strongest leads, the threat of violence will always exist. You know that."

"Even when the strongest leads, the weak will plot against them. It is only by choosing peace that we can stop the fighting."

Santiago suddenly smiled, shaking her head a little. "That's the difference between us, Pravin. That has always been the difference. You build walls, and I build weapons. I guess the time has come to see which one will prevail."

The image flickered once, then faded to blackness.

"She didn't even discuss terms," said Jahn.

"There was nothing to discuss," said Pravin. "I cannot give her the datalinks, and she cannot leave empty-handed." He looked at his son. "I tried, but Earth has repeated itself on Chiron."

"We'll see. Maybe we can end this quickly."

Pravin nodded, thinking again of the nerve gas pods, and the faceless masses dying in the streets.

Early morning

Centauri B slipped close to the horizon, letting the multitude of stars in the Chiron sky blaze forth a little brighter before Centauri A rose again. From a control room on top of the walls, Jahn's operations director spun an Earth coin on his tactical display table while monitoring perimeter cameras and sensor equipment.

"Someday you're going to spin that coin across an interface box and start a war," said Jahn lightly.

"So this is all my fault?" asked Spinner, nick-named for his nervous habit. A blinking alert light caught his attention and he leaned over to check it. "Something's happening out there. There's move-ment on the east side of the line."

Jahn bent over the monitors for a closer look. "They're moving into formation."

"I guess it's time," said Spinner, a good-natured but focused young man who had decided to enter the security forces rather than tend farms. "No more peace."

"I'll alert my father."

Victor pushed his hand forward in a slicing mo-tion, indicating that his advance force should move out. He knew that as a battalion commander he could choose to stay in camp and monitor the assault, but as a Spartan he was expected to lead his troops into battle. And he certainly needed to earn the respect of his soldiers.

Also, a part of him cared little whether he lived or died. He would lead his troops to glory, he fig-ured, or go down fighting, and let the war reach its conclusion without him as spectator or participant.

He had selected three highly trained and bal-anced squads for this mission. He had pored over the data files for hours, trying to choose the perfect balance of speed, courage, and specialized skills. The soldiers didn't seem to care; they received their orders without expression, and every one was pres-ent at the assembly point.

"Let's jog," he said into the comm unit built into

his pressure mask. "Bazzell, set the cadence." There was no overwhelming need to start at a jog, except that the early morning was cold, and he wanted this over with. And he wanted to see these soldiers run.

They set off at a fast clip, giving the walls of UNHQ a wide berth. As they ran he saw his soldiers glance back at him, their pressure masks presenting blank faces to him in the darkness. He was taller than he had been before, and a little stronger, but not strong enough. In fact Bazzell picked up the pace, moving faster and faster, and he began to gasp for deeper breaths.

He pulled out a night scope and used it to look toward the walls of UNHQ. Between his position and UNHQ lay the shadowy mass of a farm storage building, about half a kilometer from the city's walls.

"Stop," he ordered, and his soldiers stopped and gathered around him. "There are farms over there."

"Yes, sir," said Bazzell, a stocky man with a deep voice. "But there are no crops left on that farm. The Keepers took them all inside the walls. It's already been scouted."

Victor looked at the shadowy farm buildings and tried to catch his breath. Above him the mass of what the Peacekeepers called Sol Ridge loomed, a dark blot against the gray predawn sky. He started to feel very uneasy, an uneasiness he couldn't pinpoint.

"Let's continue," he said. "Bazzell, you take the point. I'll take the rear position. Don't slow the pace for me."

Bazzell nodded impassively, and the Spartans did exactly as he ordered, starting on a faster clip up the slope.

Victor started running again and fingered the

trigger on his weapon. None of the fighters looked back at him, and he wondered if they thought him a coward.

I'm battalion commander, he thought. *I shouldn't be here at all.*

Victor continued up the slope toward Sol Ridge, between the widely spaced trunks of hybrid trees that loomed in the darkness. Gradually the slope got steeper and rockier and the trees vanished. He noticed the pace slowing now, and pebbles and rocks slid down from the Spartans above.

His senses reached out into the darkness, feeling again for that sense of danger. Up ahead he saw Bazzell reach a near vertical overhang and start up it, oblivious to the possibility of an ambush.

If I were the Peacekeepers, that's where I'd put it, thought Victor. *But what do they know? They're Peacekeepers.*

Bazzell seemed to reach the top of the overhang without incident, and the others followed him. Finally Victor reached the steep face and sheathed his weapon, now lagging his troops by over a minute.

He topped the overhang and saw a stretch of long flat ground that led up several hundred meters to a broad platform carved from the rock above. Leading up to the platform and on the platform itself were dozens of stone and metal pillars, and mounted at the top of each one was a large flat sheet of glass, several times as wide and tall as a human, turned to face the approaching dawn.

Solar collectors.

Victor pulled out his weapon. His troops, who had continued the climb without him, were on the platform, staring out over the city. He moved over to the rocky edge and looked, seeing the expanse of UNHQ inside its ring of walls.

Centauri A slipped above the horizon, sending a warm light over the pale white surface of the walls. Victor felt a longing stir in him, and he thought of the Peacekeepers in their quiet city, their home.

Above him his troops started planting explosive charges around the bases of the solar collectors. Victor ignored them, letting them do their work. He stayed low on the ridge and looked at the city, at the tall tower rising from its center, and then at the Spartan forces massing in front of their camp.

Above him the first explosion rocked the stone platform, and one of the collectors toppled, shattering its broad glass panels into a thousand pieces.

The lights flickered in the command room at the same moment the sound of an impact echoed across the hills to the west of the base. Another impact followed.

"It's out by the solar collectors," said Spinner.

"Get me a visual," said Jahn. Spinner dialed up a view of the solar collectors from a long-range camera on the west wall.

Along the rocky plateau above UNHQ, the third solar collector rocked from the force of an explosion and toppled over, followed by the fourth. As each one shattered it sent a blast of glass fragments and smoke high into the air, glittering in the pale morning light.

"They're on the ridge, sir." Spinner said. "Do it now?"

"Yes. Detonate the charges," Jahn said. Spinner nodded and entered a security code sequence, then activated a detonator.

Up on the ridge above UNHQ, an array of explosives rocked the bases of the solar collectors, sending fragments of glass and stone in all directions, along with tattered forms that looked like bodies. The booming of the explosions echoed over the city.

"Fight fire with fire," said Jahn as waves of concussive force shook the high ridges, throwing more glass skyward and sending rocks and soil tumbling down from the high slopes. A cloud of dust and smoke rose off the high ridge.

"Cool," breathed Spinner.

"Any indication of damage?" asked Jahn.

"None that we can see here. But there's no more movement."

"We'll have to keep a close eye on that ridge. If they try for it again, we'll have to send soldiers up there."

"Hazard duty," said Spinner. As Jahn watched the displays, two of the damaged solar panels nearest the edge of the ridge suddenly toppled, crashing down the rocky slopes.

"Make sure Sophia knows that power rationing begins now," said Jahn.

Victor had no idea the blast was coming. One moment his primary demo woman was laying explosives around the base of the fifth solar panel and the next moment a wave of heat and force slammed across his back. He covered his face as the air filled with rocks and shards of glass.

"Get down off the ridge!" he shouted to his soldiers, while his mind whirled. *A basic ambush. They let us have the panels, knowing we would target them, and used them as bait.*

Victor ran up the slope to the top of the ridge. He could feel shards of glass in his back where the shock wave had hit him, but his injuries were nothing compared to what had happened to his troops.

Hunks of stone and metal lay scattered everywhere, and the ground was covered with a carpet of glass. Men and women lay tossed around in broken heaps, most dead, some still groaning. Bazzell staggered in his direction, clutching his face, both of his forearms riddled with large slivers of glass. Another tower exploded, sending its remains skyward, and Victor figured that the view from down on the plain was spectacular.

"Drag the wounded back to the overhang," Victor said to Bazzell. "We'll get them back down to the farm building." Bazzell nodded wordlessly. Victor looked over to see a soldier on his back, so full of glass and metal that every time Victor blinked the man's face turned into a glittering kaleidoscope.

Victor grabbed the soldier by the ankles and started dragging him down the slope.

"What's next?" asked Spinner, checking his monitors ceaselessly.

"Front and center. Here they come," said Jahn, pointing to a view of the field outside.

The wall of Spartans massing outside the camp suddenly surged into motion, coming forward like a wave. Speeders rocketed forward, distancing themselves from the jogging infantry, while Spartan gunners manned the speeder turrets, ready to fire.

"Sound the alert," Jahn said calmly. Spinner pressed an alert key and sirens wailed throughout the base, while an update of the battle condition was quicklinked to every citizen. Jahn had a fleeting thought of Sophia, hunched over displays in the council room.

"Alert the gunners on the wall." He took a deep breath. *Should I let them fire first?* It was a small distinction, to let the Spartans initiate fire, but an important one if he really did believe in peace.

Yet as a commander, he couldn't let the enemy approach the walls unchallenged. Again, he had no choice.

"Tell them . . . when the Spartans get in range, we'll open fire."

Victor reentered the west end of the Spartan camp accompanied only by Bazzell, who grimaced every time he stepped on a broken foot.

"Will we send medics back up to them?" asked Bazzell, pain now shortening his breath to tight gasps.

Victor ran his fingers through his short-cropped hair and thought of the suffering that the Spartans had taught him, how they had convinced him the beatings would cleanse his spirit and make him fit to live as a warrior.

He shook his head. "Those citizens will never recover in time to be of use to us during this battle. We'll see how Diego fares, and if there are spare medics we'll send them up the ridge."

"That seems irregular, sir," said the man, and Victor turned on him with cold, blank eyes.

"Would you like me to order you back into combat now, to remind you how much pain the Spartan body can endure?"

"No, sir," said the man quietly.

"Get back to your tent," Victor said, and then turned and headed for the command tent.

They won't blame me for the failure of this mission, he thought. No one could have known that the Peacekeepers had rigged their own solar collectors with explosives.

No. I should have anticipated. They're better tacticians than we expected, and perhaps more desperate.

He continued walking toward the command tent at a steady pace, his face blank, preparing to face his mother and Diego.

Jahn watched the field from the battlements as the Spartans drew within range of the walls. The Spartan speeders crossed the plain in great sweeping arcs, trying to confuse the defensive fire from the walls, as the infantry came forward in a steady wave, the early morning light sending their long shadows across the plain.

"Our weakest point is the gates," said Jahn. "We've got to keep them back from there. They may have a ram or explosive charges."

"We have soldiers standing by in the west and east guard towers flanking the gates, and we have the charges buried outside as well," said Spinner. "Let the Spartans get close."

Jahn nodded. "Tell the forward observers to relay positions of the largest concentrations of infantry back to the mortar crews. Let the marksmen handle the speeders for now."

"Yes, sir."

From up on the walls, trained observers informed mortar crews stationed behind the walls where to aim their munitions. Soldiers armed with rocket launchers and highly accurate penetration rifles tracked the enemy from the battlements. Jahn waited, trying to teleport himself mentally into the battle, to feel what it was like in the Spartan ranks, looking up at the great walls of UNHQ.

"Fire at will," he said, and Spinner relayed the order. From behind the walls he heard a sound like a loud *chuff,* and a smoky trail arced into the sky like a flare over a dark sea. Down toward a squad of Spartan soldiers it arced, and they began scattering, breaking their perfect formation.

The mortar struck and exploded in a flash of light, the boom rolling across the plain back to the walls. When the flash and smoke cleared, two figures lay still in the red soil.

"Got them!" shouted Spinner. More *chuffs* sounded, and trails of smoke arced into the sky, heading down into the approaching army. Tiny puffs of smoke kicked up from the plains as the marksmen opened fire from the walls, and two rockets streaked down, one whipping through a Spartan formation and somehow knocking the commander back almost fifty meters before detonating. The Spartan infantry began spreading out and accelerating their pace.

Jahn grabbed his binoculars and quickly zoomed in on the first Spartan casualties. They lay on the plain like dark blots against the pale red earth.

They would probably go down in Spartan history.
Small consolation.

The Spartan infantry had accelerated its pace to a fast jog, and they seemed to advance without tiring. The next round of mortars passed right over them, exploding in columns of fire behind the advancing warriors.

"Conserve ammo," said Jahn. "We could have a long fight ahead of us."

Speeders roared forward at top speed and cut in front of the walls. Spartans manned the gun turrets and opened fire. Shredder bolts raked the top of the wall, and Jahn said a quick prayer for the marksmen, who were taught to fire and dodge as if their lives depended on it. The fire toward the battlements increased until it seemed like a buzzing cloud.

"I hope our people know when to duck," said Spinner.

"The Spartans have lots of ammo, and fast speeders, and well-trained soldiers," said Jahn. "But I don't see their advanced weaponry yet. We know they've done research into energy weapons."

"It's out there somewhere. Just like the bullet with your name on it. You just don't know where it's coming from."

Jahn nodded and watched the Spartan advance.

"Eighteen casualties from my battalion," said Diego grimly. He looked up from the tactical display table and over to Santiago, who also looked at the virtual projection of the battle. Victor stood a little back from the table, his face unreadable. "They died with honor."

"It's still unfortunate," said Santiago. She pointed to the display. "How is your plan progressing?"

"We're hitting their defenses hard in preparation for our assault on the south gates," said Diego, and he couldn't hide the relish in his voice. "We have a demo speeder loaded with explosive charges, and there's no way for the Peacekeepers to tell which speeder it is. We'll open fire with our energy weapons to distract them, and then run the demo speeder to the gates."

"The gates are strong," said Santiago. "You'll have to get very close."

"We will," said Diego. He looked over at Victor. "Well, Commander, will you stand there with your hands in your codpiece all day? How is your side of the attack?"

"We were sabotaged, as you know," said Victor, his voice not betraying any emotion. "But this ridge is too valuable to ignore. I left some soldiers in the farm buildings in case the Peacekeepers send more troops out for an ambush. When you make your assault on the gate, we'll send two more squads up to the ridge."

"It's a difficult approach," said Santiago. "But you're right, the position is invaluable."

"When we take the position, we'll fire our heavy weaponry down into their city directly, damaging their pressure domes," said Victor. "They'll have no chance to regain the ridge once its ours."

"Good," said Santiago.

"It'll just be icing on the cake when we crack the gates wide," said Diego. He looked at Santiago. "Will your Myrmidons be joining the massacre?"

"I didn't order a massacre, and it sounds like my Myrmidons are unnecessary. I'm going to look on the battle with my own eyes. Don't forget to watch your backs." She put her pressure mask on and pushed her way out of the tent seal.

Diego looked at the battle, and then at Victor. "You'll have to go out there and fight with your citizens again," he said. "You may be a bad luck charm, but we are Spartans, and Spartans live for war. We relish it."

Victor looked at him impassively.

chapter eight

The same day

JAHN WATCHED THE MOVEMENTS OF THE SPEEDERS ON THE plain. Shredder, rocket, and rifle fire crossed from the speeders up to the walls and back down again, kicking up clumps of red dirt and churning the soil of the plain. Fallen Spartans lay at erratic intervals around the field of battle, and Jahn noticed that some of the marksmen were taking potshots at the medics.

"Don't shoot their medics or corpse bearers!" he said angrily into an open line on his quicklink. "We're not barbarians!" He closed the link crossly.

"They're setting up mortars," said Spinner, subdued. *It's never as much fun on the receiving end,* Jahn thought. As he watched, two speeders formed a blockade and a squad of Spartan infantry set up a mortar behind them. Spinner rattled off a warning, and two rockets streaked down from the walls and burst near the Spartans, but both missed. From the mortar crew came a flash of light, and then a silver shape arced up into the sky, sailing high and over the Peacekeeper walls.

"Shit. It's a high-caliber round," said Spinner,

sounding the alert inside the city. He skillfully operated cameras to follow the course of the incoming round.

"By Chiron," Jahn said. He felt helpless as he watched the round, at least twice as big as the Peacekeepers' defensive munitions, start its descent into the area inside the city walls.

"At least they can't see where they're firing," said Spinner. "They're shooting blind."

"The Children's Crèche," said Jahn, and he felt his legs go weak underneath him.

Then they watched in silence as the round fell inside the walls, near one of the many twisting hallways and pressure domes inside UNHQ, close to a small, round reinforced tent that held fifty Peacekeeper children during the day.

There was a moment between the time the round almost hit, and the time right after the round hit, and that moment seemed to draw on forever, and a darkness seemed to descend over Chiron as Jahn waited.

There was a flash of light, and a ring of explosive force that radiated outward in an instant, twisting the metal of nearby hallways and blasting the side off the Crèche tent, tearing its rubbery outer shell and collapsing its metal supports. Where a moment before there had been a part of the city, Jahn now saw a smoking crater in the earth, scorched metal, and the misshapen Crèche tent bleeding its atmosphere into the sky.

"They hit it," said Spinner.

Jahn shook his head in disbelief. "All the children must have been moved to underground passages."

"Most. There were nurses down there, organizing the evac. I've scrambled the med team."

"The tent is losing its air, and those hallways. Get the engineers down there to seal it." Jahn turned his attention back to the battlefield, where more Spartan mortar teams set up, and more rounds fired into the air. He could see two more even now, arcing like vipers into the heart of his city.

"They won't hit something every time," said Spinner, but Jahn wondered how many times they needed.

Pravin hurried down narrow metal hallways in the old section of UNHQ, toward the location where the Spartan mortar had struck the Children's Crèche. He had already put on a pressure mask, and he could hear his own breath rasping in his ears.

He rounded a corner and saw three yellow-suited engineers covering the hallway with a thick sheet of translucent rubbery material. They worked quickly, and he could see the stress on their faces already, this early in the battle.

We haven't prepared them for this kind of work, he thought.

One of them looked at him with tired eyes, which Pravin could see even through the man's pressure mask.

The man pulled up a flap in the bottom of the makeshift seal and motioned Pravin through. Pravin ducked and crossed into a world that had been turned upside down.

The narrow hallway had turned into a blackened, twisting serpent, thrown haphazardly across the terrain. One entire wall had been torn open, and he could see the smoking crater where the mortar had struck. Beyond the crater he could see the wall of the Children's Crèche, now collapsed and torn.

He made his way carefully past the tunnel wreckage and to the edge of the Crèche tent. What he saw inside was utter ruin . . . small tables and chairs tossed like doll's furniture, thick smoke in the air, and the brightly colored walls torn and melted.

He stepped over the body of a woman, one of the metal support rods thrust through her belly. She stared up at him with empty eyes, blood soaking into her simple, bright blue teacher's smock.

He saw two of his medics bent over another victim, an older teacher whose dimming eyesight had left him unable to do precise engineering tasks. The man's face and arms were blackened and his mouth was frozen open in a grimace, as if he were about to shout.

Go ahead and shout, thought Pravin.

"How are things here?" asked Pravin, as a medic walked over to greet him. The medic's face was ashen. "Is this the worst of it?"

The medic shook his head and pointed along the collapsed wall of the Crèche, where a small square trapdoor in the floor was propped open with a piece of broken wood. Around the trapdoor Pravin saw a large crack in the floor, as if the very foundation of the Crèche had shifted.

"That's the worst," said the medic, shaking his head. "There's nothing to be done."

Pravin hurried to the trapdoor and looked down. A wide ladder led down into a space beneath the tent's foundation. Jagged pieces of stone lay at odd angles, and harsh white floodlights threw the space into stark relief.

Pravin went down the ladder slowly. Two medics moved through the wreckage like ghosts, looking helpless.

The space was large and low ceilinged, and in the center of the room were rows of small plastic desks with rocks piled around them. Support beams had crashed down from the ceiling, and rubble lay strewn everywhere.

In almost every desk sat a child. Their feet were flat on the floor and their heads bowed on their desks, faces turned to one side or the other. The technicians had cleared much of the rubble away, but Pravin could still see where the broad beams from the ceiling had fallen, crushing the heads and bodies of the children.

"No," said Pravin quietly. He walked slowly toward the corner desk, where a young Indian boy lay with his head turned sideways and his hands on either side. The force of the collapsing roof had forced his small head into the desk, cracking the wooden surface in two. Pravin brushed the boy's tiny fingers, thinking of Jahn at this age.

"What have we done?"

"What has *she* done," said one of the medics, her voice loud and angry in the almost reverent atmosphere. "Santiago killed these kids." The woman stopped, choking with emotion. "I swear I'm going to transfer to the wall."

"Did any survive?" asked Pravin.

"Some did," said the woman. "Eleven of the fifty. We took them to the medlabs." She shook her head angrily. "They came down here for safety."

Pravin found himself drifting around the perimeter of the seats, as ghostlike as the two medics. He felt himself disassociating from the world outside, but knew he couldn't let that happen.

From somewhere above and far away came an explosion, sending a shock wave through the foundation. Rocks shifted above them.

"There will be more injuries," said Pravin. "There is nothing more to do here now. We will move the rest of the children into the deep underground tunnels near the medlabs."

The woman stared at him blankly, standing right in the path of one of the bright lights. It turned her face into an unpleasant relief of shadows and light.

"Go upstairs," Pravin told her. "Put this in the back of your mind for now."

"I don't think I can," she said.

"You must," Pravin replied, and turned back to the ladder.

"Where did those last Spartan mortars hit?" asked Jahn.

"Two of them missed any domes, although one of them damaged one of the storage facilities. The last one hit dead on the recreation commons on the east side. Three reported dead, five injured."

"Everyone who knows how to work a concussion hammer needs to be out there on repair crews," said Jahn. He spoke into his quicklink. "These mortars are hitting us hard, citizens. They're much more potent than we anticipated. Take them out before any other targets."

"They're still shooting blind," said Spinner. "Critical targets are the medlabs, which are underground, the water tanks, which are near the inner gates, the power capacitors, and any of the reinforced housing facilities."

"They might get lucky, but we can't help that," said Jahn. "But I think we underestimated the importance of Sol Ridge. If they get this powerful weaponry up there, they'll have the whole city laid out for them like a map."

Spinner nodded in agreement. Jahn got on his quicklink. "West battlements, report in," he said, and waited for the acknowledgment. "What's happening on Sol Ridge?"

"The smoke from the explosives is drifting down the ridge. It's thick and slow to disperse," replied a snappy voice.

"Any movement on the ridge?"

"None right now, sir."

Jahn nodded and spoke into his quicklink. "Keep both eyes on that ridge, soldier. I don't want you to blink without seeing that ridge on the back of your eyelids. If they take that position we're in for a world of trouble."

"Yes, sir."

Jahn broke the link and lapsed into thought. "If this battle continues we're going to have to go out there."

"We'd get decimated, sir," said Spinner. "We'd lose the benefits of the walls." He looked at Jahn and spun his coin across the touchpanel again. "But if they take the ridge we're in trouble anyway."

Jahn nodded.

Diego looked out through the narrow gun port of the speeder as the red soil of Chiron whizzed past.

He grinned, his hands on his weapon, relishing his presence in the battle as the mortars arced overhead and the return fire boomed on the plain.

He took out a pair of binoculars and swept his gaze along the top of the wall. The Peacekeeper marksmen had become more aggressive, thrusting their long-barreled penetration rifles through the gun ports on the battlements and taking shots at his speeders. Even as he watched a speeder blew out, rolling over and over, turning into an oily, flaming hunk of metal that crashed into a phalanx of six Spartan infantry.

"It's time," said Diego. He spoke into his quicklink. "Laser speeders open fire. Target the tops of the walls. Let's cook up some Keepers."

As he watched, several speeders with black steel turrets peeled out of formation. The turrets, which had pointed away from UNHQ, now swiveled toward it, revealing guns that were long and black and held no shredder bolts. Diego could almost hear the high-pitched whine as the energy cells charged.

"Fire at will!" he shouted, then turned to his driver. "Meet up with the demo speeder and let's head for the gates. Drive carefully." He grinned.

The speeder pilot nodded and kicked in a burst of extra speed.

"Another three speeders coming out of the Spartan camp," said Spinner. "They have no markings, but they're fast. May be command vehicles."

"Keep an eye on them," said Jahn. He stared at the tactical display, trying to see an overall pattern of movement that would indicate the Spartan plan. So far the Spartans had blasted chunks from the walls and decimated some sections of the base, but had done little else.

"Our marksmen are going to have to take more risks," said Jahn. "Order them to step up their fire. Those mortars are costing us."

"Yes, sir," said Spinner, and relayed the order.

Private Jones crouched at her position on the battlements as the plain below filled with burning wreckage and thick, slow-moving smoke.

She took a deep breath and popped up into a gun port, aimed her long penetration rifle quickly, and squeezed off several shots at a three-person Spartan mortar team setting up a hundred meters from the wall. One of them clutched his belly and staggered back. Private Jones ducked back to avoid return fire, wondering if she had disabled her target.

A short-range missile streaked up from the plain, arcing in a crazy loop and exploding against the battlements near her. The floor beneath her shook, and a cloud of white fragments sprayed up into the air.

Another missile struck, even closer, and her eyes burned from the flash. A fine white dust coated her blue uniform, and she began to glance back toward the guard towers, wondering if a superior officer would make an appearance.

"Stay focused on the field, Jones," muttered Cunningham, the burly soldier stationed to her right. She looked over at him and saw him crouched down tensely, ready to pop up and squeeze off some shots.

"You don't look around at all?" she asked him, and in another time and place might have even put a flirtatious lilt into her voice. But not here. She gripped the stock of her rifle tightly.

"That's right, Jones. I took my training to heart." He darted up and fired several shots, then ducked back down again.

"Then how did you know I was looking away?" she asked, and jumped up again, firing repeatedly at the mortar squad. This time she stayed up until she saw one of them, the crew chief, jerk and fall backwards. The next instant a Peacekeeper mortar hit the location dead on, engulfing the three in an orange-white blast.

Next to her, Cunningham looked her way, and she thought she heard a smile in his voice.

"Good one, Jones."

She started to say something else, and then noticed him pull out a small mirror and use it to look over the battlements without endangering himself. He shook his head. "They're getting more aggressive, Jones. They're getting closer to the wall. Look at all the speeders."

He slid her the mirror and she used it to look down over the wall. She saw that the Spartan speeders were indeed running full throttle in attack patterns close to the wall. A line of shredder bolts hit the wall in front of her, one of them going right through her gun portal and striking the wall behind her.

"Keep firing," said Cunningham, and he went up again and started firing at Spartans that were now almost beneath him. "Missed," he muttered angrily as he ducked again.

Jones stood up and took aim, waited for the moment between heartbeats, cleared her mind and fired. A Spartan's head jerked back once, and she thought she could see the web of cracks radiating out from the center of his visor.

"Wonder what that feels like," she asked herself as she took cover again. She popped up again for a moment just to look at the body, relishing its stillness. Another three speeders swept across the plain in front of her. Smoke bombs and thermal interference charges burst all around the field like fireworks, and she fired randomly at the spot where she thought the speeders were headed.

"Keep firing. Use that luck of yours," said Cunningham, and he jumped up to open fire into the haze. Jones gritted her teeth but didn't reply.

Just as she was about to fire again a hail of shredder fire struck the wall in front of her. Sharp fragments of the metal battlement edge flew off with pinging noises, and one of them pierced her pressure mask. She felt the impact jerk her head back, and she fell back to the ground. Then she felt the sharp pain in her face.

The metal had broken the seal on the pressure mask. She heard her oxygen-balanced air hiss out, then she choked as she inhaled a mouthful of blood. She began to panic.

"Get back," said Cunningham. He leaned over and squeezed off a barrage of shots on automatic.

"Don't order me around," she said, then gasped again. She tore the pressure mask off her face, but as she did she felt the fragment of metal tear from the skin on her cheek.

"Damn!" she said as a soft rain of red blood pattered down.

"Get back, Jones. Please," he said to her without looking back.

She nodded and pressed one hand to her face, trying to stanch the blood that was staining her blue uniform a dark red. She still held her weapon with the other hand.

"I was on fire," she muttered, then felt a wave of lightheadedness as the nitrogen-rich air got to her.

Next to her appeared a man with a red medic cross sewn into his uniform. He pushed a clean rebreather into her face. She felt herself inhaling some of the blood and heard it gurgle inside the rebreather.

As the medic helped her away from the wall, she glanced back. Cunningham looked down intently, peering over the edge of his gun port. "Some of those speeders are acting a little odd," he said, and then there was a strange whining sound from the field. As Jones watched, a blast of blue-white light engulfed the top of the wall. She cried out and held her eyes, but she could see only bright white, fading to black.

She reached out for the medic but couldn't find him.

Blind. I'm blind!

She kicked something and felt someone grab her foot. She fell to her knees and heard the medic gasp with panic.

"I can't see!" he shouted. "I can't see!"

Jones started crawling forward, though she had no idea where she was going. She could smell a horrible smell behind her, the smell of melted metal, and stone, and flesh. Though she could not see it with her eyes, her mind painted a portrait of Cunningham as a blackened shape leaning on the burned wall.

She crawled forward, into a night that would not end.

Thirteen squads of Spartan warriors converged on the walls and gates of UNHQ. Short-range impact missiles streaked overhead and slammed into the wall, sending fragments of metal and stone showering across the Peacekeepers along the rim. Shredder bolts and penetration bolts whistled back down from the wall, thumping in the earth and cracking off the Spartan battle armor, while laser blasts continued to crackle along the battlements.

Diego watched as his speeder neared the south gates of UNHQ. He traced the outline of their great arch, cut into the strong white walls, and looked at the bands of Morgan-produced steel that reinforced them. The gates had such a classical old Earth design that he almost expected to see a large keyhole in them.

But I brought my own key, keyhole or not.

Somewhere nearby, four more speeders converged on the great gates. Only one of them held the bundles of explosives, and only that one needed to get close to one of the great hinged gates.

"Get up there and fire," he ordered his gunman. "Hit the watchtowers with everything we've got."

"Yes, sir."

Somewhere above him the turret opened. He heard the high-pitched whine as the laser charged, and he felt the exultation of battle rise in his belly.

I won't stay in here! As soon as the speeder neared the gates, he would push through the hatch and fire at the Peacekeepers on the wall. And if his speeder didn't make it to the gates, then he would have a hero's funeral, with full honors.

The lights in the speeder dimmed as the laser fired, sending its burst of concentrated light toward the western guard tower. He averted his eyes as the

blue flash engulfed the top of the guard tower, out-
lining the walls of UNHQ in a brilliant halo.

The skies of Chiron have never seen anything like this!

The speeder pulled up near the gates and the top
hatch opened, discharging warriors to clear the way.

"Another laser," said Spinner. Jahn shook his
head, staring at the plains as bolts of blue light em-
anated from about fifteen of the speeders on the
plain and arced up into the walls.

"Mark it!" he said. "Stay focused. We have to
track those laser speeders and destroy them."

Spinner nodded and quickly began dispensing
orders to forward observers on the walls.

"Count seconds," Jahn said, his mind racing.
"We need to know how frequently they can fire.
And tell everyone to switch their priorities to the
laser speeders."

He used the tactical comm unit to get verbal up-
dates on several positions. He heard heavy gunfire
and the howls of the wounded.

"Reserve medics to the wall," he ordered.

"At least we know where they are," said Spinner.
He checked some reports. "The wall is holding up,
though their lasers are melting larger holes around
the gun ports, giving our people less cover. And our
people . . ." He shook his head. "Dozens dead.
Dozens more blinded."

"Whenever there's a blue flash from the field,
we'll have to take cover, then come back and try to
pick off the speeder that fired," said Jahn. "It'll be
tricky, but it has to be done." He studied the tactical map. "Look at this," he said suddenly.

"What?"

"Classic diversion. While the laser speeders are attacking, there are five speeders converging on the gates."

At that moment, a blinding halo of light struck the nearby west guard tower, and Jahn could feel the heat even through the stone walls.

"I'm going to the guard tower. Mind the gates!" he said to Spinner, and bolted from the command center.

Jahn ran along the hallway toward the guard towers overlooking the great south gates. As he approached the gates he slowed, a wave of shock going through him.

This is far worse than I could have imagined.

The hallway leading to the west tower doors was blackened from the energy blast, and the stone seemed to have warped, like liquid. As he hurried forward again he saw someone coming toward him, crawling on hands and knees. It was a young citizen, burned hands groping along the smoking floor of the hallway, his face blackened and his eyes burned.

It's just like Earth again, Jahn realized. *It's just like the Flash Wars . . . blinded people crawling in the streets.*

He called for a medic and touched the young man on the shoulder, telling him to wait and to breathe deeply. Then he hurried on through a broad metal door and into the west tower.

Diego jumped out of the speeder and took cover behind it, looking up to see the walls rising to a dizzying height above him, before two more blue flashes exploded on them. Four speeders had formed a perimeter near the west guard tower, and now the fifth one came barreling in, heading right in to the gates.

The demo speeder.

"Head for the west gate, demo," he ordered by quicklink. "Get right next to the hinges, and then you have ten seconds to get out of there."

The speeder surged forward, its engine roaring, dust churning up around it.

"Take out those high positions!" Diego shouted to his speeder troops. "All of you, drop and fire. For Sparta!"

They were so close to the wall now that the sharpshooters in the battlements had problems seeing them. He saw figures in blue lean out of cannon ports and turn their rifles down at him. A burst of automatic fire kicked up the earth at his feet.

He brought his own rifle into position, took aim, and fired. He could see the splash of red against the pale blue sky as a Peacekeeper recoiled from the shot.

All around him his Spartans dropped to their knees, aimed, and fired. Blue forms jerked and fell back from the top of the walls, and then more gunfire rained down, along with a missile that turned one of his speeders into bright chunks of metal. He took aim again and a second Peacekeeper went down, and then a third.

"Three," he said, and then realized his quicklink was still on. He turned it off but smiled to himself. No other Spartan could have taken down so many in so short a time.

A bolt kicked up smoke near his boot and he ran around to the rear of his speeder. He saw the demo speeder jam on its brakes at the west gate, the front end actually crunching into the hinges. The hatch had already opened, and Spartans leaped out.

Diego ran past a Spartan lying on her side, and he could see her chest heaving inside the armor. Her visor was shattered, and as he watched another bolt thumped into her belly.

Without thinking he swiveled up and took aim back along the line of the shot. Another Peacekeeper went down, perhaps the one who had fired the shot, perhaps not. Either way, he nodded in satisfaction. An eye for an eye.

His Spartans crouched behind the remaining speeders, partially exposed to the battlements but holding their own. It was time.

"Blow the gate," he said into his quicklink.

Jahn burst into the guard tower and ran up two flights of spiral stairs cut into the stone and metal cylinder. On the top floor he found several dazed soldiers firing down at the plain below at a severe angle. On one side of the room two citizens lay next to each other, still alive but burned beyond recognition.

"What's happening?" asked Jahn.

"There are speeders around the gate," said Hulsey, a tough woman with strong muscles and a determined look on her face. Jahn ran to the gun ports and looked down.

"They're right below us. They could blow the gates!" he said. "Where's the detonator for the buried charges? And where are the fire barrels?"

She gestured to the detonator, hanging from a wire on the wall, and next to that several small barrels marked with hazard symbols. Jahn grabbed the detonator, and as he did he saw another speeder roar up and actually slam into the gate below.

"This is it," said Jahn. The hatch opened and several Spartans leaped out. "Get ready on those barrels."

Hulsey shouted orders at two of the other Peacekeepers. All three then ripped the seals off the barrels and carried them to a covered walkway with openings directly above the gates.

"Brace yourselves," said Jahn. He pushed the control button, and nitrate charges wrapped in phosphorus detonated in front of the gates, sending rocks and debris ten meters into the air and showering the entire area with the phosphorus, which burned yellow white and stuck to anything it touched. He saw Spartans torn to pieces by the explosions, and others fleeing the aftermath, their bodies sizzling and burning to the bone. The speeder near the gate was thrown into the air and came down in pieces.

"Pour now," said Jahn, and the three soldiers shouted and tipped the barrels. More burning white powder cascaded down like a waterfall of fire, engulfing some of the Spartans and raining down around the ruined speeder by the gate.

Down on the plain, Diego felt an unmistakable instinct to jump back. He propelled himself backwards as an explosion tore the earth near his feet and then a shower of white fire sprayed toward him. He lifted his left arm to shield himself and felt it suddenly become warm as if he had dunked it in hot water, then he rolled on the ground, away from the heat.

White fire and flying debris filled the air around him like a storm. He saw the Spartan with the trigger for the demo speeder to his right, and then the man had vanished in a blast of smoke and flying red earth.

"Blow the speeder remotely!" he shouted into his quicklink, sending the order back to the Spartan base.

As the firestorm abated, he looked down to see the skin of his left arm boiling up with blisters before his eyes, and he heard a violent sizzling sound.

My arm . . .

He turned his arm, trying to get the phosphorus to fall off, but it continued to burn, eating its way toward the bone. A wave of pain like he had never felt washed through him.

He looked up to see the demo man stagger toward him, the man's plastic pressure mask melted onto his blistered face, his useless arms reaching out before him, two pieces of burned meat. At the gate he saw three more of his soldiers running for the demo speeder, which had malfunctioned and failed to detonate, and then he saw them disappear under three silvery tongues of fire from above the gates.

"Fall back," he said into his quicklink. The stink of burning flesh and metal penetrated even his pressure mask, and the demo speeder rested in pieces under the rain of chemicals from above the gates.

"The detonators are destroyed," he said to no one in particular. He could still hear the sizzling of the phosphorus on his arm . . . *in* his arm, and he bit back a sudden cry of pain. He jumped back into his speeder and waited for one other Spartan, a man burned from head to toe, eyes staring from a charred ruin of a face, to collapse into the hatch.

The stink . . .

Diego turned the speeder around and gunned it

back to the Spartan camp, noticing as he did the yellow sphere of Centauri A setting on Day One of the battle.

"Order someone out to disarm that speeder," said Jahn into his quicklink. "We've got to get those explosives away from the wall."

He looked down on the plain, where Spartans howled and grabbed their burning skin, writhing like souls in torment. He watched as they collected themselves, those that could still move and think, and headed for their speeders. He began to lift a rifle to take a shot, but the sight of the dying Spartans sickened him, and he couldn't do it.

He saw a muscular man with a burned arm climb into a speeder, stopping to cast one look back at the south gates before vanishing inside. Another burning man collapsed in after him, and the speeder took off. Around the battle plain, Spartans turned back, heading for camp.

"Cease fire," he ordered his troops, not caring whether or not they liked it. "Let them leave in peace."

Jahn watched them go, the sound of weapons from the plain suddenly quieted.

"I think the first day is over," he said, staring at the sunset.

chapter nine

Midnight

"JAHN, COME TO THE COMMAND CENTER," SAID PRAVIN over his quicklink. Jahn sighed in weariness, wanting to see Sophia and sleep with her for a few precious hours, but his father's next words energized him. "We have good news."

Jahn walked into the command center to find Pravin at the touchscreen, talking to Santiago. Jahn heard the words "cease fire" and hurried over, his heart leaping.

"Now we know how much we can hurt each other, Pravin," said Santiago from the touchscreen. "And now all of our people are suffering. Maybe this fighting is no good for anyone."

"So you would be willing to work out a deal that would not involve the transfer of the datalinks?" asked Pravin.

"If we can ultimately garrison a force of Spartans at UNHQ to ensure that neither you nor anyone else will ever use those terrible weapons," said Santiago.

Garrison troops in our city? Jahn asked himself,

looking at his father. But Pravin nodded at the touchscreen.

"Very well, Corazon. The broad outline of our agreement is that you will withdraw your troops from this area, and we will send you medical support for your injured. And we will sign a covenant never to use the nerve gas weapons on Chiron."

"A covenant we Spartans will help enforce," said Santiago. "I hope that we can work this out successfully. I hate to see good soldiers injured." Santiago watched them, her face as cool as ever.

I would really hate to meet her on the field, thought Jahn.

"Santiago out."

Pravin turned to Jahn, a light shining in his eyes for the first time in a long while. "A truce, Jahn. A cease-fire. There will be no more injuries."

"Father, you can't possibly intend to allow her troops into our research labs."

"We will have to work out those details later. But for now we have what we need. We have a truce, and a potential ally."

"Santiago will never take a true ally, Father. She doesn't respect us. She only respects strength."

Pravin shook his head. "We are strong. We maintained our ideals and our home in the face of civil war. Now go tell your troops that the fighting is over."

Jahn nodded, opening himself a little to the possibility of peace. "You make the announcement, Father, to both soldiers and civilians. You've earned it."

"We'll have to be very careful with this, Jahn. Many died during this attack, including children. Some people will be slow to forgive the Spartans."

"And this is how hatred starts that can last generations," said Jahn, nodding. He thought of the burning Spartans, crawling in the dirt outside the gate. *Will they forget?*

"What we have is a start." Pravin clapped Jahn on the shoulder. "Go and get some rest."

Jahn smiled and left the command center, but something nagged at him, something that they had forgotten in the congratulations, but he was too tired to remember. Then his father's video feed came over the quicklinks, declaring peace, and Jahn heard the shouts of pleasure down the hallways, and then music coming from one of the mess halls. He stopped in the doorway and watched as people flowed up from basement shelters and began to dance on the tables to an electronic mix performed by two musically minded citizens wearing elaborate headdresses of colored corn husks.

Jahn smiled as he watched them, and after a while headed back to the quarters he shared with Sophia. She wasn't there, and he figured she was helping his father coordinate the peace initiative. He signaled an attendant to bring their child back up from the shelters, and the man appeared shortly, holding his son wrapped in a long white blanket. Jahn took his son and cradled him, staring at the child who remained in a deep sleep, not a care in the world, and then he put him in the bed next to the one he shared with Sophia.

He set the lights on dim and removed his clothes. It was only when his head had hit the pillow that he remembered . . .

Pierson. He's still out there, with orders to sabotage the Spartans in any way he can.

* * *

Santiago sat with her advisors around a crackling fire outside of the command tent. She normally wouldn't light a fire with so many prominent citizens in the area, but she had doubled the watch on UNHQ's gates, and she believed Pravin would enforce the cease-fire.

"Peace so soon," said Messier. "And the chance to get a garrison inside their city. But we didn't get what we came here for." He looked over at Diego, who sat by the fire, sweat beading the skin around his pressure mask. Pressure bandages wrapped his arm up to the shoulder. He said nothing, appearing to share some dark inner world with his pain.

"The rest of the settlements may turn against us now," continued Messier. "I'm concerned about that. They've seen what we're capable of doing."

"We had little hope of taking the settlements by force anyway," said Santiago. She looked up at him as coals hissed in the fire. "Don't you understand that? We would be fighting Peacekeepers and Gaians and everyone else at every turn, day after day."

"Perhaps," said Messier. "Clearly we aren't invincible. At least not yet."

Diego's eyes blazed for a moment, but he still said nothing.

"I sent a squad up onto the ridge," said Victor abruptly, from the shadows on the far side of the fire. "I decided to send them when the peace celebration started in the base."

Santiago and Messier gave him appraising looks, though he still hadn't looked up from the fire. Even Diego turned in his direction.

"It can't hurt," said Santiago. "Just make sure they don't do anything foolish."

"They're under strict orders," said Victor. "But they say the base is marvelous." Now he looked up, his eyes shining. "It's laid out like a picture before them, and the pressure tents and tall buildings are lighting up now that peace is declared."

"The Peacekeepers should be careful," said Messier. "This could be an elaborate feint." He looked at Santiago suddenly, as if realizing a hidden truth, but she shook her head.

"We'll hold back for now. Everything in due time," said Santiago. She reached out with a metal rod to stir the coals. Messier remained silent, and Diego continued to stare into the fire.

Pierson sat exposed in the turret of his rover, an automatic shredder weapon cradled in his lap. He watched the shadowy terrain go by under starlight, and clenched his jaw against the tension he felt, which made his cheek wound hurt again, making him even more tense.

Around him nine more rovers drove in a loose formation. As they approached UNHQ, they drove more and more slowly, knowing that Spartans would be on patrol in the area.

From up ahead came the rattle of shredder fire, at about the location his point rover would have reached by now. "Speed up," he said to his driver. They all had their quicklinks off, traveling under radio silence on a mission to ambush the Spartan camp.

Radio silence to make sure that the Spartans don't pick up any of our short-range transmissions, he told himself, but a part of him knew that he had a deeper reason, barely acknowledged even to himself.

He liked being the rogue, operating without orders, striking the Spartans at will and vanishing into the night. He didn't need any more interference from Pravin and his council to hurt the enemy. This stealth mission fulfilled both of his needs: nondetection and noninterference.

The rovers gathered at a location ahead. Two Spartan guards lay crumbled on the ground, blood pooling around their heads. A young Peacekeeper had jumped down from the point rover and looked at them, holding his shredder rifle in a rest position.

Pierson hopped down and walked over, enjoying the cool night air for a brief moment.

"They didn't even fight back," said the young man. "They weren't really looking. I just shot them."

"Pretty lax for Spartans," said Pierson, looking at the bodies as if they would hop up again and start firing. "Let's move on. If these are lookouts, then the camp can't be far away. When you see me open fire, that's the signal."

They hopped back into the rovers and continued forward into the night. As they crested a small ridge the Spartan camp opened up below them, hundreds of small tents, glowing softly under the stars. Fires crackled, and the occasional sound of harsh laughter drifted up into the sky.

"Gun it," said Pierson, and he picked up two flame grenades and lobbed them at a lone Spartan sentry and a nearby tent. Then he lifted his shredder automatic and filled every tent he saw with streams of deadly fire.

*   *   *

The first explosion came from behind them, and not from the direction of UNHQ, where they expected it. A tent in the rear of the camp burst into flame, and then the rattle of shredder pistols followed.

Santiago was on her feet in an instant, well-trained instincts sending her rolling for the dark safety of the shadows away from the fire. Messier stood up and drew his weapon, and Diego did the same, craning his neck toward the explosion. Victor faded back into the shadows, a full second after his mother.

The roar of rovers came from the rear of the camp. Spartans shouted as the shredder fire continued, and then return fire came from the Spartans as their training and reflexes kicked in. As Santiago watched, a line of black slashes appeared in one of the tents by the fire as shredder fire raked across their position.

She didn't yell a warning. There was no time. Messier was hit, enemy fire raking his belly, and he clutched his stomach and fell hard. Diego scrambled away, curses breaking his silence, already returning gunfire into the darkness. Santiago drew her weapon and waited for the dark shape of a rover, and then she fired, putting a bullet through the skull of the woman who sat at the turret. The rover swerved toward them, gunning its engine.

Diego jumped away and crashed through the fire, sending bright orange sparks swirling up into the night sky. He ran into Victor, knocking him backwards, and the two tumbled to the ground as gunfire hummed through the air around them.

Victor felt Diego's hand digging into his shoulder. "Order your men on the ridge to shell the city,"

Diego said angrily. His face floated before Victor like a terrible moon.

"You can't give me orders," Victor said, and then clamped his lips shut.

"We're under attack by the Peacekeepers," said Diego. "They broke the truce. Now order your men on the ridge to attack before the Peacekeepers get them as well."

Victor nodded, suddenly seeing the possibility of Peacekeepers sneaking up the side of the mountain, picking off thirty citizens. *His* citizens.

"Victor to Eagle One," he said into his quicklink, contacting his squad leader on the ridge overlooking UNHQ. "We've been ambushed. You are ordered to attack the city. I repeat, you may open fire."

On the ridge overlooking UNHQ, Chavez, code-named Eagle One, ordered his soldiers to reinforce the loose perimeter they had set up in the rocky darkness of the ridge. Soldiers hopped to their feet and ran to take positions behind the shattered columns that used to be the bases of solar collectors, glass crunching under their feet.

He hurried to the edge of the ridge and looked down, right into the city, where hallways and domes had begun to light up again and a flare or two arced into the sky.

"Looks like they're still celebrating," said his chief weapons officer.

"Better targets," said Chavez. "We have our orders. Open fire." He smiled, looking down at the city beneath him. "What a beautiful sight. Target practice."

His chief weapons officer nodded and shouldered

a seismic rocket launcher. The loader slid a round into position, and the weapons officer took aim.

"Fire," said Chavez, and the seismic streaked down from the ridge and toward the west end of UNHQ.

"No dice, sir," said Spinner. "We can't raise Pierson. He went into deep cover so that the Spartans couldn't pick up his transmissions."

"We've got to warn Santiago, then," said Jahn. "Have her fly a white flag at the perimeter of her camp."

"A white flag? She'd sooner fly her own skin. If we warn her of Pierson's approach she may end up killing him before they get it all straightened out."

"We have to do it. I'll tell my father to contact her."

"Too late," said Spinner suddenly. "Something's happening out there." He pointed to one of the video feeds, where flashes of light exploded like fireworks in the rear of the Spartan camp.

"I'm going to the wall to take a closer look," said Jahn. As he ran to the guard towers he contacted his father, telling him what might be happening. When he reached the west guard tower he found Hulsey still on duty, along with one other Peacekeeper.

"Where is everyone?" asked Jahn.

"Off duty, for sleep or celebration," said the woman. "I figured they had earned it."

"*You* figured!" Jahn said, angry. "Get them back on duty!" He ran to the battlements overlooking the plain, and swept his binoculars over the Spartan camp. Behind the line of tents, so far in the distance he could see them only as a line of bright sparks against a charcoal horizon, he saw the flashes of light and fire.

"There's fighting out there. Pierson's broken the truce!" he said. Hulsey stared at him, her face shifting as she realized what was happening.

"Commander," came the voice of Spinner through his quicklink. "Look to the west, on the ridge. There's something going on up there."

Jahn ran to the rear of the guard tower where a flight of stairs spiraled up. He dashed up three stairs at a time, finally pushing his way up through a trapdoor and onto the roof of the guard tower, under the dark vault of the limitless sky.

Sol Ridge waited above the city, massive and uneven against the stars. He started to lift his binoculars, but then realized he didn't need them. He could see the streak of fire, racing down into the city, directly for the large dome that housed their food supplies.

Directly for it. They can see everything!

The rocket burst, shaking the ground and sending out a ring of fire that engulfed the pressure dome. The dome warped and rippled under the impact, and the thick skin tore, the edges burning. The sound of the explosion traveled out and across the city.

Alone on the high tower, Jahn remembered the rings of fire in the Earth cities, seen from the shuttle flight to the *Unity*.

More deaths, he thought.

Another rocket streaked down, this one heading for a junction point where several tunnels came together. Jahn linked to Pravin.

"Father, you must contact Santiago. There are men on Sol Ridge. They'll decimate the city."

Pravin's voice came on, shaky. "Pierson killed one of the Spartan commanders," he said. "Plus up to eighty more Spartans, asleep in their tents. Santiago is furious. She says the soldiers on the ridge will fire until morning, to avenge the dead."

Jahn watched helplessly as another rocket came down and exploded, rocking a medium-sized pressure tent that sheltered one of the mess halls. He imagined death in there, running rampant.

"We can't let them continue. They'll kill us!"

"What about the hospital?" his father asked suddenly, his voice shaky. *Pria . . .*

Jahn looked across the city, marking the positions where the rockets struck. "They must have hand-held launchers, because the rockets aren't reaching the east part of the city. And the medlabs are underground anyway. But we have to stop them from getting heavier armament up there." He paused and made a split-second decision. "I'm going out. We have to cut off Spartan access to the ridge."

He thought his father would argue, but only silence returned. *He knows.*

"I'm going out there with my best people," Jahn continued. "If you can reason with Santiago, let me know and we'll call off the attack instantly."

Another rocket crossed the night sky and hurled toward UNHQ. This one almost reached the central tower, but burst in an open garden instead, licking the nearby buildings with fire.

Jahn Lal stood in the courtyard just inside the south gates and rechecked the fit on his pressure mask. In front of him waited four squads of soldiers, each one with ten to fifteen members, all standing at attention. Jahn looked at every soldier, at the tension in their shoulders and how they fingered their weapons nervously.

"We're going up to the ridge," said Jahn. "We're going to move quickly, under cover of darkness. I have no secrets for getting back alive, except to be careful and move quickly. If we make it to the ridge and things get bad, we can rappel down the ridge and try to make it to the north gates."

He looked at them again. Some of them already had wounds, and the chain of command had turned into a mindworm tangle as the rockets pounded UNHQ over and over again. Soldiers now lay in smoking piles in the ruined structures of the mess tent, or under one of the barracks that had taken a direct hit.

Jahn glanced to the translucent seal that opened from the nearest pressure tent and saw a flash of white wrapped around a familiar figure. Sophia stood beyond the pressure seal, her form indistinct through the tough, rubbery fabric of the tent.

So much easier to go to your death when you can forget the life you leave behind, he thought.

He moved to the gates and faced his troops.

"Let's move out."

He heard the sound of hydraulics as the small human-sized sally port built into the wall near the west gate released and swung open. One by one his soldiers slipped out into the darkness of the plain beyond.

Jahn led the troops under cover of darkness toward the shadows of the farm buildings, which occupied the center of the wide gap between the edge of the Spartan camp and the base of the ridge. They crossed the plains in a slow jog. To the right of them the high walls of UNHQ rose, pale white under the starlight. To their left explosions and gunfire rocked the Spartan camp.

"This would be a good time to squeeze them," said Rank, his second-in-command for the mission. "We could send armed rovers and hit their camp from the front."

Jahn nodded. "Let's get to the farm buildings and see. I want to give my father time to talk with Santiago."

"Sounds like Santiago is talking with her guns tonight," said Rank, as a flash of blue light illuminated the Spartan camp. *The Spartan laser speeders*, realized Jahn. And as he looked up another rocket tore through the sky.

"We have to cut off any contact between the camp and that ridge," said Jahn. "If they get a transport up there with heavier-gauge weaponry or something like a laser cannon, the city is finished."

Santiago watched as her troops formed a loose battle line and unleashed disciplined bursts of fire toward the rear of the camp. The attacking rovers had come in for a quick strike and then turned and bolted for safety, though a number of them now smoldered in her camp.

As she watched, her soldiers stormed into three of the disabled rovers, pulling out blue-suited Peacekeepers who struggled against them. She watched a burly Spartan grab a female Peacekeeper's weapon and tear it out of her hands, then strike her across the temple with it.

More Peacekeepers were dragged out of the rovers, and the Spartans surrounded them, drawing their weapons. She saw her citizens kicking the downed enemies, and saw some more dragging them by their necks and arms and feet toward the interrogation tent. And she saw several of them draw their pistols.

She started to say something, but then she looked into the wavering ring of firelight where medics bowed over Messier, moving calmly rather than urgently, which could mean only one thing. And she looked again toward UNHQ, where the rockets still fired, flying like shooting stars into the heart of the base.

It's all like a dream, she reflected. *There is no awakening.*

A pistol shot rang out, and then another and another, and she looked over to see two Peacekeeper men and one woman slump to the ground, a ring of Spartans around them. She realized they had crossed a line, from truce back into battle, and this time there was no returning.

Diego emerged from the shadows, speaking into his quicklink, assembling his troops. "We're regrouping, sir," he informed her. "We'll open a supply line to the ridge."

She nodded, not particularly wanting to see the mindless battle fury in his eyes for the hundredth time. "Let's end this," she said, and looked around to find her son.

Pravin Lal stood in the battlements overlooking the south gates, Sophia next to him. They stared out over the Spartan camp, where the explosions and chaos seemed to have calmed.

"Pierson must be in retreat," said Pravin.

"I hope he knows how much he's cost us," said Sophia. "Breaking that truce . . ."

Pravin put his hand on her shoulder. "It's done," he said. "We all knew how Pierson felt about the Spartans. In fact I think many of us secretly shared his views. Now we must try and undo his mistake."

"The dead and wounded are piling up. We have beds set up in the hallways around the medlabs. The head surgeons are afraid we'll run out of painkillers."

I have a way to end the pain, thought Pravin. *One speeder with the nerve gas pods, and the Santiago problem vanishes. But a new set of problems begins.*

"Jahn will report back when he's taken the farm and the ridge," said Pravin. "We'll see what to do then. And maybe I can get through to Santiago again."

Pravin looked over the plain, where lights flickered out in the Spartan camp, plunging it into darkness. *I have the power to end this now,* he thought. *But I cannot do it. Not that way.*

I cannot.

Jahn reached the edge of the cornfield, which had been harvested quickly, the cut stalks taken into the city before the Spartan attack.

Now the stumps ranged all around him, dark clumps in the shadows, as he headed for the long storage building where he had once fought the Believers, years ago. His men ran like ghosts beside him, silent except for the rhythmic crunching of their footsteps. At his right hand ran Rank, his footsteps strong and sure.

The last time I passed through this field, I came out a

killer, he reflected, and wondered how many of his soldiers had ever actually killed someone, either back on Earth or on Chiron.

They reached the rear of the storage shed, and Jahn stopped to look in the window, which had long been patched up. He saw only pitch blackness, indicating that the large doors on the other side were closed. A chill went down his spine as he imagined enemy soldiers lurking in that darkness.

"What do you think?" Rank whispered.

"We should get going up the ridge, but any enemy soldiers inside this building could hit us from the rear."

Rank nodded. Jahn looked at him.

"You take all of the squads but one and start up the ridge. You're in command of taking out the enemy position. I'm staying here, to clear this shed and set up a command post."

Rank nodded, accepting the order, then reached out his hand. Jahn clasped it hard and clapped him on the shoulder. "Use that Spartan training. Remember what they taught you."

Rank saluted him and turned to the men gathered around him. Within seconds most of them headed up toward the ridge at a fast jog. Jahn looked at the twelve soldiers left behind.

"We're going through this window," he said. He took off his jacket and put it over the glass, then used the butt of his gun to smash it, motioning everyone to stay out of the window's line of sight. The muffled sound of the glass breaking made him tense up. When he took the jacket down, shards of glass clattered down inside the building.

He waited to the side of the window, breathing

heavily. He counted to fifty, and still no sound emerged from the darkness inside the building.

He pointed, indicating they should enter one by one, after him. He moved underneath the window, grabbed the edge, and pulled himself over and inside.

Rank lifted his hand to order a stop on the steep slope to the ridge. Company commander Elroy came up next to him.

"It gets steep up there above the forest, and the small rocks will slide as we scramble up the slope to that overhang, alerting them to our presence," said Rank. "It's unavoidable."

"Yes, sir," said Elroy. "If I were them I'd make sure anyone topping that slope was staring down the throat of two guns, at least. It wouldn't take much more than two to cover that position, anyway."

"If they have only two, I may be able to take them."

Elroy looked at him. "That's very dangerous, sir. If you fail we'll have a tough time following you."

"It's a risk we have to take. If we go over that overhang together, they'll kill us all." He began taking equipment off, including his pack. "Hand me a rocket tube," he said. "And prepare to charge up at my signal." He thought for a moment. "Or, if it sounds like I'm dead, at your discretion."

"This sounds like a bad idea, sir."

"I trained with these Spartans. I know where they'll position their lookouts, and how quickly they'll react to a threat. And we don't have time to argue. Have everyone take off their packs and leave them here so you can get up the ridge faster. Tie them with ropes and we'll drag them up after."

Rank tucked three rockets and a shredder pistol into his belt. He also took a knife out of a belt sheath and put it in his mouth.

Without looking back he headed up the rocky slope.

Rank moved slowly, on fingertips and toes only. As he moved he tried to imagine himself scaling a wall, where any wrong move could mean plummeting to his death. He moved like a spider, supporting his body weight with only his fingertips and toes, so that nothing touched the pebbles and rocks beneath him.

His progress was painfully slow. Every time he jostled one of the small rocks on the slope he froze as it clattered down around him, back to the shadowy watching forms of his troops below. Sweat slicked his torso within minutes, and he reached deep into himself to call forth that Spartan ability to find pleasure in pain.

Above him the slope curved up into the overhang, and he found himself progressing up an almost vertical surface.

Beyond this overhang they're waiting, he realized.

His fingers bit into the rocky surface, but his boots could find little purchase in the craggy face.

I should have left the boots behind. Too late for that . . .

Every muscle in his body trembled as he hooked his fingers into narrow crevices in the rock. His mind became absorbed in the moment; his troops lay a million miles below him, and the Spartan enemies a million miles above.

Thump.

Something hit his shoulder. He turned his head.

Sitting on his shoulder in a coil, whipping its spiked head around, lay a mindworm.

Mindworm!

He heard a pattering sound, and another fell down, and then another, hitting his shoulders and then his face. The one on his shoulder began making a hideous hissing sound that he seemed to hear not in his ears but in his brain. He could feel a malevolence rising off the creature.

It'll go for my skull, and burrow in, he thought, a wave of panic washing over him as the mindworm whipped its head up and toward him. Then a tremendous pain racked through the muscles of his shoulders and back as they spasmed from the effort of keeping him suspended.

Go through the pain . . .

The mindworm stopped short. He could feel the tiny prick of its pincers in the skin on his temple, but it had stopped short of burrowing. The hiss grew louder.

The pain gives me the focus I need . . .

He closed his eyes and sank deeper into the pain, into the cords of muscle knotted across his arms and back, into the pain that burned through him. Again he became aware of only the moment and only the agony in his muscles. A tight grin spread across his face as he relished it.

Some part of his consciousness became aware of screams coming from above him, and then shouts below, from his own troops. More mindworms pattered down around him, not nearly enough to form a full boil, but enough to kill and to terrify. With a deep muscular effort he curled his legs up to his chest and tilted his body back, and the worms on his shoulders and head let go and fell away. After a few more long moments the rain of worms abated.

He kept his consciousness deep in his body and used a hidden reserve of strength to pull himself up and over the overhang. In front of him the rocky slope leveled off into an open valley with jagged rocks on the other side, and beyond that rose Sol Ridge.

If we had stepped onto this flatland, we would have been killed for sure, he realized. But as he looked he saw thousands of squirming shadows beneath the purple sky, covering the floor of the valley and flowing slowly to the east.

Some kind of night migration. Maybe they sense the fear and anger of the soldiers, and they've come to feed. Bad news for the Peacekeepers.

Near the rock formations two Spartans thrashed on the ground, mindworms burrowing into their skulls and hanging from their eye sockets. Their screams turned to gurgles, but Rank kept his mind clear, disconnected from the fear of death. He walked through the mindworms and toward the ridge beyond.

They feed on your mind. Remove your mind completely and they don't even know you're there.

Worms coiled their way between the shattered bases of the solar collectors. At the edge of the ridge the Spartan weapons crew howled, three of them down, the last one shouting and firing his shredder pistol into the sea of worms at his feet. They flowed up his legs like a second skin. Rank calmly took out his own pistol and shot the man through the forehead.

He walked to the edge of the ridge and looked out over the city, which burned from the rocket strikes, and at the tall central tower, which had not been touched, and at the worms that flowed over the ridge like a living waterfall, heading not for UNHQ but for the xenofungus on the far side.

He felt a state of grace descend on him, an ecstasy he never wanted to lose. He felt that nothing could ever harm him again.

"This is what it means to be a Spartan," he said aloud. "It's not the killing or the suffering that matters. It's the purity of focus, without fear of death or pain."

He wondered how many Spartans really understood, as he watched the city glow at his feet.

Jahn slipped into the window, letting himself fall quickly to the cool earth inside the storage shed. He began to move to his left, and heard the next soldier hit the ground behind him.

His breathing hissed in his ears from the pressure mask. So far he heard no enemy movement, and no gunshots had hit the window. But he found it hard to believe that no Spartans had reconnoitered this position.

There could be explosives here, he thought suddenly, and hoped that the Spartans preferred a more human touch.

He pulled a small flashlight from his pack and ran his fingers along it, debating whether or not to turn it on. To do so would give away his position and serve as a target. Instead he covered the light, turned it on, and threw it away from his body.

A short spray of gunfire rattled the air, and the light bounced and rolled into the side of a storage bin, revealing nothing. Jahn's heart pounded in his ears.

He pulled out his weapon and continued to move forward, but away from the light. Behind him he could hear the breathing of the next soldier, but the darkness was like ink around him.

Using his hands to explore in front of him, Jahn suddenly felt the cold steel of a table leg. He felt up to the surface of the table, and then his hand touched something that felt like wet flesh, with something hard that he recognized as bone.

He heard a sharp intake of breath and then a shot exploded near his head. He reached out and grabbed the wounded flesh as hard as he could and heard a howl of pain, and then he pushed forward. A body crashed onto the floor, and Jahn ducked as random gunfire filled the air, ricocheting off the metal walls.

Jahn could hear the man he had dumped yelling on the floor. Suddenly he heard one of his soldiers say, "Lights coming on," in his quicklink, and he closed his eyes. A bright floodlight came on, sending a wash of white light over everything, and he could feel its brightness on the inside of his eyelids.

He opened his eyes as the light swung away, in time to see several injured Spartans, blinking against the blinding light, lying in shattered heaps around the broad metal tables. Several had pistols cradled in their laps.

Jahn and his soldiers sprang into action, grabbing pistols from blinded Spartans. "Don't shoot. We can help you!" shouted Jahn, but the Spartans began firing anyway, blindly, and Jahn heard one of his people take a hit. He and his soldiers began firing at any Spartan holding a weapon, until every Spartan was either dead or disarmed.

Jahn collected the Spartan weapons and threw them into a pile. A Peacekeeper set up a small glowlamp in the center of the shed, making sure its light didn't shine in the window.

Spartans lay on the ground and on the broad tables, badly burned, many with broken limbs or fragments of glass embedded in their skin. Pools of wet and dried blood spotted the ground. Most of the Spartans had an expression of intense stoicism warring with pain frozen on their faces.

"From the explosion on the ridge," said one Peacekeeper, who had medical training. "Good tactics."

Several of his soldiers held their pistols and looked down at the Spartans, sickened. "What should we do?" asked the medic.

Jahn looked over the warriors and at the damage done to their bodies, and tried to connect it with his order to detonate the explosives on Sol Ridge. He couldn't connect the two acts, the way his simple words had led to this carnage.

"We'll help the ones we can," said Jahn. "In the meantime, set up a perimeter and make sure there are no more of them. The fighting isn't over."

He bent over a Spartan and pulled some pressure bandages out of his pack, pressing them into a cut on the man's bicep that bled deep red.

"I'm surprised you're still alive," Jahn said to the Spartan, who stared at him with cold fury. Jahn could see no expression of gratitude or humanity in the man's face.

"Where is your armory tent?" Jahn asked, not expecting an answer. The Spartan suddenly reached out and grabbed Jahn's throat with his uninjured hand, and Jahn felt a force like a vise squeezing his windpipe. He reached up and grabbed the man's wound, digging his fingers into it, feeling the tendons slide around under his fingertips. The man continued to tighten his grip, then gasped in pain and released him.

Jahn rubbed his throat as one of his soldiers ran up to check on him.

"No second bandage for this one," said Jahn, still feeling his throat. *They won't give up.*

He walked to the large metal doors and slid one open just enough to walk outside. He wanted to locate the edge of the Spartan camp, and get some fresh air as well.

It's their hatred that gets to me, Jahn thought. *But I hate them, too.*

The night sky of Chiron had just begun to lighten when Pravin received the message from Jahn. Pravin waited in the command center, Spinner next to him, carefully monitoring movements in the Spartan camp.

"Father, we have ten soldiers in the farm buildings, and four squads up on the ridge. We must hold these positions, and my scout says that the Spartans are still sorting out their dead and wounded from Pierson's sortie."

"Why are the rockets still firing from the ridge?" asked Pravin.

"That was Rankojin's idea. He's firing periodically into the barren land to the north of the city. It might trick the Spartans into thinking they still hold the ridge. In the meantime, have Spinner get our rovers ready and we'll hit the Spartans from this flank."

"I don't like risking Peacekeeper lives outside of these walls, Jahn."

"We have no choice. If they retake the ridge and get their more powerful weapons up there, our walls become meaningless. We'll hit them quickly, gunning for their ammo dumps, and then fall back to the city. We'll never have another chance like this one."

"You are right, of course."

"Also send out some explosive charges so that we can booby-trap this area by the farm. How are the casualties?"

"Severe. Many civilians were hit in that last attack, and many soldiers as well. The rockets did not discriminate."

"Then it's time to make sure this doesn't happen again," said Jahn. "Arm the speeders and line them up at the gates. We'll attack before dawn."

chapter ten

Dawn

PRAVIN STOOD AT A CIRCULAR WINDOW OVERLOOKING the courtyard in front of the south gates. Rovers formed up in two lines, and members of the Peacekeeping Forces walked up and down the line, checking equipment and finding their assigned vehicles. They moved with grim determination.

Finally everyone had taken their positions, and the commander of each rover gave the "hands forward" ready sign from the turrets of the speeders. There would be no infantry in this attack, although several of the rovers would discharge troops onto the ground when they neared the Spartan camp.

Quick, silent, and ruthless, Jahn had told his commanders.

Quick, silent, and ruthless, repeated Pravin to himself. A warning buzzer sounded, and the reinforced metal drawbars hissed and withdrew from behind the gates. As the gates opened, Pravin could see out into the dark plain, where the first tints of dawn touched the earth.

When the gates were open, the first pair of rovers

surged forward, and then the second and the third, until they had all accelerated through, hurling themselves toward the distant enemy. Pravin saw several of them peel off toward the farms, where Jahn waited to coordinate the attack on the Spartan flank.

In moments the courtyard lay empty. Pravin looked down to see his hand on his quicklink, and he wondered why, until he realized that a thought had half formed in his mind to countermand his son's orders and call off the attack.

But what would that gain us? More dead . . .

The gates hissed and swung closed. Pravin headed for his communications room, to seek relief in diplomacy.

Santiago stood in the hospital tent, where Spartans lay about her on low metal cots, dark bloodstains all over the floor. As long as she stood there, hardly a Spartan would make a groan of discomfort. On a cot near her a Spartan medic held down a blood-spattered woman while another medic pried fragments of metal from her belly. Her face tightened and she bared her teeth, but she didn't cry out.

I recognize her, thought Santiago. It was the blond girl she had followed from childhood, the one who had mastered hand-to-hand combat so well. *But you can't wrestle a bullet.*

She walked to the woman and leaned over her. The woman opened her eyes, her face slicked with sweat.

"Sir," she stammered. The medic by her belly braced himself and twisted something out of her, then threw a jagged fragment of metal on the floor. The woman grimaced.

Santiago grabbed her hand firmly. "I have watched

you since you were a child," she said. "You will make
a fine leader. My spirit lifts when I watch you train."

The woman nodded. A trickle of blood ran down
from her lip.

"Have you taken pain medication?" asked Santiago. The woman shook her head.

"Only the minimum. I refused all else."

Santiago nodded and looked down at the
woman, at her strong body and a stomach that had
been flat and firm, but which now looked like a
bloody soup. She looked at the medic, who shook
his head slightly. *No chance.*

Santiago reached over to a tray near the bed and
picked up an injector loaded with pain medication,
which few Spartans would deign to take. She
pushed it into the woman's shoulder and fired it.
The woman opened her mouth as if to protest.

"Rest," said Santiago, and turned away from
the bed.

A message beeped on Santiago's quicklink. "The
gates are opening!" came the message from her forward observer.

She hurried through the camp toward the command tent. Inside Diego waited, pacing like a caged
animal, his bandaged arm tight against his body.
Victor waited with him, and the two saluted her as
she entered. Then they all gathered around the tactical display.

"Rovers leaving the base," said Diego. "Most of
them coming straight at us, and the rest heading to
the west."

"Do we still control the ridge?" asked Santiago.

"The crew is still firing, but I've been unable to

establish contact," said Victor. "I just sent a transport and another four squads toward the ridge, armed with heavy weapons. One squad will go up first, while the rest carry the weapons up the slope, no matter how long it takes."

"I don't like this," said Santiago.

"We still have the rogue Peacekeepers running around behind us," said Diego. "A third of my troops are gone, trying to flush them out of hiding."

"How many are left in the camp then?" asked Santiago. Diego and Victor both studied the tactical display intently. "You should know now!" shouted Santiago. "You two must speak, and coordinate your attacks! Are you children?"

Diego stared at her sullenly, while Victor held the same expressionless gaze that seemed to define his life. Santiago shook her head.

"Get your citizens to the front and defend the camp. Anchor the line with the laser scouts. Go!"

Victor and Diego began issuing their orders as the sound of the first concussion grenade came from outside.

Jahn stood behind the storage building as five rovers roared up. He flagged down the lead one and started issuing orders over his quicklink.

"There are Spartans coming up toward the ridge from the camp," he said. "We have them pinned down with suppressing fire, but I think they're moving their laser speeders into position. Don't stop moving. Sweep down and hit them from the flank."

The rovers roared around him and headed down toward the Spartan camp, which lay in the semidarkness to the south. Jahn got back on his quicklink.

"Rank, report in."

"We have the ridge," Rank replied, his voice clean and calm. "I've positioned guards to protect the approach. If thirty Peacekeepers can hold off an assault, we'll do it."

"Good. We're attacking the Spartan camp. Will the rockets reach that far?"

"Negative. And because of the terrain they won't reach your position. But we have a mortar up here, and it will reach the farms. If the Spartans approach you, I'll open fire."

"Take care, my friend," said Jahn, and broke the link.

Toward the Spartan camps he saw the first blue-white flash as the laser speeders fired against his attacking force, and he saw a ball of fire with the silhouetted form of a rover rise up into the air and come crashing down again. But he saw Spartan tents collapsing as well.

He looked up at the ridge, wondering how long they could hold it. Then he headed down toward the Spartan camp at a run.

Centauri A rose on a Spartan camp torn by an attack and a vicious counterattack. Jahn's rovers crisscrossed in front of the camp, staying in motion as the blue flashes of Spartan energy weapons filled the plain with smoking craters. Spartans stood in a staggered line, taking cover behind tents and parked speeders, as Jahn's troops raked their line with fire.

From the direction of the farm Jahn advanced with his rovers. They came down in a wave, several Peacekeepers dismounting from them and approaching quietly over the ground, firing at any light source in the Spartan camp. Jahn moved in with them, monitoring the effectiveness of the attack in case he needed to call a retreat. But so far he saw more Spartans down than Peacekeepers.

As he watched, one of his rovers swept by, heading across the line of fire of a parked Spartan laser speeder. Jahn saw the gunner on his rover take a shot to the throat and chest and slump back into the vehicle, unleashing a barrage of automatic fire as she did.

The rover continued into the darkness at top speed, the sounds of its engines receding. Jahn lifted his rifle to fire at the Spartan laser speeder, when the sound of the rover's engines returned, coming from the darkness like a train approaching.

The rover clattered over some rocks and came into view, jouncing heavily from the speed. It headed right toward the laser speeder, and Jahn saw the gunner quickly rotate the turret and unleash a laser blast. It hit the Peacekeeper rover, which jumped in the air, the entire front end melted, but somehow it steered itself back on course and struck the Spartan laser speeder head-on.

"Go!" shouted Jahn, running toward the burning vehicles. More of his security forces appeared from the darkness as well, crossing fire with the Spartan defenders, who fell back slowly. Jahn saw three of his soldiers go down, then four, but suddenly one of them reached the laser speeder. Then another was there and then so was Jahn.

A Spartan opened the hatch from the inside, but Jahn quickly opened fire, riddling the upturned Spartan pressure mask with bullets. Spurts of blood popped up from the holes in the mask.

I'm not a builder any more, Jahn realized.

Another Peacekeeper started to toss a flame grenade into the hatch but Jahn waved the man off.

"No! Don't damage it. Take them with pistols."

Two more Spartans emerged, and a furious short-range gun battle erupted around the laser speeder. Finally the superior numbers of the Peacekeepers won out, and the vehicle was clear. Jahn jumped down into the hatch and ordered a gunner in with him.

"Get this thing working," Jahn said, and the gunner started fiddling with levers. Jahn told him how the speeder responded, until the man could rotate the turret toward the Spartan camp.

"Charge," said Jahn, figuring that firing an energy weapon was a two-stage process. The gunner charged up the weapon and put his hand on the trigger.

"Fire," said Jahn, and a blast of blue light exploded in the Spartan camp from the west side, turning a long tent into melted plastic.

"Keep going," said Jahn. "Let's get this thing moving. Maybe we can get a medal."

The gunner smiled, the first smile Jahn had seen in a long time.

Noon

The sun had almost reached its zenith when Jahn ordered the fallback. The Spartan camp had taken heavy damage, but most of his rovers lay in ruins around the tents. He knew his casualties numbered at least one hundred fifty, but Spartan tents burned all around them.

His crew turned the laser speeder and headed back for UNHQ at top speed. Jahn opened the top hatch and looked around him as they ran.

The plain seemed hot and empty as the clouds of smoke drifted sluggishly across the ground. Dark bodies lay at odd angles here and there, like jagged rocks jutting from a red sea. As he watched, a Peacekeeper running for a rover took a shot from a hidden Spartan wielding a flame gun and fell. Three Spartans closed in like hyenas, stomping out the fire and pulling the Peacekeeper to his feet.

"They'll kill him," said the gunner, watching. He turned their speeder back to rescue their fallen comrade, but the Spartans unleashed a furious barrage in their direction. Jahn ordered his crew to turn back, knowing they couldn't risk losing the valuable laser speeder. They headed back for UNHQ in silence.

"How did we do?" asked Jahn finally.

"We inflicted heavy damages on the west side of their camp, and we managed to take this one laser speeder for ourselves," said the gunner. "We weren't so lucky on the east side. They put up heavy resistance there, and we had to fall back. Apparently some kind of elite Spartan fighting force is encamped over there."

Jahn remained silent, digesting this information. Was there no end to it?

The speeder reached the gates of UNHQ, which opened to let them in, and Jahn felt a weariness descend on him as if his bones had turned to lead.

"Sleep," he said, through cracked lips, and he opened the hatch as the speeder stopped.

Jahn heard the gates close behind him and he walked slowly through the courtyard, head downcast from weariness. He removed his helmet and carried it under his arm. His armor was covered with dust and blood, and he felt close to collapse.

He stepped into the barracks attached to the command center and stripped off his armor, letting the pieces drop on the floor. He nodded to the handler that picked up the pieces for examination, repair, and cleaning. When he had stripped down to the thin underbody suit, Jahn left the barracks and headed to his room.

He opened the door slowly, not wanting to wake Sophia or his son, but his rooms appeared empty. He went into the bathroom and stripped off the rest of his clothes, and then poured hot water from a tap and used it to wash himself. He washed carefully, scrubbing every trace of the heat and dust of battle from his skin, then dabbed a drop of scented cologne on his chest and put on a loose-fitting robe.

"Sophia," he called out. There was still no answer. He checked his locator and saw that she was on the battlements.

His heart pounding a little at her proximity to the battlefield, he hurried through the base until he found her. She stood in the shielded battlements, safely back from the wall, looking out over the plain. He called her name, and she turned back to him.

"I was watching you return," she said. Her face looked pure and noble, but her eyes blazed with a quiet intensity, and he wasn't quite sure to what it was directed. In her arms she held their sleeping son.

"We did well today," Jahn said, and he walked toward her. "I feel like I've been ground under the tread of a rover."

"Don't say such things," she said.

"I wish you wouldn't stand up here. It could be dangerous."

"And down there, where you stand, it's safe?" she asked, one eyebrow arching. "If my husband risks his life down there, I can risk my life here, watching him, and following him with my prayers."

"That's true." He lifted his son from her arms and cradled the boy. Then he felt a light touch, her touch, on his arm, and when he looked at her he saw tears leaking from her eyes. He didn't speak, but touched her face with one hand.

"Jahn, I can't watch this day after day," she said, her voice cracking. "When do you think it will end?"

Jahn looked away from her, down at the face of his son, and enjoyed the innocent purity there. "It may not ever really end, I'm afraid. My father hoped for a new world, but we've taken Earth's problems with us."

She moved closer to him and leaned in as if to kiss him, but instead she whispered in his ear, and he felt her long hair brush his face. "I must ask you, Jahn. Can't you stay inside, and let your troops do the fighting? If not for me, then for your son?"

Jahn turned and looked her full in the eyes, where he saw that her intensity had melted into tender concern, and fear. "I can't leave my father and my fellow Peacekeepers to fight without me. To do so would be to betray everything I stand for, and how could I face my son then?"

And then he lifted his son above him and let the boy look down on his mother and father, and the boy smiled. "He'll be a great man, with his mother's beauty and spirit, and his father's honor. I can't take those things from him, even at the cost of . . ." he trailed off, and looked at his wife again, then handed his son to her. "This base may fall. It's in the nature of the Spartans to kill. But perhaps my father will surrender before it's too late, and we can leave here alive."

"Your father can be a prideful man," said Sophia, and Jahn smiled.

"It runs in the family. Now let's go back to the rooms, and leave the smell of battle behind."

Victor entered Santiágo's tent, trying to ignore the two black-clad Myrmidons at the entrance.

She stood inside, wearing a white loincloth and kicking repeatedly at a training dummy in the corner of her tent. The sound of the impact rang out, and sweat dripped off her.

Finally she turned around, grabbing a white towel to wipe the sweat from her body. He saw dark fury shadowing her face, and her eyes looked as if she were trapped in a distant place, under the control of an unseen foe.

"Are there any more dead?" she asked him.

"Twelve. Added to the three hundred we've already found. I guess we underestimated the Peacekeepers."

"Perhaps Diego did, or Messier. It's never good to fight an enemy on his own soil."

"Will you be calling out your Myrmidons now?"

"Why? So they can throw themselves at the walls of the city, and I can add my most highly trained troops to the casualties?"

"They would turn the tide of the battle."

"They're best at close-range fighting, or for assaults requiring physical strength and endurance," said Santiago. "The walls minimize their advantage, as I've told Diego repeatedly. The council wanted this fight, and if they want it to end they'll have to vote to fall back to Sparta Command and endure humiliation before our citizens."

"The Spartans do not lose," said Victor, setting his jaw.

Santiago looked at him appraisingly. "You're small, but you're still a Spartan at heart. When you were young, they wanted to kill you. Food was short, and weakness couldn't be tolerated. But I refused."

She went to a metal trunk by the wall of the tent and opened it. He stepped forward to see the contents.

"This is my personal battle armor," she said. He looked at the pile of armor pieces, with the smooth surface of the Myrmidon armor but with a rich red cast. "When the Spartan citizens see this armor, it will lift their spirit and make them feel invincible, but I won't wear it for this battle."

She looked at the armor, and then back at her son. "You're a commander now. If you choose, you may wear it and lead the army against the Peacekeepers. The Spartans will follow you to the shores of hell if I order it. But think carefully first. Think like a leader."

"What would you do?"

"I would do exactly what I have done, which is to turn the decision over to you." She turned away from him, back to the fighting dummy. "Regardless, there is something for you on my desk. Take it." She began to kick the dummy again, grunting with each blow.

Victor walked to the desk, where he found an ID badge. It had command insignia and was engraved with the name Santiago, V.

"This morning's attack took as much out of the Peacekeepers as it did out of us. There will be no fighting tonight," Santiago said. "Enjoy the time."

She continued to kick the dummy, but behind her back he saluted her.

Victor left Santiago's tent and headed for the command tent, then suddenly changed his mind, altering his course toward the front of the Spartan camp. Around the edges of the camp, and spread out over the plain, he could see the bodies of Spartans, lying where they had fallen.

There will be no fighting tonight. He looked up at the vault of the Centauri sky, where the sun again fell to the horizon and shadows began to lengthen.

This twilight is like a death. It is a transition to a different world, but one that may share the same code of honor.

Jahn stood in the battlements above the south gates with his father and watched the Spartan camp. Tiny sparks of light dotted the landscape, more appearing as the minutes passed.

Jahn lifted his binoculars and stared at the scene for a while, then passed them to his father, who also looked.

"They are burning their dead," said Pravin.

Indeed, an honor guard of Spartans went from body to body, arranging each one where it fell and then dousing it with a flammable liquid. A high-ranking officer said some words over the body, and then flames licked into the sky. As they lit body after body, the plain resembled a sky of its own, with red fires instead of stars dotting its expanse.

Jahn and Pravin watched the scene soberly.

"We bury, they burn," said Pravin. "But we both honor our dead."

Jahn nodded. "There will be no more fighting tonight," he said. "Our soldiers must rest."

"And we have our own wounded to attend to."

Victor walked back toward the Spartan camp with the honor guard drawn from the ranks of his citizens. Around the perimeter of the camp Spartan soldiers stood at attention, watching the bodies burn, isolated pools of firelight scattered across the dark plain.

In front of the camp forty Spartans were laid out in a long line, Spartans that had died in the medical tent. Citizens doused their bodies in flammable liquid and stacked wood from the nearby forests around them.

Santiago walked forward out of the camp and joined the honor guard in front of the line of bodies. Victor took a torch from the honor guard and handed it to her.

"We came from a world of fire, and to fire we must return," she said, putting the end of the torch into the row of bodies. Fire licked up around it and then ran along the line, and finally the flames rose up into a wall behind her. They stood and watched it burn for several minutes, each lost in thought.

Then Santiago walked with Victor and the honor guard back toward the camp, the wall of fire behind them pushing back the darkness. Spartan citizens stood at attention as they approached, and Victor walked with his head high.

Santiago stopped and turned to her son. "Order them to build a perimeter," she said to him.

Victor turned to his lieutenant. "Where you see that wall of fire, dig a trench with a six-foot-high wall in front," he said. "Make it the length of the camp. Do it by morning."

The man saluted and went off to carry out the orders.

In the command tent, Diego sat in a chair, glaring out from under lowered eyelids. "I think we should leave here," he said. "We'll repair our laser speeders and return at a later time. Lal won't know what hit him."

The other members of the council sat in grim silence. Santiago looked at them all, waiting for them to speak their minds.

"Perhaps you're right," said Halleck.

A commotion outside attracted their attention, and a Spartan commander burst into the tent, the smell of blood and red Centauri soil entering with him. His arms were bare where pieces of his armor had been hacked away, but he walked tall.

"Sir," he said, saluting Santiago. "We finally cornered the rogue Peacekeepers from their second base. They ran far, but finally took a wrong turn into a closed canyon. We backed them against the wall and decimated them."

From a pack that hung over one shoulder he pulled a round object and hurled it on the floor in front of the council. "I thought you might like a souvenir," he said.

A round head with gray hair rolled onto the floor, trailing blood. The face was flushed red in life, but now faded to an unhealthy white pallor in death.

"Their leader, named Pierson," the commander

said. "He fought until the end. But we won. And we took very few casualties."

Diego suddenly grinned, flexing his one good arm. He picked up the head and held it, staring at it from every angle.

"I believe we will stay and fight after all," he said. "The Peacekeeper city will fall. There can be no other end to this."

The rest of the Spartans nodded their assent.

chapter eleven

Morning

"DEIRDRE SKYE," SAID PRAVIN, GREETING HER OVER THE quicklink.

Deirdre stood somewhere in her vast network of greenhouses, wearing a sleeveless green top, her hair pinned up off her ageless face. Behind her the colors of dawn touched the sky outside the glass wall of the greenhouse, and Jahn could see fields of xenofungus stretching to the horizon. With the earth plants framing the view inside the greenhouse and the sun touching them, Jahn could see a kind of beauty in Chiron's xenofields.

"Pravin. I'm very sorry about what happened to you and your city."

"Thank you, Deirdre. Our walls have held, but we have suffered many casualties. I want to remind you of the Charter." He stopped and let out a deep breath. "And our friendship. Settlement citizens are dying here, in what amounts to a military coup."

"Pravin, again you have my deepest sympathy. There is little I can do, having spent so much of my time in this world." She gestured to the greenhouse around her. "But I tell you again that Chiron has a way of striking back against forces that upset its equilibrium. I hope that you believe me."

"I believe in your good intentions, Deirdre. I certainly share your desire to maintain harmony on Chiron. But we need fighters now, to drive Santiago's forces back and to put her under arrest."

"Arrest?" She smiled at him. "Pravin, you are the supreme idealist. I have so few troops that I can't spare any, in case Santiago decides one base is not enough. But I'll ask you again to have some faith."

Pravin shook his head. "Very well, Deirdre. I must also tell you that if this base falls, your new Gaia's High Garden base is the closest safe location. If we abandon this base, I and my citizens must seek asylum there."

Deirdre's face grew troubled. "That seems like a drastic step."

"It is drastic," said Jahn, stepping forward. "But rest assured we'll be bringing enough of our remaining armament to defend ourselves against any further threats from Santiago."

Deirdre's expression cooled. "I understand your implication. You're always welcome here. We all need to work together. But I hope it won't come to that. My quarters are very cramped." She nodded to them. "I wish you well. Skye out."

The image flickered and vanished.

"I think she feels safe because she has scientific knowledge that can help feed the Spartans, and without her expertise her crops will die," said Pravin.

"That and the fact that she is much farther away from Sparta Command," said Jahn. "But now she must realize that the fight can come to her."

"She has the food crops, Morgan has his mining expertise, and Zakharov cooks up new technologies in his extensive laboratories." Pravin looked at his son. "What do I have, Jahn, that can make me as useful?"

"I believe it's your idealism, father. Whether they admit it or not, no one wants to repeat Earth's tragedies. The settlements need a moral rudder."

"I hope I remain the rudder they need," said Pravin quietly. "I consider that my purpose in being here."

Two days later

"They're coming, sir. I can feel it," said Spinner, flicking his coin nervously.

Jahn took the binoculars and looked out from the battlements. "They made that trench and wall fast."

"Morgan's digging tools," said Spinner stubbornly. "He's helping them, I know it."

Jahn continued to look through the binoculars. "Is that another feeling of yours, Spinner?"

"He'll sell anything to anybody. That's no way to encourage loyalty. Why hasn't he helped us, his friends?"

"He sent us two of his new synthesized metal rovers. They should help us in the next attack."

"Synthmetal? The same synthmetal that Santiago uses on her fastest speeders?"

Jahn looked at him. "You may have something there. There could be commerce occurring between Morgan and Santiago. At any rate, we have the rovers, though the weapons are nothing spectacular. I wish we had time to transfer the Spartan energy weapon to the new chassis."

Spinner nodded and lifted his own binoculars. "The wall they built is nothing more than a low embankment to cover them if we attack again."

"Though it's about as tall as a person. And it does have a crude gate."

"Speaking frankly, we would be foolish to go down there again anyway, sir," said Spinner. "The Spartans have reorganized now, and I'm sure Pierson is dead. We should stay behind these walls and read touchporn until the Spartans pack up and go home."

"Unless they attack the ridge again." Jahn looked at Spinner. "We can't let them have the ridge. You know that."

"I know." Spinner lifted his binoculars. "The Spartan gate is opening. Speeders coming, laser and standard."

Jahn felt his heart pound in his chest, but he also felt a new weariness rise up. *More deaths, only hours after the last round.*

"Alert the marksmen," he said. "As usual, laser speeders are the primary target." Spinner nodded and headed back for the command center.

"What's your feeling on the battle, Spinner?" Jahn asked as he reached the door.

"Violence destroyed Earth," said Spinner. "Violence always wins. It's just a matter of who's left standing afterwards."

Diego rode in his speeder, holding a shredder pistol in his left hand, the butt wedged into his injured arm, which still lay bound against his side. He watched the red earth go by, and he felt his melancholy leaving him, replaced by a rising battle lust. The white walls of UNHQ rose up before him.

"Hit them hard, with all lasers. Clear the top of the wall. Then pull the lasers to the left flank and take the farm buildings on my signal," said Diego.

Bolts of blue fire streaked up to the walls and flashed along the length of the Peacekeeper battlements. The lasers struck again and again, turning the top of the wall into a line of brilliant fire fading into darkness. When the lasers let up, the entire rim of the wall was burned black.

"Rockets to the gate," said Diego. "Laser speeders to the west."

The two groups of speeders broke away from each other. Diego picked up a small rocket tube and aimed it through the gun port. He fired it and watched the rocket streak across the plain toward the gun port on top of the west tower. As he watched, the rocket threaded right through the gun port and exploded inside. He could see the silhouettes of the Peacekeeper guards against the flames.

"To victory!" he shouted, his spirits lifting. He grabbed another rocket tube and pushed his torso out of the speeder hatch. He fired the rocket, watching as it streaked and detonated against the gates. Then he picked up his autoshredder and, one-handed, riddled the top of the wall with fire as his speeder turned parallel to the wall.

"The laser speeders are breaking west," said Spinner, spinning his coin nervously on the command console. "But the brute force attack is on the gates. Handheld rockets and weapons."

"Can they break through?" asked Jahn.

"Eventually, if enough of them hit. And in this attack pattern they're running they're hitting repeatedly. Plus the mortars are starting again, and although they're firing blind, they've been on the ridge and they have a better idea of where to aim."

"We killed or incapacitated all of the Spartans that made it to the ridge," said Jahn.

"So they go up but they don't come down. Good. But the Spartans are still heading for the farm."

"Order our people at the farm to move up to the ridge. We'll support them when we can."

"There's enemy movement below, at the farms," Elroy reported to Rank. "Laser speeders approaching. A lot of them."

"Without a direct line of sight it'll be hard for them to hit us, and vice versa," said Rank. "But prepare the mortars. As soon as the enemy's within range, open fire. We'll hold this position as long as we can."

"And then what?" asked Elroy suddenly. Rank stared at the man until he actually took a step back.

"Then we'll hold it no more," said Rank.

Diego had noticed a weak point in the wall's defenses and ordered his speeders to set up a small perimeter on the far east side of the wall. They continuously raked fire across the top of the wall, interfering with the Peacekeeper defenses at that location, and his soldiers had set up a mortar and were lobbing shots directly at the west tower and the gate, honing their aim and pounding it repeatedly.

"Keep firing! Keep firing!" he shouted, unleashing his own fury through his autoshredder. "At this rate we'll break through!"

Diego first heard the hissing sound against the roar of mortar explosions and shredder fire. As it grew louder, he had to shout to be heard over it, and then suddenly it dominated his mental landscape, impossible to ignore.

He saw the Spartans near him start to grab their ears and look around, sweat beading on their brows. It took Diego only a moment to discover the source of the sound.

From the xenofields to the east of the base, the vast red fields that had so far served only as an impassable obstacle, the hissing emerged, and as Diego watched the fields began to crawl with movement. As if summoned, millions of twisting, mottled mindworms rose up in the xenofungus fields and began rolling forward like a wave, washing toward and around the walls of UNHQ.

"Get the flame guns!" Diego shouted. "Remember your training!"

Spartans frantically ran to the speeders and pulled out long-barreled flame guns, strapping the fuel tanks on their back. They immediately fell into the tightly knit phalanx formations known as worm wedges, packed tight not for defense or offense but to draw moral support from comrades.

The fire from the Peacekeeper walls had silenced, and Diego could imagine them fleeing their positions in terror or watching in awe, their weapons loose in their hands. He ran and grabbed a flame gun himself and moved forward parallel with the two worm wedges.

The mindworm boil approached, rippling across the plain in a vast teeming wave, hundreds of thousands of wriggling nightmares forming the wave's crest. Diego's eyes shone with the heat of battle as he imagined victory, strength, conquering the enemy, all images that had worked against the boils back at Sparta Command.

The two worm wedges advanced, and the citizen on point triggered the flame gun. Diego advanced on his own, firing his flame gun and watching the long hot tongue of fire reach out for the wriggling mass that suddenly stretched for kilometers in front of him. He felt the body of the gun get warm in his hand, and he struggled to stop his newly burned left arm from withdrawing.

Flames.

The mindworm wave rose over him, and Diego looked up as the wave turned into a wall, cresting five meters above him, and then he felt it spinning around him, red and pulsing. He saw his flame gun wash over the first worms, and as he watched them coil and burn he shouted in anger and victory. But then the wall of red worms became a throat that swallowed him, and he felt as if he were falling a long, long way.

He was back on Earth, bound and on his back, and there were men over him, laughing at him. He tried to move his hands but couldn't, and then faces with eyes as dark as the sun was light bent over him, and silver blades cut into him, peeling his skin back layer by layer and cutting off his tongue and fingers.

And then the ropes fell away and he lifted his fist, but it was a worthless stump, and the red of his own blood flowed around his ankles, and these men, who then became women and children, laughed at him and tore at him and cut him, and he felt tears of shame roll down his face

They cut off his skin and then cut out his muscles, piece by piece, and he watched his flesh fall away in bloody chunks that were swallowed by black rats beneath his feet. And the children cut into his tendons, on his arms and his legs and around his neck, until he was nothing but bone and nerve.

Then he fell on the ground and he saw the red blood around him, his enemies' blood that had become his own, and then the children's blades came down for his eyes.

And after that, the darkness.

"Diego is dead," came the report.

Santiago nodded, but needed no report. She stood on the wall and watched the wave of mindworms consume her soldiers, breaking their phalanxes. She shouted at her citizens, trying to keep their line intact.

"They're going to kill us all," said her operations director, standing next to her with sweat beading his forehead. "Sound the retreat!"

"If I sound the retreat they'll decimate us," said Santiago. "I must stay here and direct a slow fallback, until we can dig in behind this wall. If we're lucky, we'll come through alive." She issued more orders to the citizens on the plain, her own voice starting to crack with the wormfear. "This is the largest boil I've ever seen."

"Colonel," said the voice of Victor. She looked down from the wall to see him standing there.

"We have to rally the citizens, or this camp will fall."

"What do you think I'm doing up here?" she almost shouted, angry at his interruption. But then she saw something in his eyes, a kind of stubbornness.

"Your armor, sir. Our warriors need to see it."

"I can't leave my position," she said. From the

other side of the wall, someone turned a flame gun on his own phalanx, the blackened skeletons of his own squad dropping to the ground in burning pieces. "Get out of here," she spat at Victor.

"I want your armor, sir. You promised it to me."

She started to turn away, then looked at his badge, which now read Santiago. She had made a vow to her son. She nodded once and gave him the key to the armor chest from around her neck.

"Do it," she said.

The speeders pulled up to the camp wall first, and Spartans jumped out and tried to enter the gates, but the gates were closed. The orders came at them through quicklink, breaking through the screams that rang in their minds: take your flame guns and turn back the worms.

The infantry reached the wall next, and then the mindworms came, again rising up and sending living tendrils out to consume the human sources of terror that attracted them. Another Spartan phalanx broke, and the lead gunner went down, screaming as he died. Two more phalanxes collapsed at the sound of the screams, and Spartans began kneeling on the ground or throwing themselves into the worm boil in terror.

"Look up!" came a voice through the quicklinks, and the living Spartans who heard the voice looked up.

On the top of the wall a figure emerged, a figure in the gleaming red battle armor of the Spartan supreme commander. The troops on the field, delirious with terror, looked up to see the image of that figure in red above them. The sight lifted their spirits, and the phalanxes tightened.

"Forward!" shouted the figure, its voice magnified by the soldiers' quicklinks and echoing strangely in the psychic fields set up by the worms. "Citizens, do not fear. The worms feed on fear. But we are Spartans, and they will find no food in us."

The figure of their supreme commander jumped down from the wall, activated a flame gun, and walked forward into the worms, which parted like a sea, and now the Spartans could hear the shrieks of the creatures dying.

Flame guns activated down the Spartan line, and phalanxes moved forward relentlessly, step by step. The worms turned and coiled like burning paper and receded like a rushing tide, back into the xenofungus from which they had come.

The figure in red turned as the Spartans shouted their approval, and pointed wordlessly at the ridge above the Peacekeeper city. Roaring their approval again, the Spartans remounted their speeders and headed for the ridge, a deadly tide of focused killing energy.

On the lead speeder stood the figure in red, commander of the Spartan armies, in the battle armor of Santiago.

And the son of Santiago led the troops of Sparta from terror into exultation.

"They turned the mindworm attack," said Jahn. He pushed his hand into his ear, trying to shake the echoes of the psychic assault he had felt even from his position on the battlements.

"It was fortune smiling on us anyway," said Pravin. "Surely we didn't expect them to win the battle for us?"

"It would have been nice. But at least it killed a few of them, I think."

"Look," said Pravin, his voice hushed. Jahn looked to see the Spartans at their low wall massing together and shouting their victory cries. And as he watched they turned en masse toward the northwest and began heading toward the ridge. In their lead a figure in red rode in a speeder, and the Spartans ran and rode behind it.

"Is that Santiago herself?" asked Pravin.

"It doesn't matter," said Jahn. "They're heading for the ridge, and they look very determined. But they're ignoring our troops here in the city. We must hit them from the flank while they're trying to scale the ridge."

Pravin grabbed at Jahn's sleeve, turning him around. "Jahn, I don't want you to go out there."

"I must. Look at them. They have victory in their bearing."

"That is why you must stay," said Pravin.

Jahn looked at his father, looking into eyes that mirrored his own, yet perceived different worlds. His father had grown up in relative peace, and Jahn in constant war.

"To stay here means suicide for all of us. I'm going." He gripped his father's shoulder hard, and then suddenly found himself in an embrace and felt his father's face on his shoulder.

"I'll be all right," he said, then broke away and headed for the courtyard, not looking back.

* * *

Victor reached the farms and ordered a quick and brutal attack. His Spartan warriors—all loyal warriors who would follow him to the death—surrounded the building. He saw them going through the back windows and tearing open the front doors, fearless. Speeders pulled up and established a quick perimeter.

"Sir, the enemy has abandoned this position," came the report as a lieutenant came sprinting back out the doors. "There are Spartan dead and wounded in here, from the assault on the ridge."

"Keep moving," said Victor, feeling the momentum of battle carrying them forward to victory. "Leave a complement of troops here to cover us. The rest, to the ridge!"

The ground troops and speeders turned back up the hill and continued through the trees and onto the sloped earth.

"They're coming, sir, a full battalion from the looks of it, with lasers."

Rank looked down the hill and then turned to look over at the walls of UNHQ.

"Look. The Peacekeepers are coming out to hit them from the flank. We'll assist from up here. If the Spartans keep coming, they'll be walking into a meat grinder." He looked around at his subcommanders. "You take a full squad and fire down the overhang at anything that moves. You prepare the mortar and start lobbing shots as soon as they're within range. Make it tough for them."

One soldier stared at him, white-faced. "Sir, we can't hold that many of them off."

"It's fear, soldier. They brought every speeder and a mass of troops so that you would hand them this ridge with only half a fight. We're going to give them a full fight, and then some. And their speeders will never make it up those slopes, so don't be fooled."

The soldier nodded. "I came here to start a new life, sir," he said suddenly, as if in explanation.

"And here it is, my friend. Take comfort in the fact that if you stayed on Earth you'd be dead, so every moment up here is another moment borrowed from the grave."

He looked at his command staff, who watched him silently. "Get to work," he said, and they hurried off.

Victor felt the speeder grind, its wheels gripping for purchase as the slope increased. Finally it came to a standstill in a small clearing, wheels slipping and sending rocks clattering down the slope.

Without a word Victor jumped to the ground and hefted his autoshredder to his shoulder.

"Here they come, sir," said his second-in-command, and he looked back down the slope to see several Peacekeeper rovers coming their way at full tilt. The first barrage of gunfire clattered into the nearby rocks, not quite reaching them.

"Wait until they get close and have the speeders by the farm open fire," he ordered.

From the ridge above came a whomping sound, and something arced into the air. Victor looked up to see a small dark shape at the head of a comet trail descending toward them.

"Incoming!" shouted his second. The mortar struck, turning a speeder into showers of hot metal. Spartans slipped back down the slope, and a small rock slide started.

"They're turning our own mortars against us!"

shouted the second. Victor said nothing, feeling secure in his armor, but a tiny part of his confidence slipped as he wondered if he had misjudged again.

Another mortar blast landed nearby, and a body hurled through the air and struck Victor on the torso. He grunted and nearly fell, then regained his feet.

"Attack them," he said, pointing to the Peacekeepers coming from the base. "Hit them with everything and stay in motion. When we get close enough the mortars will stop."

The high-pitched whine of the laser speeders split the air, and then flashes of blue fire arced across the slope and into the approaching Peacekeepers.

"Evasive action!" shouted Jahn, and his rovers split in various directions as the bolts of blue fire ripped toward them.

He could see the mortar fire hitting the Spartans, and then the Spartans turned away from the ridge and came toward his approaching force.

"We're going uphill into a moderate slope," he warned his troops. "Be very careful. And we need to get close to them to neutralize the laser fire. Drive like demons."

The rovers swung around as another wave of blue fire scorched the earth around them. One rover took a hit broadside and the entire right side turned into a twisted black mass, a burned figure of a soldier falling from the wreckage. Another rover, one of the new armored ones that Morgan had sent them, took a laser to the front and bounced up on two wheels, then fell back down again and kept going.

"Be careful," Jahn said to no one in particular. He

looked up toward the highest of the Spartan force and saw the figure in red battle armor, pointing at his approaching Peacekeepers.

That's the leader, he thought, and a competitive instinct honed in years of hand-to-hand combat training made him yearn to meet the Spartan commander. He thought of his Peacekeepers lying in hospital beds, burned and broken, more human wreckage transplanted from Earth to the new world. And he wanted to kill that leader, and make him or her pay.

The Peacekeepers hit the Spartans like a blue wave crashing onto a red shore. Gunfire erupted and filled the air with a steady drone, and shouts and cries of pain echoed up and down the ridge. Bolts of blue energy crackled and melted rock and metal and flesh. And Jahn laid fire all around him.

"They're really mixing it up on the slopes," said Elroy, and Rank nodded.

"The fighting is unusually tight. We'll have to be careful with the mortar fire. What are the Spartans near the farm doing?"

His second-in-command looked through binoculars down the slope as another mortar fired and arced over their heads.

"They're coming up to join the fight."

Rank considered. The sensible thing would be to hold this position on the ridge with as many people as possible. But he felt that the battle taking place below him marked a crucial turning point. And the element of surprise never failed to give an advantage.

"We're going down," he said quietly. His second

stared at him as Rank called all the troops around him and spoke to them.

"We're going down the slope," he said. "We're going to hit them from above, with everything we've got, and turn the tide of this battle. And we're going now," he said, and he met the eyes of every last soldier under his command, and they all saw that his eyes held no fear.

"Get your weapons and say your prayers. Move out!"

Jahn looked out the gun port of his rover as the chaos of battle raged outside. A Spartan appeared right in front of him and he opened fire, unconsciously gritting his teeth as the body jerked wildly and fell underneath the tires of his vehicle.

Suddenly an explosion jolted him to the bone, and the metal beneath him warped from the force of a concussion grenade beneath the rover. The cockpit around him spun as the rover went up and crashed down on its side. Jahn's head slammed into metal.

"Get out!" he shouted. He punched the emergency exit switch and the hatch blew open, revealing the cloud-sprinkled pale sky above. He immediatly began pushing members of his crew outside, following the last one close behind.

Two suns blazed down on the slope as the battle raged. Speeders and rovers turned in tighter and tighter circles as soldiers on foot tried to incapacitate them or jam flame grenades through the gun ports.

He saw Spartans and Peacekeepers shooting at each other point blank, and then shooting the corpses. Shouts of anger and pain rang out.

There's no turning back now.

From the direction of the farms came more arcs of blue fire, and Jahn saw even Spartan soldiers staggering blindly from the aftermath of those attacks.

Then suddenly from above them a long, frightening battle cry sounded, and Rank crashed down into the fray, cutting into the Spartans from above, sending flesh churning into blood.

Jahn felt the battle cry lift his spirits, and he surrendered utterly to the chaos of the battle. Hatred and fears that had been with him for his entire life, since the rattled streets of New Delhi on Earth, rose up and were burned away by a pure focus on the kill.

Victor looked around at the torn-up slopes, at the Spartans and Peacekeepers lying dead all around him, and saw that in many ways the Peacekeepers had become Spartans, fighting with the same ferocity and focused rage.

The Peacekeepers had caught them in a classic flanking maneuver. With the Peacekeepers from the city hammering them from the east, and now the attack coming down from the ridge, he could see his citizens' pure battle rage becoming a disorganized free-for-all on the slopes.

I led them into this, he thought, remembering the explosives on the ridge, and how he had failed to see that trap.

He looked down at his armor, the gleaming red armor that had saved the Spartans from the mindworm attack, and he remembered that fleeting glory.

But for that one moment, I had it. I was a Spartan to the core.

He nodded, and at that moment, on the slope below him, he saw the Peacekeeper commander.

Ahead of him Jahn Lal caught a flash of red and headed for it. He ran through a column of smoke that rose off a burning speeder and found the leader in the red battle armor, leaning against a tree as if bewildered or in need of a rest.

Jahn aimed his shredder pistol as the Spartan's blank faceplate turned toward him, then suddenly the Spartan was in motion, jumping not away from him but toward him, rolling under the barrel of the gun. Jahn opened fire and saw several of his shredder bolts hit the Spartan in the arm and glance off the highly compact material of the armor. The Spartan tumbled down from the impact, but then climbed up again and jumped on Jahn.

Jahn could feel the tension in the wiry muscles as they rolled on the rocky ground. The smooth hard armor pressed into Jahn, and he could find no place to land a blow. The Spartan hit him hard across the face, and Jahn felt his head snap back.

Fights like a demon.

Jahn moved tight against the Spartan's body, trying to minimize his opponent's leverage, but the blows still came like hammers. Jahn tried a kidney punch but only bruised his knuckles against the surface of the armor.

Better change tactics, he thought, and felt panic mingling with anger. He slumped a little, feigning unconsciousness, and slipped down the Spartan's body. His opponent, sensing the weakness, got his feet underneath him and pushed up. Jahn slipped down the Spartan's ankle and grabbed it.

I learned my lesson about mercy, he thought. He took the ankle and twisted it hard, putting every bit of strength and leverage into it. The ankle turned and he felt it give, then he felt the cracks as bone splintered, and still he kept twisting.

Victor felt his ankle turn and crack in the hands of the Peacekeeper, and he closed his eyes as an ecstasy born of the sudden pain shot through him. The world around him became preternaturally bright, and he looked again at the red armor, the armor of his mother, the Supreme Commander.

I wear it well.

And maybe it was better to remember himself as Victor the slayer of mindworms, son of Santiago, and take his place in the hall of heroes.

He dropped his guard and let go.

Jahn never heard the Spartan make a sound, but his opponent fell back to the ground silently. Jahn looked around and saw his autoshredder, which he lunged for and picked up. The Spartan stood up again, and Jahn realized that he had picked up the barrel end of his weapon.

He swung it hard, calling on a deep primitive instinct to fight, and knocked the Spartan's helmet from his head. He swung again and felt the butt of his gun crunch into bone, then he reversed the weapon and fired, letting his rage carry him.

He fired point-blank into the chest of the Spartan, and the shots struck the smooth red armor, the sound echoing ferociously across the slope. He saw the armor take the shots and then begin to splinter

and finally split open, and now his shots tore into
the exposed flesh below.

"The commander is down," came the message to
the command tent in the Spartan camp.

Santiago looked up, and her operations director
noticed her face pale slightly. "What do you mean,
down?" she asked, her voice cracking across him
like a whip, and the phrase *don't kill the messenger*
flashed across his mind.

"No more details. A citizen saw him fall in combat with a Peacekeeper commander. He's been shot
in the chest."

"Bring him back!" Santiago said, and lunged toward the communication panel. The operations
director fell back, breathless from her fury. She
opened a link and spoke to every Spartan on the
field.

"Bring back the body of your commander, alive
or dead!" she said, anger crackling through her
voice. "If any Spartan returns before that body, I
will shoot you on sight!"

She closed the link and stormed from the command tent, leaving a stunned silence in her wake.

Jahn released the trigger and looked at the dead
body of the Spartan commander, the man he had
just defeated, and suddenly the fight left him.

What have I done here?

"Get the armor!" shouted Rank, pointing to it.
Jahn shook his head, a confusion setting in.

It's just a boy. Underneath the helmet that he had
knocked off, he could see the face of a young man,
eighteen or so, with a short crop of bright red hair.

The boy stared up into the pale blue sky, his face expressionless.

"The armor!" shouted Rank. He ran up and began pulling the damaged chest piece off the fallen commander. "This is valuable. I think it's Santiago's personal battle armor."

Jahn nodded and bent down mechanically, pulling pieces of the armor off. As they worked, three Spartans burst onto the scene, and Rank rolled to the side and opened fire, cutting all three of them off at the throat. A Spartan laser speeder suddenly pulled into view, and Jahn looked up in time to see a Peacekeeper jump onto the turret like a pouncing lion, firing down into the top hatch with shredder fire. The laser speeder jerked and kept on driving, plowing into a lone tree.

"They're converging on us, I think," said Rank. He got on his quicklink. "Concentrate your fire on Spartans approaching my position," he said to his men.

"Maybe it's time to fall back," said Jahn quietly, and he noticed that his troops seemed to lack any focus other than to kill or be killed. He pulled the chest piece off the corpse and then saw something on the thin uniform underneath. He touched the boy's chest.

"Santiago," he said. "His badge says Santiago."

"It's her armor," said Rank, pulling off a glove. A concussion grenade landed nearby, and he turned his head away from the blast. "They're coming for the body," he said. "Get out of here." He grabbed Jahn and pulled him to his feet, and the two of them ran from the body back toward a Peacekeeper rover.

"Get inside, sir," said Rank, shoving the pieces of

armor into Jahn's arms. "I'm taking my men back up on the ridge. Things are going to get ugly."

Jahn looked back at the clearing where the body lay. Spartans and Peacekeepers fired at each other, the combat crossing back and forth over the fallen boy. As Jahn watched, a barrage of stray gunfire struck the body. It jerked on the ground and then lay still again, the young face staring up into the sky.

"Fall back," said Jahn into his quicklink, as he saw more and more Spartans converging on the clearing.

Jahn threw the armor up to the rover pilot and then climbed in himself.

"Let's get out of here," he said, a bitter taste in his mouth. As they rocketed across the plain, the empty eyes of the Spartan commander haunted him.

chapter twelve

Twilight

JAHN AND PRAVIN STOOD OVER THE STURDY TABLE IN THE military research section of the tech labs. On the table were laid out the pieces of hard red armor from the Spartan commander, in the rough shape of a body.

"It's marvelous stuff," said Ella, her long hair tied back with something that looked suspiciously like the hose from a Bunsen burner. She walked around the table, picking up each piece in turn. "It's lightweight but very strong. As you found out, it can even turn shredder bolts, except at very close range."

Jahn looked at the chest piece of the armor, torn open by his ruthless attack. "We'll sew that up somehow," Ella said calmly.

Another man stepped forward, small and balding, with light, darting eyes. "The armor will also have a psychological effect on the enemy, of course," he said.

"Who are you?" Jahn asked curtly.

"Military psych," the small man said. "This is the armor of the Spartan commanders, and any Spar-

tan soldier knows it by sight. Plus, they know it can
turn bullets. The tiniest hesitation of the enemy
when seeing this armor, coupled with the fear and
obedience effects, will give us a slight edge in any
battle to come."

"Are you saying someone here should wear this
armor?" asked Jahn, and deep in his mind disgust
at his behavior in the day's battle warred with a
small excitement at claiming this prize.

"Naturally," said Ella. "We'll take 3-D images of it
and keep a few pieces to study, but it'll take years to
duplicate. Right now it will help the Peacekeepers a
lot more out there than in here. Unless the Spartans make it into our labs," she added thought-
fully.

*We must destroy the datalinks and gas pods if that
happens,* Pravin realized. *I will talk to Ella.*

Jahn nodded, reaching out to touch the armor's
smooth red surface. "If it'll help us, I'll wear it,"
said Jahn.

"Clean off the bloodstains first," said Pravin. Ella
looked at him curiously.

Santiago sat in the darkened command tent. Her
two remaining advisors, Halleck and Gruber, sat in
their regular chairs, which were also the farthest
from Santiago. Empty chairs sat around the table,
where Diego, Messier, and Victor had once sat. Santiago looked at each advisor in turn.

"I will speak first," said Gruber. "I withdraw my
vote for the attack. It's time to regroup. We can use
our remaining forces to take Peacekeeper Base Two
with little effort, and—"

"The battle will continue," said Santiago. Halleck

looked at her and saw the terrible shadow that masked her face.

"We must have council," protested Gruber.

"Our attack is not finished," said Santiago. "Since both commanders are dead, I am the only person qualified to finish the attack. Do you doubt it?" She looked at both of them.

"No, sir," said Gruber, and Halleck nodded.

"Do you know who the Myrmidons are?" asked Santiago. Halleck nodded again.

"Have you ever seen them fight?" asked Santiago, and they both shook their heads.

"You are dismissed," Santiago said, and left the command tent before they could salute.

Outside, dusk fell across the Spartan camp. The gates in the Spartan embankment were open, and just outside a large pile of wood waited under the emerging stars. On top of the pyre lay a body.

Santiago stepped through the gates and to the body, which lay dressed in uniform. She looked at the boy's face and at the ID badge that shared her name, and something she never anticipated twisted in her gut.

She shook her head angrily, pushing her pain back down into her core, where it would feed the battle rage that drove her. She took a long torch from the honor guard and thrust it into the pyre with no fanfare.

"We came from a world of fire, and to fire we must return," she said quietly, and watched as the flames licked up, obscuring the shape of UNHQ on the dim horizon. Grief twisted in her belly again and turned into rage.

Night

Santiago stepped out of her tent and looked at her Myrmidons, assembled before her like phantoms in the darkness. They stood utterly silent, their blank faceplates looking straight ahead, but she knew their finely tuned senses absorbed everything around them.

Santiago wore the typical black armor of a Myrmidon, since her red armor had fallen into the hands of the enemy. She held the broad helmet under her arm so she could address her troops and let them see the determination in her eyes.

"We're going to end this conflict tonight," she said. "The Peacekeeper defense is weak from the fighting, and we are fresh. We will divide into two forces. One will attack the gate head-on, the other will carry the pieces of a heavy laser cannon up to the ridge, destroying any remaining Peacekeeper resistance up there. We will use no speeders and will carry the cannon in pieces, so the surprise will be total. When the gates are open, we will let in the other Spartans, and UNHQ will fall."

She swept her elite troops with her eyes one more time, her face smooth and hard. Then she put on her helmet and led her Myrmidons forward into the night.

Jahn stood on the battlements, staring across the dark plains toward the Spartan camp as Ella fitted the Spartan armor to his body, taking her time wrapping the pieces around his chest.

"It feels good," said Jahn, moving his arms. "It's

light but strong. I feel as if I can lead the troops to Sparta and back."

Pravin nodded, watching his son. *Lead the troops to Sparta.* He had never heard his son talk that way, back when his biggest interests had been the expansion of the base and his new wife.

He looks so sure of himself, thought Pravin. *His face has an intensity I remember in him even as a child.*

He walked over as Ella fastened shin plates over his shins. Jahn seemed to straighten up in the armor, to stand taller and move more precisely.

"Can you activate any of the Spartan technology?" Pravin asked.

"Not yet," said Ella. "But there does seem to be some tracking equipment in there that may allow you to get past Spartan sensors. Still, they know the armor is gone, and that's a great risk."

"I see," said Pravin.

"We might be able to confuse them," said Jahn, holding his hand up toward a lightbank and turning a polished red glove before his face. "This is truly beautiful. I feel strong."

"Just remember you're not invulnerable," said Ella. "Don't get cocky, or someone will surprise you with a flash grenade up your ass." She stood back and looked at him appraisingly.

"Maybe the Spartans will retreat and none of this will be necessary," said Jahn.

"Maybe a cloud of magic fairy dust will appear and kill them all," said Ella. "Sir," she added belatedly.

"Until we know, keep pushing," said Pravin quickly. He stepped back and watched his son move crisply in the elite armor.

Is that the armor of my enemy? he thought. So far

he had managed to hold the thought that he fought for a unified humanity. But now he thought of the dozens of Peacekeepers lying dead, burned, wounded, and dying inside the medlabs. And when he looked at the Spartan armor on his son he felt a bitterness turn in his stomach.

This is how it begins, he reflected. *The ancient hatreds all have their roots somewhere.* In looking at the red of the Spartan armor and seeing his own dying soldiers on their beds, he was conditioning himself to hate.

He took a deep breath and let it out into the chilly night air. He walked to the battlements and looked out into the darkness.

Something moved out there. He had seen it, but now the darkness seemed solid.

"Spinner, are you there?" Pravin asked through his quicklink.

"Yes, sir,"

"I think I saw something on the plain."

"Hadn't noticed, sir. I'll have to do some scans."

"Then do them," Pravin said, suddenly agitated. Jahn and Ella walked over and looked out at the plain.

"Would the Spartans attack so soon after today's fighting?" asked Jahn.

"Look," said Ella.

Under the starlight, they could see a broad phalanx of troops running toward the base at a phenomenal clip. The figures wore black armor that reflected the night sky, and on their heads elaborate helmets with faceless masks.

"No speeders," said Pravin, his heart sinking. "I've never seen Spartans like that before."

"Scramble the defenses," said Jahn. "Everyone on alert."

The black figures ran on, not firing, just approaching the gates with single-minded purpose.

"They keep running under the mortars," said Spinner, scanning copious readouts from the battlefields. "The shells are just lighting them up."

"How about the marksmen?" asked Jahn.

"Somewhat effective, but I believe these are the infamous Spartan Myrmidons, which means they have the strong armor like yours, and they fire back with deadly accuracy. Looks like they're drilling shots through the cannon ports at two-hundred meters on the run." He checked another readout. "They're at the gates," he said.

"I'm going up to the tower to coordinate the attack," said Jahn.

Jahn reached the window in the west guard tower in time to see Hulsey directing four other Peacekeepers poised with fire barrels, ready to pour. Hulsey also had her hand on the trigger switch for the explosive charges, which Peacekeeper demo techs had replanted earlier.

Jahn ran to the window and looked down. The figures in black seemed to emerge from the darkness as if they were part of it, closing in on the gate. Suddenly several dozen small canisters rocketed out from amongst them, sending thick clouds of white smoke billowing up from the battlefield.

"What's this?" asked Hulsey, a curse in her voice. The smoke spread out quickly, choking the ground in white and lapping all the way up against the gates. Jahn could see nothing and quickly lifted his binoculars, switching them to an infrared view.

"I can see them," said Jahn. "They're still coming. Prepare to trigger the charges."

As Jahn watched, several of the Spartans bent down and seemed to dig in the earth, and then stood and began pulling. In the monochrome green-and-black view of the infrared, he saw dark strings being torn from the ground.

"They're pulling up the detonation wires!" shouted Jahn. "Detonate them now!"

Hulsey triggered the switch but nothing happened. "They pulled the wires from the wall," said Jahn. He shook his head. "Prepare the barrels." The smoke rose up around them, dissipating.

"They won't be able to breach the gates," said Hulsey. "They couldn't possibly carry enough explosives."

"The sally port," said Jahn, thinking about the smaller gate in the wall next to the west gate that would allow only one person to pass at a time. As he looked down he saw six of the warriors pull out a small hydraulic ram of some kind. "They're going to try and break through the sally port."

"If they come in one at a time we'll massacre them," said Hulsey, but she didn't look too sure.

"I'll order our best fighters to the inner courtyard," said Jahn, his heart thumping. "Now dump those barrels!"

From narrow walkways atop the guard towers and battlements overlooking the south gates, a waterfall of white fire cascaded down onto the heads of the attackers below.

* * *

Wilson lay on his belly at the top of the over-hang leading up to Sol Ridge. The ground felt cold beneath him, and he kept shifting uncomfortably, counting the moments until dawn arrived, along with his relief.

"They won't attack tonight," he said, and his own voice startled him a little. "We fought them too hard today."

"Shut up," said Pace, his bitter companion at arms, who held the position on the other side of the slope. "No talking on watch."

Wilson shook his head and sighted through his scope, then on a whim swiveled it toward Pace's position, using the crosshairs to sight along the man's shoulders and head. When he grew bored of this game he swiveled his rifle back.

Rising up from the darkness at the edge of the overhang came a faceless mask, then a quick movement and nothing.

He looked up from the scope, his heart pounding. Every sound around him seemed magnified, and he felt afraid to call out to Pace, afraid to give away his position.

He heard a soft chuffing sound, and then the darkness closed in around him, sending him into an infinite night.

Rank could feel the death force closing in on the ridge around him. He could see its purple field surrounding him, lighting up the faces of his soldiers, and he didn't need anyone to tell him that something bad was coming his way.

He stood up and looked around the ridge. The clear night seemed now to close in around him, stifling him, and the silence roared in his ears.

"Have everyone check in," said Rank, drawing his pistol. The wide dark eyes of his second-in-command looked up at him, reflecting the emptiness of the sky. "Do it."

As he suspected, no one answered. Rank walked calmly to the edge of the solar collectors and stared down the hill.

The black figure was upon him like a shadow. Rank saw the barrel of a pistol and heard the muffled sound of silenced gunfire, but he turned away, his reflexes lightning quick. He lunged back into the attacker, realizing suddenly that it was a Myrmidon, one of the ruthless elite Spartan fighters. His heart pounding, he wrapped himself around his enemy, tangling his arms and legs.

Hers, not his, he realized, feeling the form underneath the armor. Something hit him in the belly like a pile driver, forcing every ounce of oxygen from his lungs, and then it hit again. He rolled away and gasped for a breath.

Cold black metal descended on him relentlessly. He felt something grab his left hand and twist it, and he heard bones crunch. He struck out with his right fist and hit nothing, then a cold grip claimed that right fist and he felt it twist and break.

He pushed away, his hands held at unnatural angles, sweat pouring down his face. Heat and cold washed through his body.

"I will not . . ." he said, and then realized he had no idea how to finish the sentence. He got up and turned to face his opponent, but she came at him suddenly from behind, pushing him to the ground. He felt an ankle break, and then the other.

She's breaking my bones one by one.

He turned and saw the faceplate again and lunged forward, wrapping his arms around the Myrmidon's neck, unable to grab her with his broken wrists. He pushed forward with all his strength, tightening his grip on her neck as something struck him over and over in the chest. He felt his ribs break and collapse with every hit.

He twisted away and her helmet popped off. Underneath was the shaved head of a woman, her face smooth and calm and covered with a myriad of small scars. She stared at him without emotion.

He felt something give as another blow forced his ribs deep into the soft places inside his chest. His will kept him going, forcing his muscles to wrap around her, to drive his fingers into her eyes, but then he realized that his muscles would no longer respond.

As he watched, the woman's face seemed to fall away from him, but actually it was him falling, down onto the ground, and then onto his back. He looked at the stars above and wondered what waited there for him.

Way too short was his last thought.

Six Spartans stood at the sally port and directed the hydraulic ram. The ram struck the gate again and again, in a terrible rhythm that Jahn could hear and feel in the guard tower.

The burning phosphorus cascaded down around them, and twelve other Myrmidons lifted up large shields made of the same black material as their armor. Jahn saw two of them fall, collapsing into white fire, but two others stepped forward to take their place.

The pounding on the gate faltered for a moment, and then started again.

"Their armor resists the chemicals, and we don't have much of it left," said Hulsey. "If they get the gates open we might need it."

"Then save it," said Jahn, angry. *At the root of anger is fear,* he remembered, and he knew what he feared now. *These Spartans won't stop.*

"I'm going to the courtyard," he said. "Prepare for an assault by the rest of the Spartan forces. Do what you can against these."

"Do what we can," Hulsey repeated blankly. Jahn left the guard tower and headed for the courtyard below, while the ram continued to boom.

Pravin Lal stood alone in a section of the battlements east of the gates, looking down at the figures in black that were pounding the ram into the sally port. He watched the white fire cascade down around them, and watched them keep working, the booming of the ram shaking the stone even beneath his feet.

It won't be long. This could be the end.

He looked beyond the waiting Myrmidons, who fired back at his sharpshooters with deadly accuracy, crouched behind their shields. And beyond that, across the plain and in the Spartan camp, he knew hundreds more Spartan soldiers waited to storm his city when the gates fell.

"Ella," he said into his quicklink, and she responded immediately.

"He's coming," she said. "And we have another pod loaded in a speeder. We can sneak it out the north gate and into the Spartan camp. It won't matter if it's destroyed, because the payload will be delivered. Just say the word."

At that moment a man in the white uniform of the science staff hurried onto the battlements, carrying an odd-looking rifle with a large pneumatic chamber.

"Sir, I'm ready," he said, and took position at a gun port, aiming the rifle down toward the Myrmidons. "Just say the word and I'll fire."

Pravin looked at the man in his white clothes, his finger on the trigger of the nerve gas rifle. *A small pod, minuscule, but enough to wipe out the Myrmidons in an instant. And then another pod for the rest of the Spartans.*

"Sir?"

He closed his eyes, seeing the video footage in his mind, the thrashing rioters dying in the streets, hurling themselves from windows. He opened his eyes again to see one of the Myrmidons fall, swallowed in the blast of a rocket from the walls. The figure fell, and even as it fell it looked up with its blank faceplate and continued firing, like an unstoppable spirit.

Inevitable. Unstoppable. Human nature. But everything that happened would be different, if only we had chosen differently.

"No," Pravin said, then activated his quicklink as the scientist looked at him, confused. "Destroy it. Ella, destroy the nerve gas pods and the datalinks too. We will find another way."

She hesitated. "Are you certain? Because you know I'll do it, and there's no going back."

"Do it, Ella. As fast as you can."

"Consider it done," she said, and broke the link. He looked at the scientist in time to see the man slump down to the floor, a Myrmidon bolt in his forehead. Pravin went to him and picked up the nerve gas rifle, ejecting the tiny pod and hiding it deep in his pocket.

Below him the ram pounded into the sally port, and suddenly the gate cracked. One more shot from the ram and the gate flew open, opening his city to the enemy.

Jahn stood in the courtyard with every soldier he could muster, staring at the sally port as it shook from the impact of the ram. They fingered their weapons and shifted nervously, crouching behind a perimeter of parked rovers.

"They can only send in one at a time," said Jahn. "Remember that. Keep up your fire, and aim for the chest and head. Their armor is strong."

He looked over to where their one stolen laser speeder waited as well. *This could get ugly.*

He started to say something more, something to reassure his soldiers and let them know they fought for the right reasons, when the gate buckled in, torn off its hinges. The next strike of the ram sent the gate crashing into the courtyard, and the sally port of UNHQ opened. The first Myrmidon entered, the beginning of a black tide.

The Myrmidons came through faster than Jahn could have imagined. Some rolled through, some ran through, and every single one cut off in a different direction. The Peacekeeper fire was unrelenting, and some Myrmidons fell a few steps into the courtyard, but others took cover behind the bodies that piled up.

The return fire was deadly accurate. Jahn saw Peacekeepers hidden behind metal barrels or parked rovers go down from a single bullet to the forehead. He leaned out to open fire and felt a bullet ricochet off the shoulder of his armor, and he felt the bruise forming underneath.

Keep firing . . .

He concentrated his fire, trying to hold the enemy in the gate with a barrage of shredder bolts, but the Myrmidons behind them pushed their comrades forward, using their wounded as cover once they were hit. And once inside the gate those faceless masks turned left and right, and everywhere they turned a Peacekeeper fell.

One Myrmidon got to the laser speeder and cut his way through the hatch, and Jahn heard screams from inside. The turret swiveled, and a blast of blue light hit the Peacekeepers' strongest defensive grouping, melting bodies into the pale white stone of the courtyard.

We're losing . . .

The black tide continued to come, and then Jahn looked over to see three Myrmidons pushing into the pressure hatch of the dome adjoining the courtyard.

"They're inside!" he said. "Spartans in the base!"

He ran after them, the part of his brain that created his nightmares seeing them walking through the base, killing citizens until they found the mechanism that would open the gate.

And killing his father on the way.

Jahn entered the pressure dome in time to see the three Myrmidons split up. He pursued one, finally catching him at a locked door. Jahn aimed and fired, and as the Myrmidon whirled and drew Jahn thought he caught a split-second hesitation as the Myrmidon saw his red battle armor.

Jahn rolled as shredder fire passed over him. The Myrmidon snapped back from Jahn's shot, and then Jahn felt shredder bolts ricocheting off his arm and shoulder. He opened fire again, right at the Myrmidon's ankles, and the Spartan went down.

Jahn kept firing, hitting the feet, chest and throat, and finally the Spartan stopped moving. Jahn kicked off the Myrmidon's helmet and put a bullet in the center of the man's head.

Better to be sure, he told himself. He got on his quicklink.

"Spinner?"

"They're inside for sure," said Spinner. "I've sealed the doors to the command center, and I'll coordinate the defense for as long as possible. Your father has signaled the retreat code, which means people like you head for the escape train."

"Where are Sophia and my son?" Jahn asked.

"They're heading for the train. Your father was up here on the battlements, and he's heading for the train as well, with at least two Peacekeepers for escort."

"I'm right below that position. I'm going to accompany him to the train."

"You get out of here, too. Someone's got to rebuild this place."

"Hold on," said Jahn, not knowing what else to say. Mercifully, Spinner broke the link first.

Jahn ran up a flight of twisting stairs, toward his father's location.

The Myrmidon commander stood atop the ridge and looked down at the city through the dark faceplate of her armor. She saw it not as a city but as a tar-

get, with weak spots and strong spots; places not
worth striking, and places where a hit would cripple it.

She turned to look down the ridge where more of
the Myrmidons pulled on heavy cable that dragged
the Spartan cannon up to the ridge. The Myrmidons pulled rhythmically, never breaking their pace
even though the cable itself strained from the
weight of the equipment they dragged up the slope.

She looked at the city again as her second-in-
command carried a piece of the cannon base over
and let it drop onto the ground.

"First target, sir?" the second asked, his black
faceplate staring at the Myrmidon commander ex-
pectantly.

"The central tower is the obvious choice," said the
commander. "It's well within the cannon's range, and
it probably holds important Peacekeeper intelligence
or staff. Probably." She studied the base again, combing every square inch of it for locations of tactical significance. "If we could hit the medlabs, it would cripple them, both emotionally and tactically."

"We don't know the location, except that they're
underground and probably on the far side of the
base," said her second.

"Then look down there. Tell me where they
could be."

The second studied the city blankly. *This man is
just a killing machine,* she thought. *Even he doesn't
see the big picture.*

"The big building," said her second.

"Go get the rest of the cannon base," the commander said, and the second saluted and jogged off
without complaint.

No pattern recognition except in the heat of hand-to-

hand, thought the commander. But she had pattern recognition. Santiago had ordered her to study tactics and everything else she could get hold of, and so she had. Including architecture.

The medlabs will need to be near a power source, have easy access to the gates and major cross tunnels, will need extensive ventilation, and will be large enough that no surface structures could have deep supports in that area.

She saw it. A rectangle of unusually flat land near the central tower, dotted with small ventilation shafts.

It's there. And it will be the first target.

The second-in-command returned with another piece of the cannon.

Jahn found Pravin on a narrow staircase leading down from the battlements, with two Peacekeepers he didn't recognize as escorts. The two escorts, a man and a woman whose nameplates read Remy and Chan, looked angry and jumpy, duty warring with self-preservation as they escorted Pravin down toward the escape trains near the medlabs.

"Father," said Pravin, and Pravin's eyes lit up as he saw his son. To Jahn, it looked as if he had chased dark shadows from his father's face. "We have to get you out of here."

"You will have no argument," said Pravin. Jahn took the lead, taking them down the narrow staircases and into a network of surface tunnels.

"Pressure masks in place," said Jahn. "Many of these tunnels aren't secure." In fact, as they ran forward they found the tunnel collapsed, blocked by piles of debris.

"Can't go that way," said Jahn.

"To the council room," said Pravin. "There is access to the underground tunnels from there."

Jahn nodded and led the way back through a twisting network of surface tunnels leading to the core of the original UNHQ, where the tunnels became narrower and darker.

There is where I awakened, thought Jahn, passing a metal door where the curtains to his recovery room had once been located. He wondered for a moment if Paula was among the living or the dead.

Down several more hallways he ran, and then he saw moonlight around a curve ahead, and they found themselves in the glass hallway of the Planet Walk. To the south Jahn could see the large expanses of base facilities and the great wall beyond, while to the north lay flat land and another curve of wall beyond which the xenofungus waited.

The hospital is beneath that flat land, thought Jahn. Once they got into the underground tunnels, it wouldn't be far.

"Go!" said Jahn, pushing his father and the two escorts into the long glass tunnel for the run to the council room at the base of the central tower. He ran after them.

Pravin reached the door and threw it open, when a burst of gunfire exploded all around him. Jahn felt an impact against the solid back of his armor, and he fell to the ground halfway down the hall, the wind knocked out of him. Remy shouted as a shredder bolt hit him in the shoulder.

Jahn looked back. Standing behind them was a Myrmidon, in gleaming black armor.

"Stay where you are, Pravin," said a woman's voice with a clipped Latino accent that both Jahn and Pravin recognized.

"Corazon," said Pravin.

Jahn rolled over with an exaggerated groan of pain. His hand found his shredder pistol. *I'll only get one chance at this.* So far Santiago had ignored him.

"Step down from that door, Pravin. I'm sure you can lock it from the other side. If you try to get away everyone here will die."

Pravin lifted his hands, remaining in the doorway. Santiago took steady steps toward him, her pistol at the ready.

Now.

Jahn leaped to his feet and took three steps directly toward her. He felt a shredder bolt slam into his forehead, and his head jerked back, but the bolt didn't penetrate his helmet. Then he reached her, and the two of them tangled and fell on the ground.

She regained her feet more quickly than he could have imagined. He turned and fired, and she rolled past him and to the other side of the hallway. Another shot hit him in the side, and he gasped in pain.

"Keep coming, Jahn," she said. He sank to one knee as if spent, then lunged forward, not at her but low and to her left, praying she would dodge in that direction.

She jumped left with catlike reflexes and he plowed into her, pushing her to the ground. His shredder pistol went off, and the glass wall behind her shattered, then suddenly he felt himself lifted off his feet as she grabbed him and threw him over her body, out into the dead space beyond the glass wall.

Pravin still stood in the doorway, watching his son. The woman, Chan, opened fire, but Santiago also dove outside of the glass wall, returning a shot that hit the woman in the chest and sent her sprawling to the ground, blood spreading out over her uniform. Pravin hurried to give her aid.

No, Father! Leave! Jahn thought.

Santiago had turned on Jahn again and kicked him low three times, the kicks hitting his shins and thighs like hammer blows. She jumped on top of him as he fell, and they both rolled farther away from the Planet Walk.

Keep rolling, Jahn thought. He felt her gun and tore it out of her hands as they rolled. She suddenly reached down and pulled his helmet off, and he found himself staring into her blank faceplate. He reached up to grasp her faceplate and felt her helmet slip off as well. He saw her features, perfectly composed, but with fury radiating from her eyes.

"Do you hear it?" she said to him, and he saw relish at her own fighting prowess in her face. He shook his head.

"The worms," she said. "They're out there, beyond the wall, inside the fungus." And indeed he heard a distant hissing sound, like a rattlesnake nesting inside his skull. "They're furious at our cannon fire and our fighting."

"Can *you* hear them?" Jahn asked. He felt a terror gnawing at the periphery of his spirit as the hissing rattle grew louder and louder. He struggled, then suddenly realized that she had him pinned in the darkness, his movements neutralized.

"Yes. I hear them. But I don't fear the worms. They

bring nightmares, and I have already lived mine."

She tore the shredder pistol from his hand and then wrenched his right arm behind his back.

"Let go, Jahn," she said. "Face them like a warrior. What are your nightmares, that the worms bring to you? Tell me, you who cost me a son."

He closed his eyes, shaking his head against the visions that crept into his consciousness on the back of the sinister hissing.

I used to be a builder, he remembered. *And I could never hear the worms.*

He tried to struggle against Santiago, but she had him utterly bound. The wormfear washed over him, and he saw . . .

Sophia, surrounded by Spartans tearing at her clothes and bruising her perfect face. He saw his son, his infant child, hurled from the burning walls of UNHQ that he had helped build so high. He saw fire consuming the faces of his loved ones, and his father and mother lying not in graves but in piles of corpses burned by their enemies. And he saw Santiago, her face cool and angry above him, reaching for his face.

She took his head in her hand and twisted it, until his neck snapped and she could press his face into the dirt. And Jahn Lal, son of Pravin Lal, died at the hands of Corazon Santiago.

The glass wall shattered as shredder bolts exploded from inside the hall, striking Santiago. She ducked and turned away, disengaging from the body of Pravin's son as she tried to reach her helmet, which lay on the ground nearby.

The barrage of gunfire continued relentlessly. She felt it hitting her chest plate as she tried to protect her head, and the impact sent her falling backwards. She felt a seam of the armor opening, and she shouted a curse and rolled farther away, returning shredder fire toward the enemy.

Pravin and the two escorts hurried past the shattered wall, drowning Santiago in a hail of autoshredder fire.

"Keep her off balance or we are dead!" shouted Pravin. The faces of his escorts were masks of fear. As Pravin watched, Santiago disappeared further into the darkness, her movements as perfectly graceful as ever.

Damn her, she won't die. His grief at seeing his son's still body had yet to overwhelm him, and for now he felt it as a bottomless rage and hate.

"Get the body and get back to the council room," said Pravin. He and Remy picked up the body of Jahn, and Pravin averted his eyes at the sight of his son's twisted head. *That was my son.*

They ran back quickly to the hall, climbing through the broken glass, the white-faced Chan covering their retreat.

"Turn your fire ninety degrees," said Pravin. "She'll circle behind us." The woman turned her fire just as another plate of glass shattered from Santiago's fire.

Pravin lunged up the three steps into the council room, and his escorts piled in after him. He slammed the door and hit the lock stud.

Shredder fire pummeled the door, deforming the metal, but Pravin had built it strong and it didn't puncture. After a few moments the gunfire stopped.

Pravin slumped, his heart pounding. He looked toward his son and then looked away from the twisted face, knowing he couldn't take time for grief yet.

"Where is the helmet?" asked Pravin, not wanting to see his son's face in death.

"It's outside, sir. But surely we can't go out and get it?" The man, Remy, sounded terrified.

"No, of course not." Pravin suddenly looked at his quicklink, where an emergency message flickered. "They're evacuating the medlabs," he said. "I must get down there. You follow, and bring the body."

"You want us to carry that?" asked Chan, pressing a bandage into her bloody side.

"You must," said Pravin, looking at them both intently. "It is more important than you know. It is everything we are fighting for." He turned to a narrow door in the back of the council chamber. "I must hurry. Meet me at the trains, as quickly as you can."

"Yes, sir," said Remy, staring after him.

Pravin hurried to the medlabs.

The Myrmidon commander looked down from above the city as her second-in-command activated the laser cannon. She took pleasure in the high-pitched hum as the cannon charged, ready to rain death down on the city.

"What's the first target?" asked her second.

"The flat area to the north of the central tower," said the commander. "I believe the medlabs are underneath, so hit the ground hard, like a pile driver."

"Yes, sir. Preparing to fire."

"Fire at will," said the Myrmidon commander, staring down at the city.

"Move the ones with the head injuries last," said Pravin, directing movements through the medlabs.

"Perhaps the Spartans will have mercy on them, but we cannot afford to favor them over the others."

"Spartans and mercy are not on speaking terms," said a sweating medic, helping a wounded Peace-keeper from a bed. The medlabs were in chaos as citizens were wheeled, guided and carried toward the long narrow hall that led to the evac trains.

Pravin had turned to the bed of a severely wounded child when the first impact rocked the earth over the medlabs. The impact almost knocked him off his feet and sent several trays of instruments crashing to the ground.

"What was that?" shouted one of the attendants on duty.

Pravin shook his head, knowing that whatever it was would only bring more death.

Another impact rocked the medlabs, and he saw an unconscious soldier fall out of his bed. Several emergency monitors began beeping, and pieces of stone fell from the ceiling.

Another impact hit, even harder, and Pravin stumbled into the child's bed, and then looked up to see more stones clattering down from the ceiling. Someone began screaming. Another impact, and Pravin threw himself over the child's body as a cascade of dust fell from the ceiling and one of the support beams buckled. The explosions were loud and hard, as if a battering ram were striking the ceiling above him.

He looked up and saw a massive dark crack forming, tearing the ceiling apart. *Everyone in here will die*, he thought, and then he saw the point of impact, where the crack had begun.

Right over the small room where Pria's cryocell lay.

He ran across the room, jostling surgeons who tried to drag patients out into the hallway to safety. Pravin reached the door in a moment of breathless silence, when the sounds of the world seemed far away and yet he knew they would come crashing in again with another round of destruction.

He threw the door open. Pria's cryocell rested on its platform, the pale blue glow still suffusing the shadow of the body inside. A stream of rocks and dust fell from the shattered ceiling, and a support beam had broken through the wall, torn by the massive force.

He stepped toward the platform, reaching out to it, when the next cannon blast hit. The sound hit him like a sonic hammer, deafening him completely, and the ceiling tore open from the impact, knocking him to his knees. He felt his world turn wildly as the support beam came crashing down, smashing into the glass cocoon of the cryocell that held his wife and shattering it.

No . . .

Pravin reached out his hands as a torrent of blue liquid gushed from the shattered cryocell and washed over his feet. He slipped and fell to his knees, his nose and throat filling with the smell of the noxious suspension chemicals. Struggling not to slip any farther, he reached out his arms to catch the body of his wife.

A dark form came tumbling out of the cryocell and into his arms. His heart pounded as he caught her, his wife, and as the fluids receded around him he saw her face, blackened from decay, pieces of the skin and skull partially rotted away. He looked down her body, and everywhere it was the same: her breasts, her stomach, her legs, all were covered with patches of the black death. And her back, where the bullets had hit her on the *Unity,* was a decayed mass of dark, angry flesh.

What happened here? I thought she would be all right . . .

She moved her head a little and her lips opened, but no sound came out. He felt her pulse, and found it just in time to feel her last heartbeat.

No . . .

He started to gag and stood up as another cannon blast hit, knocking him backwards from the room and collapsing the ceiling. He saw her body half buried beneath the debris.

"Sir, get out of here!" shouted a medic, pulling him back from the room. Pravin stood up, his clothing drenched with the cryogenic suspension chemicals that had once held his wife, his Chosen.

He ran from the medlabs as the ceiling collapsed, burying the wounded and the dead, and one surgeon who had stayed too long. A medic pulled him down the hallway, and then Pravin regained his feet and started running, letting the chaos bear him away from the horrors he had seen.

He reached the train platform in a rough underground cavern and found Peacekeepers in all states boarding train cars that amounted to no more than metal boxes on a rail. The train would carry them out of the base and into a hidden clearing up in the xenofungus overlooking the battle plain, where several old rovers, including a colony transport, awaited them.

Pravin crossed back and forth on the platform, looking for Sophia and his grandson, and the two escorts with the body of his son.

Jahn's body. My last connection to Earth, he realized. He had lost a son and a wife, all within minutes, and the sense of this loss overwhelmed his anguish at the parade of wounded he saw boarding the trains.

The Spartans will never treat those left behind with honor, he realized. *We have surrendered them to a terrible fate. What have I done?* He thought again of the nerve gas pods spreading wanton death, and he wondered again what kind of world he had created through his decisions.

"Sir, we need to launch the train," said a voice, and Pravin realized that the people he passed probably saw nothing in his eyes. He had retreated to a distant place, and only seeing the two escorts with the body of his son would pull him back. "The Spartans have entered the tunnels."

"Yes," said Pravin, but he didn't really hear, and he felt the man push him toward the train. The platform had almost emptied.

"Wait!" said Pravin. He saw Remy and Chan running from the tunnels, now with two more medics assisting them. They ran for the train, and Pravin could hear shredder fire down the corridor behind them, from the direction of the medlabs.

"We got it, sir," said Remy, and he turned toward the train.

"Where?" asked Pravin. "Where is the body of my son?"

"The body?" Remy asked. Pravin looked around, and saw that Remy and Chan and the other medics held no body, but only the pieces of the red Spartan armor, the armor that Jahn had worn.

"Where is my son?" he asked, and felt weakness descend on him.

"We thought you wanted the armor!" shouted Chan, her voice rising in pitch. "We couldn't carry that body all the way down here. Look at me!" She gestured at her chest wound with a blood-soaked hand, until one of the medics moved her firmly toward the train.

"We have to board, sir," said the other medic to Pravin. He picked up the armor and pushed Pravin into the rear car of the train. Pravin let himself go, all resistance gone. Inside the train were no seats, just a large space packed with standing and lying Peacekeepers.

The medic slammed the door shut, and the train jerked into motion.

"The tunnel will collapse behind us," said the medic. "If we can get out of here, we'll be safe."

The train picked up speed, and Pravin looked back to the empty platform and the tunnel beyond, which led to the surface where his son's body lay at the mercy of the Spartans.

"That was my son," he said quietly, and grief began to wash over him like a terrible wave.

The tunnel swallowed them, and the train rocketed its way out of the Peacekeeper base to safety.

Midnight

Pravin Lal stood at the edge of the tiny Peacekeeper camp and looked out over the fields of xenofungus to the battle plain beyond. He saw flames still smoldering inside UNHQ, and the flash of the cannon from Sol Ridge as the Spartans destroyed any last pockets of resistance. The Spartans had moved their camp forward on the plain, and their translucent tents clustered near the base of the walls, glowing softly.

Sophia came from behind him and stood at a distance, also looking out over the plain. Her lustrous hair was still matted around her face, and her normally clean uniform was spotted with filth.

After a while she turned back to him, and he saw the graceful lines of her face in profile underneath her translucent pressure mask. There were bruises around her eye and cheek. Spartan warriors had caught her and beat her mercilessly before she managed to break free and escape.

A very resourceful woman.

Her infant son hadn't been so lucky, and Pravin felt a deep remorse rise up in him again, a bottomless remorse. He had lost his son, his wife, and his grandson in one terrible act of war, his entire life shattered in a single day.

Yet the stars hadn't changed at all.

"This isn't the way," said Sophia.

Pravin moved closer to her, wondering how much she blamed him for all of this.

"I thought it was all inevitable," she said. Her voice remained steady, but he saw a tear tracing its way down her cheek inside the pressure mask. "What have we done here?"

Pravin reached out to touch her, but she pulled away, shaking her head. She turned and headed back into a small pressure tent.

Pravin looked down on the plain. Somewhere

down there, Santiago gloated in her command tent, her warriors defacing the body of his only son.

Or did she gloat?

He remembered Pria, and her desire to change things for the better, no matter what the cost. Her unlimited faith. As he had told Jahn: if he didn't try to save her, he might as well not have made the journey from Earth at all.

Pravin turned, went into the small armory pressure tent, and asked the attendant there to leave him alone for a minute.

He had one thing he needed to do.

The figure came down from the xenofungus-covered hills to the east of the Spartan camp largely unnoticed. Sentries patrolled the area, but they were weary from battle and hated the xenofungus and wouldn't go near it. And when they did get near it, the fungus seemed to call to them with a strange humming sound, floating like the voices of the dead across the moonlit plain.

And so the sentries sat down and stared into the fungus as if seeing a mystery there, and the figure slipped between them without incident.

Onward into the Spartan camp it went, passing between the outer tents and slipping around the dark area at the edges of campfires and glowlamps. And when a Spartan glanced over and saw the figure, the Spartan saw only the shadowy form of a Myrmidon, and none seemed to notice under the soft moonlight that the armor of the figure had a deep reddish cast.

The figure slipped past Spartans that celebrated and Spartans that sat grimly, recounting the battle in their minds. It walked past the medical tent, the tent strangely silent as the stoic warriors inside swallowed their pain, even to their last breaths. It went past the darkened armory, where killing forces slept, and past fleets of battered laser speeders that waited to unleash their fury again.

The figure went deep into the Spartan camp, into a ring of tents where the Myrmidons remembered their dead, their faces revealed beneath their black faceplates as human but inhuman, expressionless even in joy or grief.

None of them looked up as the figure passed around the ring of tents like a shadow and reached the one tent from which no glowlamp was visible through the walls. And no Myrmidons waited there, standing guard.

The figure slipped inside, wearing the deep red armor of Santiago herself, but with the grieving eyes of Pravin Lal beneath the mask.

Pravin pushed his way into the tent. It was dark inside, lit only by a single glowlamp, and he had to look around before he found Santiago.

She stood in the far corner of the tent, leveling a shredder pistol at his throat.

"Don't think that armor will protect you," she said. "I know the weak spots, and I can hit them."

Pravin lifted his hands to his head and took off the helmet and pressure mask, revealing his face to her.

"Pravin Lal," she said.

"Corazon," he answered. "I know you can kill me any time you wish. I only wanted to speak to you first, before what happened here goes on for a hundred lifetimes."

"You are my sworn enemy now," she said, her voice tight with emotion. He saw the pistol trembling in her hand. He looked up and around the small, sparse tent, wondering if he would die here, and he nodded.

"May I sit down?" he asked. "I am very tired."

She thought for a moment, then motioned him to the battle chest against the wall. He noticed how she moved when he moved, keeping a safe distance between them.

"I have no weapons," he said as he sat down. "And of course you can have your armor whenever you wish, whether or not you choose to kill me for it. I have only one request."

"You are in no position to make requests," Santiago said. "You killed so many of my people."

"And you killed my people, Corazon. My wife, my son, and my grandson, among others. So many others."

"That is war," she said.

He nodded. "That is war. But after war we must bury our dead, and try to remember why we fought in the first place."

"What do you want, Pravin? Sanctuary? Safe passage for you and your trusted advisors? You want me to turn you over to Deirdre Skye, so that you and she can plot against me? What is it?"

Pravin looked at her through the shadows. "I want the body of my son."

She stared at him, a look of shock settling on her features. Pravin continued.

"I only want his body. I want to see him again and

to bury him properly." He started to choke, and fought to keep from crying in front of this proud woman. "You Spartans honor your dead, so I know you understand. He is all I have left. There is nothing more to fight for, that others won't struggle for in my absence. But no one will look out for him."

Through the darkness Santiago watched Pravin struggle against his tears, an old man crossing through an enemy camp to ask for the body of his only son. And she wondered if her father, whom she had never seen, would have journeyed so far if he had known her.

She knew she would go that far for the body of her own son.

She sat in a small chair behind her desk and looked at him. "We were friends once, long ago," she said. He nodded. "I had a son too, who died in this very battle."

Pravin looked at her, stunned. "I am very sorry, Corazon."

She shook her head. "He was nothing to me. He was weak. I only tried to give him the smallest fighting chance. The chance to become as great as I was."

Pravin looked at her, wondering what to say, searching her face for signs of humanity.

"I gave him the chance that my father gave me, and more. I hardened myself to his struggle, as we must all do. But when he died . . ."

He heard her voice catch, and suddenly she lifted her gun, her hand trembling as if she would kill him rather than let him see her emotion. He lifted his hands.

"Just promise me you'll bury my son," he said quietly.

She slammed the gun on the desk and stood up, her voice shaking. "When he died, I felt a terrible sorrow. He was my son."

Pravin stood up and crossed to her slowly. He reached out with one hand, toward the desk, and touched not the gun but her hand.

"Tell me what we were fighting about," he said. "Please."

She looked at him, into his aging features and his strong eyes. Then she lifted her hand and struck him across the face, plunging him into blackness.

Pravin awoke to sunlight on his face and two dark shadows looming over him. He found himself lying in the vast plain outside of UNHQ, alive.

He looked around carefully, not wanting to move. His head ached, but otherwise he felt all right. Above him stood two Spartans, hefting a long, narrow load between them. They barely glanced at him as they carried it away, and then behind him he heard a transport start up and gun its engine.

He rolled over carefully and looked around. To his north about a hundred meters away he could see the great walls of UNHQ, the gates wide open. Inside smoke still twisted in the air, and one Spartan straggler walked in his direction.

To his south he could see the vast plain, emptied of any trace of the Spartan camp, except for the last transports that Spartan soldiers packed. Toward the horizon, he could see the Spartan army marching slowly away.

"Don't approach the gates," said the lone Spartan, drawing near. Pravin started to ask why, but the Spartan kept on walking.

Suddenly a loud boom echoed through the valley, and as Pravin watched an explosion rocked the south gates, knocking them off their hinges and destroying the two guard towers. When the dust cleared, Pravin could see UNHQ behind it, buildings and pressure domes damaged from the fighting.

I guess the Spartans are leaving themselves a way back in. Yet a calm floated over the city, the calm of the aftermath.

Pravin turned back and saw the last two Spartan transports start up and move away, going around something that blocked their path. As they pulled away, Pravin could see a dark shape left in the middle of the plain, alone.

Pravin started walking toward it as the transports receded into the distance, and then as he drew closer he broke into a run, his feet carrying him across the red plain. And when he reached it he slowed and looked at it in wonder.

It was a platform built of wood, about six feet long and three feet high, and across it lay a Spartan war banner. Pravin took the edge of the war banner and pulled it. It slipped off to reveal the body of his son, arms folded across his chest, face turned to the bright sky.

Pravin touched the boy's face, and then his hands, and then he fell across the body and wept.

And when the Peacekeepers came down from the mountain, and out of their hidden shelters, there was a funeral, and the son of Pravin Lal was buried with full honors under the Centauri sky.

epilogue

CHAIRMAN YANG SAT IN A CHAIR THAT HAD BEEN CARVED for him out of an odd yellow stone from Chiron's surface, and smoothed for him by hand over the course of a hundred hours. He took pleasure in sitting in the carved seat, and he knew his workers took pleasure in the accomplishment of such a painstaking task. It demonstrated to them that they did not yet need the luxuries Morgan churned out in his production lines and showered on his greedy citizens.

Yang watched his monitor banks through dark eyes. One of his hidden surface cameras was aimed at a field of xenofungus outside, to the south of the rise under which this small base lay. Crawling around that field of xenofungus was a small rover emblazoned with the rose-and-thorn symbol that Deirdre Skye used to identify her people and equipment. Walking next to the rover were several Gaian scouts holding shredder pistols loosely.

"I suspected that we were too close to the Gaian stronghold," said the blue-robed young man next to him. Yang looked at the man, Ming-Hoa, his top advisor, who stared back with a calm, chiseled face.

"You were right, Ming-Hoa, though this location had the natural underground tunnels we needed to build a base. Still, I didn't expect Deirdre Skye to explore so much."

He switched the view on the monitor to a video feed from one of his surface scouts, trained for years to explore the fringes of the human settlements without detection. This scout crouched deep in a field of xenofungus overlooking the battle between Lal and Santiago, his body buried to the chest in the strange red tubules.

"It appears the Spartans have left the city to the Peacekeepers," said Ming-Hoa. "I wonder if that was a tactical or a political decision."

"Either way, if the settlement leaders continue to behave this way, we won't need to fear conquest."

Yang stopped, his eyes catching an odd movement on the monitor. He sat forward in his chair, tense and alert.

"What's that?"

Ming-Hoa leaned forward, looking at a flicker of movement inside the xenofields by the Peacekeeper base. The scout had seen it too, and swiveled his camera toward the movement, zooming in.

Kneeling in a pocket of the xenofungus was a tall woman with long dark hair, wearing a tight pressure suit that looked Gaian in origin. As Yang and Ming-Hoa watched, the woman swept her hands around her, and thousands of wriggling mind-worms swept through the nearby xenofungus. She seemed to be playing with them, directing their movements as if directing a symphony.

"She's controlling them," said Ming-Hoa. "She directed their movements."

"Perhaps the mindworm attack on the Spartans was not a coincidence," said Yang. He stared at the monitor, considering every ramification of this new information. "Have her followed for as long as possible," he said finally, and then he rose.

Painted red dragons flanked the doorway out of this chamber, and he glanced at them as he pushed open the broad double doors.

The mindworms snake like these dragons. They would be a very valuable ally.

Yang left the chamber and walked down a short but broad hallway, still deep in thought. He reached a bigger hallway that circled a large center shaft. He leaned over a railing and looked up. At the top of the shaft, some eighty meters above, pale light came down past huge, slowly rotating fan blades.

"Those Gaian scouts have left the area," said Ming-Hoa, coming up next to him like a shadow. "They won't find us this time. And our observer will follow the worm woman."

"I'm not yet ready to rejoin the settlements, and Deirdre's explorations are getting more far-reaching," said Yang. "Perhaps we should leave this place."

Ming-Hoa nodded. "The xenofields don't seem to frighten the Gaians as much as the others. But why think of rejoining the settlements at all? You have safety and security and loyal workers now. We're fashioning a virtual utopia across the sea."

Yang leaned back and looked past Ming-Hoa to where two quiet young women with shaved heads polished a length of railing farther down. "Because we could use their resources, and eventually they'll find us anyway."

"If they don't kill each other first."

Yang nodded. "True. But they seem to genuinely want to survive. And perhaps some of their citizens will see the wisdom of our way of life."

He thought of the Gaians and of the woman who moved her hands and watched the mindworms do her bidding. These were creatures that terrified even him. He would have to work on that fear. But in the meantime, perhaps he should also work on Lady Deirdre Skye.

"Go and bring me some of these mindworms," said Yang to Ming-Hoa. "And leave me alone for an hour. I want to think."

Ming-Hoa nodded, his face twisted with reproach at the task.

Yang turned and headed back to his chamber, where dragons slept beneath the surface of Chiron.

To be continued in *Book II: Dragon Sun*

About the Author

Michael Ely has lived all around the world and worked as a multimedia designer, a computer game producer/designer, a filmmaker, and an author. You can drop him a line at *bookthoughts@yahoo.com*.